Dedicated to all the people in my crazy life
that even remotely made this book possible,
to my Mentor in life Daisaku Ikeda

And to Chris Parsons … wherever you are, I
love you and miss you man, we all do.

Also:

Art Direction | Graphic Design: Taisha Okata-Ohira Cover Illustration: Anthony Picone

Intro:

Hi! Welcome to my slightly off color view
of the world! Before you read this, please
know that I haven't participated in the
consumption of large quantities of
hallucinogenic substances, nor do I plan to
start any time soon. This book came purely
from my imagination. That's right; all of this
came right out of my head and onto the page
without any chemical stimulation!

We live in a world that as of this intro being
written, is filled with strife and conflict that
seems to pervade the human spirit, leading
us ever closer to our own extinction based
largely on superficial conflicts rooted in our
own fundamental lack of understanding that
at our core, we are all human, we all
experience the same range of emotions, and
all have similar desires, but we insist on

focusing on the external. What religion are you, my God is better than yours, have and have-nots, etc …

In short, we're killing ourselves for nothing. I imagine if this book has a shot at existing for a thousand years, or even a hundred for people to read, we will have to focus more on the internal, on polishing our inner lives and seeing ourselves for the beautiful people we are despite our external differences. Once we love ourselves, I think that loving each other, and creating a productive society will finally be possible. Until then … Veni, Vedi, Vici … over and over again.

CONTENTS

The Drifter

I opened my eyes and saw the light … it
hurt a lot, and my head was throbbing. I
rolled on my side and puked. It was the most
awe inspiring vomiting I'd ever experienced.
The heaving was unbearable, the
convulsions were violent and I felt like I was
drowning in between them, but the pattern
on the floor briefly looked like two girls
making out, and this gave me a modest
moment of enjoyment. I finally stopped, and
took my first gasp of real honest to God air.
It filled my lungs and gave them an elated
feeling. It was a feeling which permeated
my body. It was a feeling of incredible
jubilation and joy. All told, it sucked a lot
less than vomiting. Then I saw him, my
maker … the Head Honcho, God himself
was standing in front of me.
My first thought was "Am I dead?"
My second thought was, "God's a lot shorter
than I thought."
And finally, "Did I leave the oven on this
morning?"
"Christ!" I said without thinking.
God answered, "No but he's gallivanting
around and about here somewhere".

All I could come up with in response was,
"Crap … I mean, well, yeah, crap is
appropriate for this situation."
Continuing with the theme of being
inappropriate in front of my maker, I
continued, "You're short, and I'm dead!"
In my mind it was a little more sincere, and I
meant it, but shit I should have thought it out
a little more.
"I am dead … right?" I began.
"Yep" he said.
"I mean, was it the …" I began again.
He finished for me, "… That last shot of
Goldschlagger put you over the top … but to
be fair, I'd say that poor diet, and countless,
endless nights of drinking and smoking
would have eventually done you in.
Speaking of which, want one?"
He pulled out a pack of Cigs, "God's Finest,
All Natural" it said on the pack.
After a New York minute of contemplation I
said, "Sure … what the fuck, not like it's
going to give me cancer now, and besides
how often do I get to have a smoke with
god?"
They were good too, but I guess it's only the
best for the big man.
    A few awkward moments passed. He lit
up; mine just lit up by itself.
"Damn these things are smooth." I said.
God stared at me, as if he were sizing me up
to decide which part of me had the best cut

of meat, he took a few drags, and then he spoke.

"Well?" he said.

"Well what?" I replied.

He stammered out, "Jesus you're thick"

He winced a little at this and looked back a little concerned as a large black man with an afro came out of a door that was suddenly there and like a puppy dog blurted out, "Yes Father? You beckoned for me?"

God rolled his eyes and said, "Sorry son go back to whatever it was you do back there!"

Jesus looked a little like a kid who'd been told he was going to the toy store only to find out he was tricked into going to a dentist appointment and just shuffled off dejected back into the door.

God shook his head and said, "I really have to learn not to do that so often."

He looked at me and continued, "Well?"

I just took another drag off the best fucking cigarette ever made and stared at him, a little puzzled, and a little pissed.

He mumbled to himself, "Never was the brightest one."

God went on, "What do you want to ask me? Everyone comes to me with questions, I could just answer them for you because I already know them … but I just like to see the look on people's faces when they ask them … it amuses me."

I took one more deep drag, I sighed and put out the Cig on a cloud, it immediately turned

3

dark; underneath it I could feel rain coming down.

"First of all, is that how rain is created? You put out a cigarette and suddenly a cloud puts out rain?"

He smirked, "Yeah, pretty much … luckily for you saps it's a lifelong habit … Just so long as I'm happy anyways … you should have been there when my girlfriend Janis broke up with me. I chain smoked for days, lucky I had that woman, Nora make that ark. It would have been curtains for most life on Earth if I hadn't made her do that."

"Whoa!" I said … "Nora? A woman made the ark and her name was NORA?"

He rolled his eyes, "Yeah, it was a long time ago, and all those religious texts you study are kind of like the history books you study: Incomplete, and with a lot of typos. Not to mention horribly contradictory. Sadly, she was just kind of a rebound girl for me, but I guess it was a defining moment in human history."

I remember at that moment taking a look at god. Was this really god? I mean I had a lot of expectations for what god would look like, but this was bizarre! He was about 5'4" and dressed up as a very sad looking clown. Big red floppy shoes, a giant colorful onesie, which had all the colors of the rainbow on it, but the dominant color was kind of a lime green. He looked … I don't know what the word I'm looking for here is. He had on

pancake makeup, but it couldn't hide the
bags under his eyes, the crow's feet, the
lines on his forehead. He looked tired, he
looked ancient, and he looked strange. But I
guess that's one way to keep us on our toes.
Also heaven looked odd, well at least what I
could see. It was like a desert of clouds,
there was an old torn up leather seat next to
a table with a remote, but no TV. There was
a heavy metal band playing in the
background, at least they looked like a
heavy metal band, but the music came out
like Mozart with an opera singer singing Hip
Hop, or Rap, or whatever the kids call it
now a days. And to the left of the band was
what I can only describe as a psychedelic,
multicolored, glowing octopus who was
incredibly happy, and dancing to the strange
music like he was high as a kite.
Which led me to my next question,
"Don't you think that everything here is ... I
don't know ... a little weird?"
God looked around chuckled a bit and said
"Yeah. But the really trippy thing is that
everyone who comes to heaven sees it as it
is in their mind. So as weird as this all may
look to you, it's all from your head dude."
I absorbed this thinking, "Did he just say
dude? Yes, yes he did."
I looked around, took another cigarette,
which lit itself, and decided he was right.
This is exactly what I always thought

5

heaven had looked like, or at least what I'd
hoped it would.
I took yet another drag and laughed as the
origins of my vision of heaven came rushing
back to me,
"Oh yeah … 5th grade. Mrs. Delaney"
And god in all his infinite wisdom chuckled,
and understood.

    Finally I gave into my simpler self and
asked "So here it is … the questions that
everyone asks, and I'm sure that you get
sick of answering … but here goes, why am
I here? What does it all mean?"
God sat down in his old chair, propped up
his feet and picked up the remote, turned on
the tube, and suddenly I had the answer to
my first question … I don't know how, but it
just popped into my head … last night. I was
drunk, again, and I was about to take that
last shot of Goldschlagger … and I said it.
"Here I come God!"
Or it could have been, "Come and get me
fucker!"
But the intended meaning was the same.
Then I took that last shot, and fell on the
floor, my drunk friends just looked on, and
ordered another round, one of them put out a
cigarette on my arm … I'll have to have a
talk with him at some point. I mean
assuming I get to talk to him again. Then
god put his fingers together and closed his
eyes …

"As for the other question … well, that's easy to answer … but difficult to understand." He continued "You see, it all means whatever you make of it."

"What? That's, absurd?"

God replied, "So is life, but you all have absolute and complete control over your lives. I pretty much have no control over what you do with your lives … so life is what you make of it. You see I refer to you as my creations … but you're really much more than that. You're my equals. You are all my brothers and sisters, if you figure out life, you die, and you get to move on to this higher plane … where there are, other challenges."

I looked at God a little dumbfounded, and judging off my response he said, "What can I say … my life is … complicated. I'm sure you'll understand one day … when you get to be where I am today."

He paused for a couple minutes, stared at the dancing psychedelic octopus, and let me soak this in for another few moments.

I sat on a cloud thinking about this new reality that had been thrust upon me … "Maybe this is how Adam felt after the fall of the Garden of Eden." I said.

An eternity passed, or maybe it was a few minutes. It didn't matter … obviously I had all the time in the world. Finally god spoke …

"Adam wasn't called Adam … actually he didn't have a name … you guys did that. Besides, why the hell would I call him Adam? I mean, if I were going to create the first ever human on Earth, wouldn't I at least give him a cool name like Ezekiel?"

He went on … "And actually, the whole fall of the Garden of Eden thing … well that one was actually my fault. You see I was new at the whole supreme entity thing, and I was having so much fun making all these new creations all those billions of years ago … in case you were wondering about my age, but I know you and you weren't really, sometimes I just like to brag about how good I look for my age."

God left an odd and awkwardly long silence apparently fishing for a compliment and not getting one before continuing, a little disappointed.

"Anyhow, I was so excited with this whole garden of Eden thing, Man in my own image, etc … that I wasn't paying attention, and I let my pet dog out, and he sort of ran amok, and destroyed the whole thing … since you don't know their real names, we'll just call them Adam, Eve and company."

I gawked and said, "So many questions! Let's start with this whole dog getting loose thing, it wasn't a snake? Is your dog SATAN?"

God grimaced underneath the pancake makeup a little. "Hey let's start with giving

8

me a break here, I mean everyone makes mistakes … even me … OK, especially me. Yes it was a dog, yes he is the devil, but actually his name is pronounced Santa … not Satan. I always found that to be a curious turn of events, but then look at what Christmas has turned into in most parts of the industrialized world and … well are you really surprised? Also, it isn't fair to characterize him as "The Prince of Darkness" … when really; he's just a very bad dog. Actually he can be very sweet sometimes … oh shove it, he's my dog and I love him. What else?"

My jaw hung open; I would have drooled had it not been for the burning questions that were flowing into my head and subsequently drying up the aforementioned drool.

I blurted out "Are we all really descended from Adam and Eve … or whatever you call them?"

God laughed so hard I think he almost peed in his big clown suit.

"No, ha ha ha … not at all, OK sort of. In fact, I find the whole origins of mankind thing a funny story. It's soooo off the mark! Actually Adam and Eve were sort of an um … how do I put this so you can understand it … they were single celled organisms … in fact science has it a little more correctly than anyone else. They were my first creations. What? Did you think I was going to start with bipedal mammals? That's like asking a

five year old to build The Empire state
building with his first set of Lincoln Logs. If
I'd started off with creatures like yourself,
you wouldn't have lasted 5 seconds in
Earth's early atmosphere ... no I started off
with something simple, something that could
grow and develop into the complex and
brilliant, but moronic creatures you are
today."

"Turkish delight?" He suddenly asked
holding out a candy box.

"Sure, they're my favorite!" I said.

"Duh, I know." He replied.

"So what did the garden of Eden look like?"
I asked.

He blew a smoke ring and replied
nostalgically "It was one of the most
complex places you've ever seen ... it was
so full of life, different organisms of all
shapes and colors, swimming around and,
well, then Santa had to go and pee on it, and
it just sort of disintegrated in front of my
eyes ... I'd describe it in more detail, but
there's no need to resort to potty humor,
then there was the struggle to evolve from
what was now a polluted mess of life and
dog pee. I guess in the long run it was a
good thing, he peed on Eden. If you had
stayed there without any incentive to
change, you might not even be dinosaurs yet
... but there would be an awful lot more of
you, and you'd all be about a foot taller.
Anyways to answer your question ... to you

10

it would have looked like … well, do you remember that green slime they used to have on the early Nickelodeon shows?" he asked. I replied apprehensively "Wait, it looked like green slime?"

"What?" he shot back … "just because you don't appreciate it doesn't mean it wasn't beautiful … besides, it was my first creation, and from it all life eventually evolved, I'd like to see you do the same!"

I smirked, "Sure, just get me drunk and give me a bag to barf in. I'll bring back the garden of Eden."

God thought about this for a moment, and then he laughed and said, "Yeah I guess it's kind of the same thing."

Then I asked a bigger question, one that burns in the mind of all humanity.

"God, is there any hope for us? I mean humanity, are we doomed to a world of vice, sin and destruction? Or can we redeem ourselves?"

He replied "First of all that's two or three questions depending on how you slice it. Is there any hope for you? Yes, of course there's hope, there is always hope. Hope is the one resource that you all have an unlimited supply of … well that and electricity, but you still haven't quite figured that one out yet, but I think you will once you realize just how powerful one grain of pasta can be when used properly. But, getting back to hope, hope is all around you,

11

all you have to do is reach out and grab it.
But that's up to you. As for the whole vice,
sin, and destruction thing … well first off
look around you, I'm a chain smoker who
still hasn't settled down with anyone, and
likes to watch …"

He looked at the remote for a minute, then
said "Well it's a little more complicated than
a TV, it actually puts images in your head
and … well, I'll let you guys figure that one
out. The thing is that sin, vice, and
destruction is a vital part of creation … the
bigger the boom, the more interesting the
history that comes afterwards. There is no
sin, the only thing that is going to doom
mankind though is if you people can't
realize that you're all related, what religion,
how much money you have, or what family
or nation you came from is un-important.
What's important is that you all learn to
work with each other harmoniously, and I
don't mean like a big hippie commune or
anything like that. You don't even have to
necessarily like one and other to realize that
you're all working toward a common goal.
All you have to do is cohabitate and work
with each other every day, then you can go
be with the people you do like and play
soccer, or football, or whatever you want to
call it. In fact, you people call them sins, I
call them hang ups. The worst part is you do
it to yourselves. Stop punishing yourselves
and realize that the goal of humanity is to be

happy! Start enjoying your life, don't let any of your fleeting problems bug you. So what if something kills you, you can always go back down there and try again. I keep copies of all the people you knew up here anyways and they form a big carefree collective. In some ways, a little piece of us goes to heaven with each passing life; you just have to enjoy it!"

This was a lot to take in … God was deep. But I found it hard to take him seriously when he was dressed up as a clown, or maybe that was the point.

I went on "So what about heaven and hell?"

"What about them?" he asked, smoke coming out of his mouth from what had to be the 66th cigarette he'd smoked since I got here.

"Are they real? I mean I think this is heaven … and through the powers of deduction I would assume there is a hell, but since so far everything I seem to have thought I knew up till this point is all wrong … well?"

He flashed a devilish grin and said "Yes they're real … but no, this isn't heaven. Heaven is the perfect day, it's going to the beach and meeting your wife and your mistress at the same time and having a great time, heaven is finally losing all that weight you wanted to loose, and have tried for all those years, only to finally lose it. In correlation, hell is self-defeat. Hell is a place

we all take ourselves when we feel like there is no hope, no reason to go on. Hell is a cold day with no sweater and no hot chocolate. The short answer is that heaven and hell are places that you put yourself into. They exist all together in us all at the same time. They are self created, self determined states of existence we all go to when we are down, or up on ourselves."
I was confused, but oddly satisfied.
Then I added "So where am I now?"
He looked at me and said "This is my house."

Suddenly a German Sheppard popped out of a trap door in the sky, walked down invisible stairs, jumped into god's lap, and proceeded to lick him in the face on his left cheek, this smeared his makeup a little, making the left side of his face look somewhat older than it had a moment ago. He was old … and I'm talking Rolling Ugly's, party every night for 600 years old. He reached into his pocket, pulled out a piece of what looked like Broccoli, and threw it up into the air. The dog jumped up after it, what must have been a thousand miles or more. Then landed on his feet next to god's chair and went about gnawing on this green afro-like vegetable.
"Is that … well, Santa?" I asked.
"Yes, that's my little devil!" he replied while vigorously petting him.

I thought about this for a while, I like German Sheppard's, a lot! Does that mean I have evil tendencies?

As if he read my thoughts, god looked at me and said, "He's just a dog, you're thinking about this way too much."

He went on … "I do have some good news for you; it's not your time to die."

"Wait … what?" I asked.

"Then what is all this, Purgatory?"

He thought about this for a while, longer than I think god should have had to think about it.

"No, it's not purgatory, just my house. Most people when they die don't get to come here. It's just, well … I like you. I wanted to meet you, I mean like this, not like after you die. Actually I rarely get to meet you people when you die, too many of you, and too few of me. You either ascend to a higher plane or move on to your own part of the universe, or you haven't quite figured the whole life thing out and you go back down to earth to try life one more time."

He said, the last bit coming out sarcastically.

"Man, you live thousands of lifetimes making the same mistakes over and over again, and you always come back here and act like it's your first time being reborn. You have access to all your old memories, but you still choose to act like it's the first time, or ignore those memories."

Suddenly I knew what he was talking about, I looked into my mind and saw countless lifetimes, all coming back to me, always making the same stupid mistakes, and learning very little from lifetime to lifetime … what really surprised me is how many lifetimes I'd lived as a drag queen, what was even more surprising is how much I missed it.

I said "Huh … we are silly creatures aren't we?"

God replied "Don't worry, so am I, I should know, I made you."

I went on, "Well I guess I could go on drilling you with questions for all eternity, but, I guess the real question now is … what next? Where do I go from here? I mean if I'm not supposed to die yet, then, what am I doing here?"

God looked at me, smiled, and said "My son …" he called me son "you are being given a gift."

I replied "Ooh goody! I like presents! So what have I won?"

God laughed "You are getting what I can only describe as the choice of many lifetimes. You can either go back to Earth to live countless lifetimes with unlimited wealth and luxury, or …"

I interrupted "There is an "or" I like that option!"

God sighed for a moment and then went on "Or, you can have the opportunity to talk to

all those in your life that have passed on …
people who by the way, you've known for
countless lifetimes, but have never actually
gotten to meet from the perspective of
themselves after having passed on."

I thought about it and said, "Before I make
this choice, which seems like an easy one, I
have to ask you about my other option …
what is so valuable about meeting with all
these people I already know? I mean, other
than goodbye, and how ya doing these days?
What possible value could meeting these
people have? I think the guy in The Matrix
said it best … ignorance is bliss!"

God did not speak; he only stared at me for
as long as it took for me to continue talking.
"There has to be something I'm missing
here. I mean it'd be great to see all those
people again … maybe … shit, OK, OK!
You've convinced me …"

I cringed as the next few words came out of
my mouth "… I'll meet with all my dead
comrades."

God smiled and spoke the last words I'd
hear out of his mouth for a long while,
"Congratulations, you've made a choice
which could be the first step towards a life
which countless souls can only dream of,
and by the way, I don't like being called
God, it's too formal, call me Sid." Then
there was a blinding flash of light.

Suddenly I was in darkness, a glowing …
well I could say light here, but it was more
than that, it was light, it was color, it was
sound without noise, it was feeling without
touch, then suddenly the psychedelic
octopus descended upon me. It never spoke,
but I knew instinctually what it wanted … so
I took its hand and we were off! The
universe flew by me, faster than the fastest
car I'd ever been in, but yet I saw every
detail with crystal clarity as it went by. I
spanned entire universes in seconds, all the
while the octopus, whose name I derived as
Nich, at my side, always communicating
with me, sharing his interesting life as a
Ferryman of unique souls, but never
speaking a word. Then, when I thought we
could go no further, we came to a clearing, a
giant marble floor laid out before us, it
reminded me of the floor at St. Peter's
Basilica in Vatican City, only … I don't
know, it seemed flawless, and completely
solid. On the other end lay a large set of
Double doors, Nich looked at me, his beak
expressionless … he somehow smiled, and I
knew he could go no further, but that when I
was ready, he'd be there waiting. I sucked in
my gut, straightened out my hair, and took
the long walk to those beautiful … I want to
say they were oak … doors, doors that were
bigger than the World Trade Center, when it
was still standing. I stood in front of them,
imposing and inviting, took a deep breath,

pulled back my immensely tiny fist, and knocked with no fear in my heart … the sound I made could have shattered the solar system … but it was harmonious, like old school rap, it made me smile, it filled me with purpose. The doors began to open.

The doors swung open silently, as if they were incapable of making noise … after a brief flash of darkness, suddenly the inside came alive. The scene before me was, I'm not sure how to put it into words, I guess the best way to describe it is … nothing at all like I expected it to be, which was easy considering I had no expectations to begin with. It was … a dirty old diner, like Denny's, or Du-Pars in Los Angeles, only … well, more run down. There was a distinct smell of stale cigarette smoke, mixed in with fresh, cheap cigs … that coupled with the smell of stale, artery clogging food. The carpet was green shag, and was worn down in places, the ceiling and walls had stains on them from … well everything, the place looked like it got cleaned every day with more dirt, but it was never enough. It was exactly my kind of place, and it was about to get better. A very young looking woman in a very short skirt/low cut top combo and fishnet stockings came up to me. She had perfect tits! Wow they were great … maybe a little too great, because the first thing out of her

mouth to me in that ooh so sweet voice was
…
"So can I help you, or if I let you stare at my
tits for another five minutes will that have
helped you enough?"
I jumped a little, "Oh, um … I'm sorry I was
just it's just, I didn't mean to stare … I was
simply, I mean I respect women too much to
think of them purely as sex objects."
She just smiled at me, got really close and
said "That's too bad, because you're really
cute … but too late, what can I do for you?"
I think my heart stopped for a moment, then
the other major organ in my body returned
just enough blood to my other head, or my
lesser organ as I like to call it, so that I could
say …
"I'm here for … wait …"
What the hell was I doing here? I turned
around to look at Nich hoping he'd have the
answers, but all I saw in the absence of what
had been giant doors and churchlike flooring
was … well a gas station with an old
redneck in overalls drinking a beer while
sitting out front and tending shop across the
street from the Diner on an otherwise empty
desert road. The old redneck lifted his beer
and pointed at it, and I remembered, I think
he caught on to this because he gave me a
thumbs up before I turned back around to
see what I imagined I wanted to spend the
rest of my life with and said
"I'm here to see my friends."

20

She laughed, "Sure you are sweetie, I'm just messing with you, they're right this way."
I followed her much like a stray dog who wants desperately to find a home with whomever he's following, watching those beautiful legs float over to an adjacent room, where they were waiting, this was enough to get me to stop thinking about sex for about eight seconds … and realize, that for better or worse … here they were, some of the people who had mattered most to me in life, and had hurt the most to part with were now sitting at this distant diner, waiting … smiling. Then I thought about sex again, and sat down. The woman of my dreams spoke, "Luis will be your server today, he'll be with you in a moment … enjoy!"
I called out "Wait! You mean you can't serve us today?"
She giggled a little "No sorry sweetie, I'm just the hostess, and besides, judging from your reaction when we first met, I think you only want me to serve you, and that wouldn't be fair to your party. But don't worry; we'll see each other again!"
She walked off, I suddenly yelled out "Wait, what's your name?" but she didn't hear me and kept walking.

A voice called out, "Well partner, I guess we can make you stop thinking about sex for 8 seconds or so!"
Everyone laughed … even me. I took a look around, wow … there were the five most

influential people in my life ... well that had died, I guess there were a lot of living people that have a great impact on my life, it's just that you don't realize it as much until they've passed on. To my right was my Grandfather, former Princeton man, Navy man, Flew for the airlines for 20 years when they were in their heyday, and then worked for the FAA for another 20 years, all the while doing theatre, and constantly getting into trouble. He had just passed recently, and as was in his character, had made an embarrassing comment about me in front of everyone to break the ice ... and I appreciated it. Next to him was my best friend, who had been with me through everything since college and beyond ... then one day he was just gone. I guess that happens to us, you never know when it's your time to go ... but damn, for some of us more than others, that time seems too close at hand. Then there was my Great Grandmother and Great Grandfather, sitting next to each other, holding hands, and smiling ... and finally my Grandmother ... sitting on the complete opposite side of my Grandfather ... leering a bit at him ... their marriage didn't end on the best of terms, and that was compounded by the fact that she got sick afterwards, and slowly passed on over six years from a rare and incurable disease. To be fair though, so had my grandfather, it was kind of a Montezuma's revenge sort of thing. Even if it wasn't, it was really tough watching them both slowly pass on. I sat there for a moment staring at these five people, it was like staring at Mt. Rushmore ... only with 5 People I guess, and not as statuesque ... oh and more colorful, let us not forget colorful. After a long, uncomfortable pause, I decided that I was going to have to be the one to break the silence ... I hate being the only kid in class to raise his hand.

Then like the voice of ... well not God he actually sounded nothing like this guy, but maybe some lesser deity ... with a Mexican accent,
"Hello sirs and peoples, I am Luis and I take your order?"
I turned to look at him and his eyes got really big
"Hey! Signor! You remember me? Luis!"
I wanted to say I did, but for the life of me I had no idea who this man was beyond what our hostess had told us ... I think she said his name was Luis, but I was too busy watching her lips, and imagining all the things they could do to me to actually understand what was coming out of them.
"No, sorry" I said.
He had a very sad look in his eyes, like I had just given him a puppy and then taken it away ... for good, so I went on "Um ... but maybe if you refreshed my memory I could

remember, see I'm not that good with names and faces." This was a lie, I forgot a lot of things, women's phone numbers, Birthdays, how to stay sober, but a name and face I rarely ever forgot. His face brightened up, this was progress.

He said "Oh! Si signor, it has been a very long time, I'm Luis!"

He paused, maybe for effect, I'm not sure but we were no closer to solving the mystery here.

"Go on I said …"

He went on "Oh yes, more information is good, we were in Kindergarten together, remember, and I was the only Mexican boy there, and you were the only person who was nice to me, you said hello, and once you even let me have your blocks when all the other toys were gone. So … Remember me, Luis?"

Oddly enough, I did … sort of, I do remember a kid in Kindergarten that was sort of smallish and well, I suppose he could have been Mexican, but he never wore a flag on his forehead so it was hard to tell. He would come up to me with a big grin and say, "Remember me, Luis?"

All the time … in fact I'm not sure he said anything else, come to think of it, after that school, which was made up primarily of African American kids, with the assorted white and Latino sprinkled in for diversity … We moved to an almost exclusively white part of town. I went for several years thinking that most Mexicans had a very limited vocabulary ... then I got into high school, which was pretty well mixed, and started noticing girls of south and Central American heritage the most ... and realized that not only wasn't their vocabulary limited ... most of them spoke 2 languages, and it wasn't until my hormones died down a little that they even realized that I spoke one language.

"Luis! You old Son of a gun! How are you?"

I answered this question almost before I finished asking it ... if he was here, then not as well as he could be.

"Well I actually have you to thank for a great deal ... I would not have been able to make it to where I got in life if it wasn't for you. I was so depressed throughout school, but I decided that if someone like yourself that had everything in the world could be nice to me, then I could go on. So I did, through High School, College, and eventually I got a good job, got married, and had kids! It was a good life!" he said.

I stared at him, dumbfounded at my divine accident of sorts.

I answered "Wow! That's pretty cool! So, uh, what ... you know ... happened to you."

I said this as if I had Down syndrome; I found it funny how even in the afterlife you have a hard time talking about death. He just looked at me and smiled, his face got a little flush. "Well, it's actually a little embarrassing, you see I was always very careful about my health, I worked out, ate right, I would never drink and drive, but you see … one day I was on my way to the living room in my house, and I slipped on a step, I fell hard, and the next thing I know I was applying for a job here. But it's OK, because I do so well in life that I don't have to go back again, most people aren't so lucky. Well I just want to say thank you for your good thought, I may have had a horrible life if it hadn't been for you. I go put in your order now."

Before he could turn around I said "Wait, but we haven't ordered yet …"

He just looked at me as everyone else laughed.

Then he smiled and said, "It's OK, I already know what you want, but she's busy."

Everyone seemed to chuckle at this for a moment.

"But your food, it will be here soon." Then he was off.

My Great Grandparents got up, came over and both gave me a great big hug. My Great Grandmother spoke, "We can't stay, we both have to go back down to Earth and try life over again, but don't worry, we both love you, and in the grand scheme of things, we'll see each other again! Now

26

listen I'm not preachy, but you need to get yourself a wife down there!"

My Great Grandfather looked at me "Yeah Kiddo, you're pushin' 35 and you're still single, not that I can fault you for the boozing so much, but settle down a little!"

I looked at them a little embarrassed and said "Yeah I guess I just haven't felt all that motivated to find the right woman yet, but I suppose it is getting a little late in the clock of life to be partying so much."

My great grandfather looked at me and said "Well for Cripes sake, at least try and get laid once in a while! Jeez!"

I wanted to crawl into a hole and be alone now … that was probably one of the most embarrassing things anyone had ever said to me, until … my great grandmother leaned in, gave me a peck on the cheek, held both of my arms and said,

"Maybe if you didn't whack off as much, you'd be a little more motivated."

"Right" I said back to her.

Maybe the unlimited wealth option was the better one after all … I couldn't help but feel like I'd taken what was in the mystery box instead of the cash prize, only to find out it was some sort of fish, or nothing! They both gave me a big hug and told me they loved me, and said farewell. I would have cried … but I was too embarrassed.

I sat down … where was the food? More importantly, why were there no condiments on the table, I had no idea what was coming, it could be some sort of baked octopus guts for all I knew … I mean I might want to put ketchup on octopus guts. As I sat there pondering the pros and cons of eating the insides of Octopi, then thinking about how Nich would feel about us eating one of his brethren, my attention was snapped back into reality as my Grandmother grabbed on to my hand and said

"Hey, I won't repeat it, but your great grandma is right."

This startled me, not because of the content of her speech, but because I hadn't heard her talk much, even when she was alive … Lou Gehrig's disease does that to you though.

"I know, I know, and I promise that the first woman who's moderately attractive that shows any interest in me will be the object of my desire for all eternity assuming she says yes."

My Grandmother laughed a little and said, "I don't appreciate your sarcasm, but hey, your attitude is all right, just be a little more particular than that."

She leered at my Grandfather as she said this.

I changed the subject, "So … how's er, the afterlife?"

She just smiled at me, "I've been perfecting my Mrs. Pac-Man skills, I can now get to the end without losing a single life, and I can get all the ghosts with every power pellet!"

28

My Grandmother in her later years found
herself with a lot of free time, and for some
reason developed a love of video games,
good to see she was moving on in the
afterlife "Pac-Man" I said.
"MRS. Pac-Man" She corrected.
"Right" I said.
"Um so I guess I'll skip too it, any life
altering advice you want to give me whilst
I'm here?"
She thought for a long while, then her eyes
lit up, and she made a paper football out of
her menu, propped it up and said
"THINK FAST!"
Then she flicked it right between my eyes …
it hurt a lot.
"What did you do that for?" I said.
She looked at me confused for a moment
and said,
"Well don't you get it?"
"No" I replied.
"Geez Louise, have you seen my grandson
around here anywhere? He looks just like
you only smart! The point is, think fast, and
try and have fun in life."
"That's it?" I said.
"That's it!" She replied.
Unlimited wealth and it all could have been
mine I thought to myself …
"Well, thank you Grandma … it's just good
to get to talk to you again."

Her eyes got big again, "Oh! One more thing! You know those dollar bill slots on vending machines?"

There was a pause, and it occurred to me that she was awaiting an answer.

So I said, as understandingly as I could "Um, yeah …"

She went on, very excited, "Well, if you pour salt water into them, then it messes up the mechanism in the machine, and it gives you all of its money, and soda!"

She smiled, quite proud to have been able to impart this knowledge to me, and after a short, confused moment, I smiled, kissed her on the forehead, and said

"Thank you Grandma and I love you so very much."

She gave me a big enthusiastic hug and said "Thank you for listening to me, I have to go now."

"Wait, why so soon?" I said.

"Yeah" she replied, "I've been waiting here for almost 17 years now … it's time for me to move on. But, I love you too, and we'll see each other again … I'll just look different. Bye!"

And just like that, she was off. I wondered if the last supper was anything like this.

Next there was my Grandfather. A big guy, both in stature, and in his personality, man he'd just died like a week and a half ago, but he'd been sick for 10 years, you see

30

he really hadn't been there much for a while now. It was good to see him healthy and alert again ... and wearing what I can only describe as 80's style parachute pants, a t-shirt that said "I'm with stupid" on it, and his American Airlines cap ... I wondered if this had contributed to my Grandmother leering at him.

"Partner" he said, "I've been around the world and back again ... and I've only got one piece of advice for you."

"What's that?" I replied ... already knowing the answer.

"Watch your six ... always watch your six."

My grandfather being a flying ace of the early days of aviation, had always given me this advice ... why did I come here again?

He got up to leave.

"Wait!" I said.

"Grandpa, tell me one of your stories before you go."

He always had the best stories of anyone I'd ever met. "Well, OK partner ... did I ever tell you the one about the new stewardess, and the hazing ritual?"

Now, he'd only told me this story about a million times ... but yet, I never got tired of it, so I replied

"Maybe, but tell it again, just so I remember it."

He got a big grin on his face, the old man loved telling stories ... although it was a little odd with him telling them in Parachute pants, but hey this had been a slightly unusual day for me anyways, so I just went with it. He told the story.

"Well we were flying out of DCA down to DFW on our daily route in a 747, best damn airplane ever built as far as I'm concerned. Anyways, we had a new stewardess on board, pretty little brunette number with legs that went up higher than the airplane … don't tell your grandmother that. Well she was a pretty little thing, but greener than the grass at Buckingham Palace, so we decided to initiate her into the AA family. Understand that in those days this was all fun and games, but now a day's I'd end up flying Cessna's out of the North Pole if I did any of this. So we told her all her normal duties, you know smile, make the passengers smile, serve coffee, bend over once and a while. But we decided to let her in on her most important duty, you see there was a little lever at the beverage station in the back of the plane, didn't do much, but we let her know that she had one of the most important jobs on the plane … she had to turn that lever right when we made our descent into DFW, because as we explained it, that lever made the rear wheels on the plane go down, and if she didn't turn it, we'd all crash because the plane wouldn't have the rear wheels out. She said she understood, and we all had a good laugh about it. So we all went about the business of flying the plane, it was

32

a pretty uneventful flight as I remember it. We got ready to land, you know fasten seatbelts sign and all, then as we were landing, about 20 seconds from wheels down on the tarmac, this pretty young greenhorn, skedaddled on into the cabin with explosive force, her face white as a ghost, screaming hysterically "Cap'n John, there's an emergency, and you can't land this plane!" Well I took this all very seriously and immediately pulled out of the landing, much to the chagrin and surprise of the good folks at the tower at DFW. When we were finally at a safe distance from the airport and in a holding pattern, I looked at this poor girl who was in tears now, and asked her what was wrong, what happened? She looked at me tears streaming down her face and said "I'm so sorry, but I forgot to turn the lever to let the wheels down on the back of the plane, and almost killed us all! I promise I'll never do it again!" Well we all took a moment to look at each other and realized that we'd put ourselves in this ridiculous situation, and laughed so hard we all had tears in our eyes too."

At this point, I did too.
"Well partner, it's time I got to the business of flying bigger and better things … but I'll see you on a flight some day."
With a pat on the back and a slow walk on out of the restaurant, he was gone from my life again … just like that.

"Then there were two" a familiar voice said from right in front of me … but sounding like it was a million miles away. But he was right; there were now only two of us. I looked at him for a while, Mike, one of my best friends, and one of the best human beings you'd ever meet in your life. He was in a suit and tie, and had lost some weight since I last saw him. I didn't know what to say … I mean all the other people at the table had had a chance to live out their lives to some extent or another, but not Mike. Here was a guy that was one of the best examples of humanity that I had ever known. He would have sacrificed everything he had to help anyone, whether he knew them well or they were a complete stranger. He always made you feel like smiling, and was one of the best damn performers I had ever had the privilege of seeing perform. Yet at the young age of 27, he was taken away in a senseless act of nature that stopped his heart in his sleep. He never had kids, or got married, but if anyone should have … it was him. I was speechless. He just looked at me, more somber looking than I had ever seen him in real life, even when he had his heart broken by his ex-girlfriend in college who decided she was a lesbian. Worse than that was the fact that he hadn't been invited to help her in this discovery.

He looked at me with grim, piercing eyes, reached out his had to me and said "Pull my finger."

That snapped me out of melancholy … he went on …

"No, dude, really … the longer you wait the worse the solution."

I reached out and pulled his finger … the sound as he farted and burped at the same time was almost ear shattering, the smell was worse. Everyone in the restaurant went quiet … all eyes were quietly judging me and Mike … sorry, Mike and I. After what seemed like an eternity of judging silence … everyone slowly stood up out of their seats, and began to clap! The clapping became more and more intense, until a monkey in a tuxedo came running out of the back room screaming, and slinging poo at everyone who was clapping, this abruptly ended their standing ovation, and all went back to their pre applause states, some with feces on their persons, as if nothing had happened. Mike smiled at me and said "Well that'll make you stop thinking about sex for about 8 seconds!"

"Hey!" I retorted, "That's my Grandfather's line!"

"I know" he said, "he told me I could use it … he's a good guy!"

I thought about this for a second … then I stopped thinking about it. I immediately shifted the conversation to more important things.

"What's the deal with the monkey?"

Mike just smiled, "Oh he's the manager. He can have a temper at times, but he's usually very pleasant. Just, if he comes by with our food … be sure to pat him on the head … it'll keep him from doing that again."

I was confused … but what the hell, it was about par for the course today.

There was always a question I wanted to ask Mike … the circumstances surrounding his death had always been a little bit hazy. I mean a perfectly healthy 27 year old goes to bed one night in his bed and just dies in his sleep from a heart condition? I know that's what his parents had said happened, but it never made sense to me, I mean there was always some question as to whether he had been using prescription drugs to self medicate himself … something he might have been crazy enough to do. He was more than just the guy who was drunk dancing on the table with the lampshade on his head … he was the type of guy that'd do it sober, and run electricity through a wire that ran up his spine to make it look like he had lit up a bulb in his mouth … just for a laugh. He was my friend, he was my hero, and he was a nut-job.

"So what did happen?" I asked.

He looked down at some imaginary paradox and concentrated really hard on it.

"What do you mean what happened?" I looked in his ocean blue eyes … he had a beard now … it looked cute, but I didn't swing that way.

"Mike … how did you die?"

He looked at me, a little tear forming in his eye (this was a very un-manly moment, the kind you only had with guys you were VERY close too, and never admitted to anyone, not even yourself sometimes) he answered me.

"I should have taken better care of myself … I, I should have maybe drank a little less, or not partied as much … maybe seen a doctor more often … fuck what am I doing here? I should be back on Earth doing a sitcom or something, this is insane!"

I interrupted, "so it wasn't prescription meds?"

He looked at me like I was speaking Klignon.

"What?" he said astounded.

"Well I just, I mean there was a rumor, I mean I know you didn't have health insurance or anything, and you worked at a clinic … and I just meant, someone said that maybe, uh you had taken something for your um … we'll say allergies, and that maybe that had killed you."

He just looked at me for a long moment,
then he started to laugh … hard, in between
his gasps for air, he talked to me …
"You mean … ha ha ha … you thought I …
ha ha ha … oh shit, oh Christ, that's
awesome dude! It might be the dumbest
thing I ever heard, but that's a way cooler
way to die than what really happened! Oh
man that's great! You always knew how to
cheer me up man … I missed that."
I felt so stupid … but relieved at the same
time.
"OK, so it was just … poor health then?" I
asked.
"Yeah", he replied, "just poor health mixed
with a crazy lifestyle, and an undiagnosed
heart condition."
  I could have used a cigarette or food or
something at that point, I felt like I needed
something to do with my hands, so I started
making an imaginary crop circle on the
table. "So, what happens now?" I asked.
"Now … we eat. Suddenly the manager
came leaping out, wobbling on his two hind
legs with two silver platters covered in silver
domes in each hand. He was grunting a
little, but as angry and disgruntled as he
looked, he took the utmost care in placing
the platters on the table. I looked at them,
one of them was labeled "knowledge" The
other one was labeled "nourishment".
Everyone in the restaurant stood up out of
their seats and turned their eyes towards me,

suddenly they all started shouting in competitive unison either "Knowledge" or "Nourishment" I even think I heard someone say "take the money" in the background, and I wondered if this was an option, as it sounded like an excellent choice.

I started thinking, albeit slowly as the contrary shouting got to be overwhelmingly annoying … this has to be one of these pre-college SAT style test questions, if I choose Knowledge I might get some sort of eternal wisdom that would help me ascend to a higher plain where I get to smoke great cigarettes and watch over my own planet, on the other hand I can take nourishment and live out a satiated and happy life with all the blissfully stupid things we all desire as human beings. That was sounding like the better choice … but then I blurted it out … "I'll take them both Alex!"
Everyone broke out into applause, and cajoled me with reassurance.
Mike looked at me with wide eyes and said "The monkey's name is Pete!"
I looked over to see a very angry monkey, his arm cocked back in a position of fling! He was ready to strike at me with all his fecal might! Then I remembered what Mike had said earlier and I reached over and patted him on the head.

All the anger immediately went out of his face … he even smiled a bit. He then gestured at me to hold out my hand.

"OH WOW!" Mike said, "He wants to give you a gift! This is a rarity, I'd take it!"

So I held out my hand, and he gently placed the poo inside of it. All I could do was smile … god I wanted another cig. He then looked at me intently in the eyes and made a flinging motion with one hand, while pointing over to a table occupied by what I can only describe as giant lime Jell-O molds, with eyes and ears.

"What the fuck." I said, as I proceeded to fling the poo with all my strength at the family of Jell-O molds, hitting one of them dead on, and splattering it on all the rest. I don't know if this upset them or not. As they didn't seem to have much of a face with which to make an expression, and they didn't seem to really even notice what I'd done. All I knew was that the monkey … er, Pete, was rolling on the floor laughing his ass off. When he finally stopped laughing, he came up to me, and with a deep Clark Gable sounding voice said,

"You're all right kid!"

Then he slapped me on the back and went out of the room, grunting and howling as he left.

Mike looked at me amazed and said "The monkey has spoken! The monkey never speaks. You must be very special."

40

I couldn't decide if by special he meant stupid or just unique … either way, I just shrugged and said,
"Whatever."

I looked at those two platters and contemplated in silence which one to open first … as if to answer my question for me, the platter labeled knowledge, spoke … or rather something with a Scottish accent spoke from inside it.

It said, "Ach man, are ye goin ta open me today, or should I wait another lifetime in here?"

With this new information, I did the only rational thing I could, I opened the platter labeled "Nourishment" first. In it was a pot of tea, with two tea cups, sugar, cream, honey, and of course dog biscuits, finally in the corner was a pack of cigarettes, labeled "God's Holy Smokeless Brand Cigarettes."

"Huh" I said, "smokeless cigarettes, what will they think of next?"

Meanwhile, the other platter continued to issue a stream of curse words, which I assumed, were in English, but with such a heavy Scottish accent, I couldn't be sure.

Mike looked at me and said bewildered, "Well, aren't you going to open it?"

I looked at it, looked at him, and nonchalantly answered, "No … not yet."

Then calmly through a stream of incoherent insults, I picked up the pack of Cigs, took off the wrapping, packed the

41

cigarettes, pulled one out, watched it light up, and took a drag. It was incredible … I felt the nicotine going right into my blood, I felt the smoke come into my lungs, but it never exited my body, though I felt it leave. Man, Cigs after death are the best … they taste better, smell better, and you don't have to worry about cancer. Then out of my nicotine induced glee, I remembered the insulting silver Scottish platter of knowledge. I place my hand on it gently, took a moment to look at Mike and said, "Now I'm ready."

I slowly pulled the lid off the platter and lifted it to reveal, a very angry Scottish terrier. The smell was immediately apparent (anyone who's ever owned one of these dogs will know what I'm talking about. It doesn't matter how many times you bathe them, they still have that Scottie dog smell.) I immediately recognized the dog … it was my old pet dog growing up, appropriately named Angus … we had a limited sense of humor in my family.

"Angus?" I asked.
Like I said, I was sure it was my dog, but Scottie's all pretty much look alike, so I wanted to be sure.
"Aye laddie, It's me." He said.
Then he walked up to me and licked me in the face … his breath hadn't changed either. I took another drag; that was better. He immediately started nudging the tea over

towards the other end of the table. He stopped after struggling for a couple minutes, looked up at Mike and said, "Well, are ye goin' te help or just watch an old dog struggle?"

Mike looked confused for a moment, then he leapt into action, moving Angus's bowl and the dog biscuit's to his place at the table. Angus went up to him, licked him on the face, and said "Good boy! Who's a good boy? You're a good boy"

I looked at Angus markedly confused. Angus just shot me a look back and said "What? This is the only example I ever had of how to reward good behavior. I'd rub his belly, except that I'd fall over in the process."

I thought about it … it made sense.

Mike and I reached out for our tea and biscuits. It tasted excellent, like a minty, fruity, bitter sort of taste, and with the honey and cream, it was positively delightful. The Biscuits were just as I liked them as well, stale and tasteless. I know that sounds weird, but I like stale tasteless biscuits, it reminds me of my first girlfriend … she was British.

Angus sat at the end of the table on what I can only describe as a really high booster seat. He began to sloppily lick up his tea. After we had all finished, I was amazingly still smoking the same cig I had first lit up. I looked at Angus as he sat there with his coal black eyes staring back and wagging his tail, and said "So what now? Is that it, do I have a few words with some dead folks from my past, and then have tea and biscuits with my long lost dog and deceased best friend, then what? Because I haven't learned much at all except just how ridiculous dead people can be in the afterlife."

Angus looked at Mike who looked back at him and just shook his head.

He looked back at me and said "Ach You humans are such funny creatures, you're so self important and you think that the entire universe depends on your existence. Well the truth is that you're just another cog in the wheel of the universe. Sure we need you, sure your existence is meaningful, but the truth of the matter is that your spirit is sent into a body, and if you're lucky you get 80 or so years to play around down on that paradise you call Earth. What you do down there is all up to you, but what you really need to do is relax more. Enjoy the wonderful life you're given. Stop wasting time worrying about how whether this moment or that moment is more important than the next, stop worrying about what people think of you, and for God's sake, please stop worrying about what other people do with their time on Earth … it's their business, not yours! Be kind to each other, spend time creating things instead of destroying them … in time you'll discover the true power of the human race lies in your kindness and creativity, not in your ability to wage war or get more stuff. Like it or not when life is over, you have to give all that stuff back, but all the things you did, all the people you helped along the way … that never disappears. I know, I know, it's easy to understand, but a lot more difficult to practice. I promise you, if you can live your life with joy, and just be happy no matter what happens, well then the rewards to you and humanity will be greater than your mortal existences can comprehend."

I never thought that the deepest conversation I'd ever had, would be with my dead dog and my deceased best friend in a diner at the end of existence as I knew it, over tea and biscuits, while smoking the most amazing cigarette I had ever had the privilege of smoking, indeed my existence was complete.

I looked intently at Angus, and asked him, "Why the Scottish accent, I mean, I get it, you're a Scottish terrier, but I'm half Irish, Half Italian, and I still speak American English …"

Mike put his hand on my forearm and said in Angus's voice "Ach Laddie, I dunno … this is after all, your afterlife, not mine."

I looked at Mike and Angus, not sure who to address and said, "That was a cool trick, freaky, but cool!"

Then Angus looked at me and said
excitedly, "If Ye want te see a real trick,
pick up that stick and throw it!"
"What stick?" I answered.
But as soon as I said it, the stick was there,
just as sure as if it had spent its whole life
there. I thought I knew what was coming,
and I was hesitant at first, but Angus's tail
was wagging so excitedly, and I figured,
why not … I mean, when will I get to do this
again? So I picked up the stick, from a
Silver Maple I believe, maybe an Oak tree,
but seeing as how I know absolutely nothing
about trees, it could have come off one of
those plastic Christmas trees in the mall for
all I knew; and I threw the stick as far as I
could. The Diner stretched out to
accommodate the throw, clearing a path for
Angus to run out for what must have been a
600 foot throw (maybe I'm exaggerating for
effect here, but it was a really long ways).
Angus plucked the stick up off the ground
and ran back to me as fast as his little legs
could carry him, the Diner returning to its'
normal size as he ran. He came up to me,
stick in his mouth, tail wagging, and waited
patiently for me to pull the stick out of his
mouth. He had always done that when he
was alive, he knew how to fetch something
and bring it back to you, but then you had to
fight him for it once you got close to him.
So I reached down like I had so many times
before and grappled with him for the stick

46

… but this time he seemed a lot stronger, and I closed my eyes and pulled really hard, only to feel the stick being jerked out of my … my mouth?

When I opened my eyes I was about a foot tall, standing on 4 legs looking up at … myself in black and white.

Without any control, I opened my mouth and said as Angus, "So laddie, did I fetch the stick, or did you?"

Then suddenly I was myself again, holding the stick, dumbfounded once again. This called for a new cigarette.

I lit my cigarette, or rather it lit itself. Mike said to me, "All right dude, it's about time me and Angus hit the road."

"See you guys back on Earth?" I asked.

There was an uncomfortable pause as Angus and Mike looked at each other.

Finally Mike spoke "Er, no actually. You see Angus and I have succeeded where most fail. We'll be moving on to another plane of existence."

I nearly shit my pants, and wanted to cry at the same time.

"What? Why?" I asked.

"Well" said Angus "We did live our lives like you should be living yours … carefree, and happy … in a sense, we won. But that's what we're here to tell you … you're so close to winning yourself … you just need a gentle nudge in the right direction."

"What are you talking about?" I asked.

47

"I'm sorry, our time here is up." Said Mike "I love you man … if you've been listening, we'll see each other again."
Then he gave me a hug, and Angus gave me a lick, and like that they were gone forever … well, Mike did pop in to say one more thing.
"The bill's been taken care, of … take your time man, but whenever you're ready, you can go."

Go where I thought … I wasn't sure of what I was supposed to do next. So I did what every good diner patron does, I sat there for a long time, and made up new drinks with the cream, sugar and honey, along with Tea refills that just magically appeared whenever I asked for them. I kept hoping that cute hostess would come back … but she never did. So eventually I just got up and left.

I stepped through the giant … I'm still going with Oak doors, which re-appeared where they had been in the first place, out into the churchlike marble floor, with a view that would make the richest person on Earth pee in their pants … then of course they'd probably pay someone to come and change their pants and clean the floor for them, but then I guess it's people like that who keep the economy going. Nich, my psychedelic octopus was there waiting like he said he would be … he was hitting on one of those lime jell-o creatures with eyes … I guess

48

beauty really is in the eye of the beholder. Seeing this reminded me … how did I manage to hold and fling poo and not have any on my hands … I decided it was best not to think about it … besides it wasn't really going to kill me, was it? Nich saw me, then looked at the Jell-O person and immediately spit on it … what I can only describe as a giggle came from the creature, and it immediately evaporated. I wanted to ask Nich about this, but I figured that like the poo, it was probably one of those things best left unspoken of.

I looked Nich in the eye and thought "Where to now?"
The answer appeared in my head, and within a few moments we were on our way back to God … with one quick pit stop at that gas station across the way from the Diner. The redneck looking guy that ran it got to talking with me … he was a cool guy, very well educated, but he never moved or looked up from the spot he was sitting. It was as if the smallest motion was too much for him to expend the energy for. His name was something very Russian sounding, and very unpronounceable to me, but he just laughed and told me to call him Gus, because it rhymed with gas … it didn't, but I didn't want to argue with him, so Gus it was.

As I watched Nich place a long hose into a place on his body that I'm pretty sure was someplace that you generally didn't talk

about in public … I started to wonder and
asked Gus

"So what's this place for?"

Without averting his eyes from the invisible
TV in front of him apparently running the
final episode of Dallas, and revealing once
and for all who shot J.R.

He said "It's a place to rejuvenate one's self,
it is a pit stop on the universal highway to
…" he stopped.

"To where?" I asked.

"Where would you like to go today?"

I hated all these riddles. "I dunno, I'm new
to this part of town." I said.

He just smiled and pointed out that I had
been here many times before, and would be
back many times in the future.

"Great" I thought," I'm at the cosmic
refueling station playing "Who's on first"
with a philosophical vegetable."

I think he sensed my agitation with his
philosophy, so he turned his head to look at
me, and stared at me as if he could see every
cell in my body individually and said,

"I have a gift for you, something that'll
change your life forever."

He held out his hand, and said "take it" his
eyes never leaving mine. I looked
apprehensively at his outstretched hand,
there was nothing in it.

"There's nothing there." I said.

"NO!" he replied in a voice that was
suddenly stern and reprimanding, yet still

caring. "It's there; you just choose not to see it. Now concentrate on what you really want in life."

Trouble was I wasn't sure of what I wanted in life. But after a moment, I started thinking about that waitress in the diner, I started really thinking about her, how beautiful she was, and how a life with her would not be such a bad thing to have. Actually the more I thought of it, the more I imagined, not just a night in the sack with her, but a life, kids, marriage, hopefully not in that order … except for the night in the sack thing.

Suddenly not only did it seem like a good idea, but the fear vanished out of me. For the first time I was clear on what I wanted out of life, and the more clear I was, the more his palm started to glow … brighter, and in a golden, hopeful hue … until finally I was filled with hope and joy and I saw the gift … a well cooked French fry.

"OK" I thought … "I guess fast food really is good for you then?"

I stared at it for a while and then tentatively took the fry from his hand, which was really soft for such a leatherneck looking guy. He smiled as he recoiled with great effort his body and closed his hand, he went back to Dallas.

"Who did shoot J.R.?" I thought to myself. Without looking up, Gus said "Kristen Shepard, who was played by Mary Crosby.

51

She was his sister-in-law and mistress who shot him in a fit of anger."

He paused and then added in "Everyone in the universe has watched Dallas."

"Huh, I'll have to be more careful what I think around you."

"It's all right, I already know everything about you."

I contemplated this for a while and then decided I didn't care all that much.

Finally I decided to ask out loud, as he didn't seem to want to read my thoughts on my next question.

"What is this REALLY, and what am I supposed to do with it?"

He smiled some more and said "It's REALLY a French fry, and unless I'm mistaken about your planet's customs ... you eat it. If you're wondering what it represents, which you are ... well you already know, you'll just have to realize its significance later."

"OK" I said, and popped the fry into my mouth.

To his credit; it was a really good fry! Nich came up to me, apparently having filled up on whatever ... wherever, grabbed my hand and we were off.

The trip back to God was as smooth, and as amazing as the trip there ... I was just disappointed that I wouldn't get to see all those places in person.

"Yeah" said God "It's a bummer for me too;
I rarely get to go on a vacation, although I
suppose I could find someone to watch the
place for a bit, but I have too much fun
here." I was back in God's home again, Nich
was off in a corner dancing again, and there
was God, sitting in his easy chair, smoking a
cigarette as usual, only he'd changed his
makeup … he didn't look so sad.
"So what now?" I asked.
He looked at me and said, "Now, you go
back."
Suddenly the clouds dissipated behind me,
and God reached his foot out to push me
back down to Earth.
I grabbed on really quickly to his foot and
said in a panic "WAIT WAIT! ONE MORE
THING BEFORE I GO!"
God paused, took a drag and said "All right,
but make it quick, Dallas is on."
I wanted to ask him about the significance of
the fry, but I was panicked and couldn't
think of the question, so I just blurted out the
first thing that came to my head
"Has the human race ever been visited by
aliens, and will they have a significant
impact on our lives in the future and did
they in the past?"
God just stared at me hanging on the end of
my foot with a look that said "You stopped
me to ask this?"
Finally he rolled his eyes and said, "Yes
they have, yes they will, but none of the

53

government conspiracy theories are correct.
The truth on that one will be revealed to you
in a few years. Goodbye!"

Before I could say another word, he
shook me off his foot and I fell, it was a long
fall, and I had a smoke on the way down.
Finally I hit the bottom, and then complete
silence and darkness, then light, then
cajoling and finally a blinding headache.
"Holy shit, he's alive!" said a familiar voice;
it was Walt the owner of the bar.
"Christ kid, you had a hell of a fall last
night, we thought you were dead, so I put
you in the back room to lie down, but here
you are alive and well!"
He sighed, "Guess I owe everybody five
bucks!"

The pain from the sound of his voice was
intense, it made me vomit.
I finally said "Wait, I had a severe fall, and
you just put me in the back room overnight?
What the hell Walt? What happened to
calling an ambulance?"
He looked at his feet and just said "Well, I
just thought that maybe you know …
hospitals scare me."
"Jesus!" I thought … then I reached into my
pocket and pulled out a pack of Menthols …
not what I wanted to see, but I guess it'd
have to do. I put one in my mouth and
waited … "Oh yeah"
I remembered, "I have to light them myself
now."

This last part must have come out of my mouth a little too loud.

Walt stared at me disapprovingly and said "Well look who's the new Queen of Sheba! Sorry I don't have a light for you princess!"

I just stared at him and said "I almost died here Walt, Gimme a break already."

"Yeah, yeah, come on into the bar when you're ready, I'll have someone get you something to eat."

"You're a Prince." I answered as he walked out.

I took a moment to straighten my hair, and my clothes in what was left of an old mirror that lay haphazardly against the old, wood-paneled wall. Something in that office smelled like it had died … wait … was that me? So I looked around, and on an old shelf that looked like it was held on the wall by nothing … I saw an old dusty bottle of Brut for men. I applied it liberally, and went out the door, which didn't really have a knob, it was just a metal rod that had been put into the hole where the doorknob used to be, and it pushed open creaking with ease.

The bar was well lit for a change, and dingy as hell, plus it smelled of stale beer and cigs … my kind of place. Still it looked different in the daylight, depressing, dank, quiet. I liked it better at night, when the darkness hid all its flaws. I'd never been here at … what time was it, 9:40 AM? I couldn't remember the last time I'd been up this early. I sat at the bar, I put out my cig in the Ashtray. Suddenly a beautiful waitress came out, one that I had never seen before … she must work days. Wait, hadn't I seen her before? More importantly, do people work days at bars like this, and if so, why?

Fuck she was beautiful … my heart was racing like a jet engine, where had I seen her before? She came out, smiled at me and put down a basket of fries. I took one out, put it in my mouth, and it all came back to me … the girl from the diner! The life I had imagined! The French fry! Holy crap this was my big chance, so I collected myself, and did the only thing I could do … I freaked out. My mind was going a mile a minute … faster even, what would I say to her? What was her name? Oh crap I can't even remember my name! She sensed my discomfort, grabbed my hand, with her incredibly soft hands, and looked me in the eye.

Suddenly I was calmer than a Buddhist monk at the sanctuary on the tallest mountain in the world.
She looked at me and said in that calm clear voice "I'm Julie."
All I could do was smile and thank God there was a bar in front of me hiding my erection.
I just smiled back and said "I'm Steve."
God Damn those were some good fries.

The Businesswoman

Susan Smith looked at herself in the mirror. Susan saw nothing … not that she was depressed, or some sort of fatalist, just that the mirror was fogged over. She tried to remedy the situation by cleaning off the mirror with the towel, but as she noted, the damn thing was probably wetter than the mirror. What she saw was a distorted version of herself, smeared by the lines of water created by the inadequate towel's tracks … exactly what she felt she looked like, an ugly, disgusting excuse for a human being. She wanted to smash her hand through the mirror, grab one of the broken shards and claw her face out until she looked like what she felt she was worth, but that would have hurt too much, and considering her line of work, it just wouldn't have been practical Susan shook herself out of it, "No time to wallow in self pity."
She thought to herself, as she continued her daily grooming ritual.

In reality Susan was everything a man could possibly desire in a woman … small waist, large bust, clean, long auburn hair with just a little bounce to it, and a business skirt suit that screamed, I'm in charge in bed! But this was the point, as Susan was a prostitute. Of course she preferred call girl … she was far too expensive to call herself a prostitute. Besides, prostitutes walked

around the streets at night, begging for a
John. Susan waited for them to call her, and
more importantly, she never walked … she
drove.

She was finished grooming herself by
8:30 AM, just enough time to sit down and
enjoy a nice breakfast and a pick me up
before her service called with today's
assignment. She walked into her living
room, which was almost exclusively
decorated by Pier 1 … one of her many
obsessions in life. It even smelled like the
cilantro citrus candle she got a few years ago
… it was her favorite scent, and when she
found out they weren't going to make it
anymore, she bought the rest of the stock
she could find, this basically meant that she
had an entire closet with a little over 100
cilantro citrus candles … which meant that
even when she wasn't burning them, the
house still smelled like them, and probably
would long after she had died … just the
way she wanted it.

Breakfast consisted of a tangerine coated
in fat free peanut butter, and a glass of water
with a multi-vitamin, she did after all need
to keep slim and healthy looking if she was
going to continue working. She sat down at
her black iron counter length kitchen table,
and admired the flower etchings, probably
done by some eight year old in a sweat shop.
In the back of her head she thought that this
should bother her, but she was after all a call

girl, if anything, they should be passing laws to make what she did legal as much as they should have done something to make what the eight year old did illegal, but oh well, "we all have to make a living somehow" she thought.

She pulled her citrusy peanut butter encrusted meal close to her, and positioned the latest issue of Healthy Happy Body Magazine up to the right of the plate … she liked things to be specific. The magazine was open to an article about how to lose ten pounds in ten days with ten simple exercises you could do in ten minutes. Interesting article she thought as she leaned down close to the picture of the smiling, happy woman who had just lost ten pounds and apparently gotten a six pack in the process, and proceeded to do a line of coke off the proud young woman's flat sexy abs.

"How's that for a weight loss plan?" she thought to herself.

"I can lose ten pounds in half that time you skinny bitch."

She then did a line off of the smiling woman's new, and obviously gay boyfriend's abs. "Wow!" she thought, "this is good stuff!"

She then proceeded to eat half of her tangerine, burp, and exclaim
"Well I'm full."

Then the phone rang, fun time was over, time to get to work.

The woman on the other end went by the name of Phyllis, and that's all Susan knew about her, other than she probably had smoked way too many cigarettes in her lifetime. Her voice was raspy as all hell … it wouldn't surprise Susan if the woman was 100 years old. All she knew was that Phyllis called gave her the assignments for the day, and she was expected to turn in a large percentage of her pay (35% in cash) in exchange for finding her work. The less people involved, the better was the company's philosophy. That way, when she got caught, they could keep doing business. A crappy arrangement to be sure, but she cleared about $10,000 a month tax free, so what was she complaining about? Then again, this was America, if she wasn't complaining, then she wasn't fitting in.

Only three clients today … what was the world coming too? An eventual end she supposed. Luckily one of them was a couple looking to spice up their relationship, they paid a little more, and they were usually grateful and tipped better. The other one was an old guy, it was a little gross, but they tended to get it over with faster, if at all. The last one was some young guy, which either meant he was new at this, and she'd have to do all the work for him, or he was some ass hole that would go forever just to prove a point. If it was the latter, she hoped he at least had a small cock … that way she could sit down later.

The day went pretty well, the first two clients were as she expected, the old guy just sort of laid there and stared at her, then she rode him for a couple minutes, and spent the last 55 minutes telling him he still had it … but he really didn't. The couple was predictable … mostly he wanted to watch his girlfriend getting it on with her, and mostly this is what she wanted because really she was just way too in the closet to admit it, and at least this way she could convince herself that she was still straight. Maybe she really did like guys too, Susan didn't really know, all she knew was that more than half the time they were lesbians, and the other half were usually at the end of their marriage. Of course she swung both ways, but really she thought of herself as asexual. She didn't really care who she slept with as long as they paid her. In fact she couldn't think of the last time she had actually enjoyed sex with a man or a woman. Not that she never had an orgasm, biology being what it was, it was bound to happen now and again, but usually it only happened with herself.

Susan was depressed, so what did she do when she was feeling down, she went to a bar and had a few drinks … and probably some more coke to take off the edge.

Wigglies bar was for lack of a better word, a dive. It was as if someone had taken an old wooden shotgun shack, cleared out everything from it, and put a bar and some tables with mismatched, dirty chairs in some random order into the middle of the room. She went right for the one against the wall in the far corner. She picked this seat for two reasons. First, if she sat in the same chair all the time, she could pretty much rationalize in her head that the only dirt on it was her own, and secondly … because Luke was sitting in the other seat. Luke was always there, and he was the best company a girl like her could want … a vegetable. Not to say that he was a large stalk of broccoli, it was just that after the car accident he got into a few years ago, he was only half the man he used to be. His brain was fried permanently rendering him with the intelligence of a 5 year old. He just sat there, and listened without judgment.

She sat down across from Luke and just met back his half vacant gaze. Most people would have assumed he was just high out of his mind, and that he wasn't in any way connected to what we call reality, but Susan knew better. She could look into his eyes and see a soul, just a little obscured by the clouds, but it was there. Besides, he was still cute. She asked, "How ya doin' Luke?"

He responded the same way he did to most of her inquiries … he just sort of leaned back smiled and laughed a little.

"Hi Susan!" he said.

She just smiled back at him and said, "Hey Luke, so anything new today?"

He answered, "Yeah, Tom Let me do dishes today, but I broke a few and he got real mad at me and I thought he was gonna hit me, but then he told me to go sit down."

"I see" she replied.

"So Tom isn't talking to you today?"

Another voice beamed in "No he's talking to him again, just got a little pissed off. But everything's all right now, ain't it Luke?"

It was Tom, Luke's older brother, and now sole caretaker. Tom sat down next to Luke and gave him a big pat on the back … about the most physical affection he was able to show another human being. Not that he wanted to take care of Luke, but seeing as how his parents were both dead, and managed care cost a surprisingly large amount of money considering how little a dive like this brought in, Luke was now Tom's permanent responsibility, dishwasher, and headache.

Tom Spoke, "Susie, come on by the bar, there's something I wanna talk to you about." "Sure Tom", she answered.

"Any way a girl could get a …"

Before she finished, he slid the beer he'd had with him over to her and said,

"On the house my dear."

He chuckled and wandered off to another customer on his way to the bar.

"Hi Susan!" said Luke.

Obviously the only conversation she was going to get out of him today was the dishwashing incident, it was more than most days … but less than she wanted to talk about with him. She downed her drink, and hopped over to the chair next to him.

"You take care of yourself Luke."

With that she squeezed his hand and gave him a quick kiss on the cheek. He laughed and smiled a little. While she was glad she had made his day, it made her shed a small tear, which she immediately wiped away as she swaggered up to the bar.

Tom while not at all unattractive, did not look like his brother, as he took after his father and Luke took after his mother. Tom slid her another drink, and started the conversation.

"Susie, it's been a couple weeks since I've seen you around here. What'cha been up too?"

Tom asked, but he knew the answer, and Susan knew that he knew, so she did what any self respecting call girl would do, she lied.

"Oh its terrible Tom, I had to single handedly fight off a band of wandering gnomes, armed only with a box of Keebler elves cookies, and a wad of used tissue. I nearly lost my house to the little buggers, but then a regiment from the Ethiopian army stepped in and turned the tide at the last minute. There was a lot of mopping to do after that, do you know that gnomes defecate where they stand?"

Tom just leered at her for a while.

"Right … that's about the dumbest lie I've ever heard, but creative … even for you."

She quickly responded "Yes, well that's the dumbest question I've ever heard. What do you want from me, the Truth?"

Tom stopped her, "All right, already … I get it, you were out saving children from collapsing bridges, no need to draw me a picture. Still, the truth would be nice once in a while, even if we both already know it."

She responded, "Oh Tom, I'll not let the truth screw up a good relationship like ours."

Tom just stared off into the distance for a while … drying a glass behind the bar, with a white apron on. Finally Susan broke the silence.

"You know Tom; you look like a stereotype when you do that?"

He looked straight past her … barely hearing what she had to say … she knew what he was thinking. She answered his prolonged stare again.

"Tom … TOM! Hey look at me … you've got to stop doing this … it wasn't your fault." He looked at her visibly agitated and said, "Yes it was ..."

She rolled her eyes.

"Oh my God Tom, how many times do we have to go through this ... the fact that you weren't driving wasn't your damn fault."

He snapped back, "Yes it was Susan, and you know it ... it should have been me."

He dropped the glass on the floor, shattering it into at least 27 pieces. Susan put down her drink and grabbed his hands, gently looked into his eyes and said,

"Tom, it could have been any one of you driving that car ... you know that as well as I do. It was just the luck of the draw. Besides, we both lost someone in that crash. I'm just glad it wasn't all three of you."

"Come work with me." Tom blurted out.

Susan rolled her eyes, "Tom, don't start this again. We've talked about it and ..."

He interrupted, "I know we've talked about it Susan, come on! We have this conversation every time we see each other ..."

"And I always say no!" replied Susan.

"Why not?" asked Tom.

Susan chugged down her drink and got up to leave.

"Goodbye Tom." Tom grabbed her wrist.

"Let go of me, unless you want me to charge you with assault!" Susan said.

Tom held fast and said "Sit down and talk with me or so help me I'll tell the authorities you're a whore."

"Fuck you Tom, go ahead, see if I give a shit."

Tom sighed "Either you sit down and actually talk to me for a change, or I'll tell my brother you're a whore every day, and I won't let you come in and see him no more." Susan looked at him like she was ready to kill.

"You do and I'll fucking burn down your bar."

Tom shook his head "No, you won't, and we both know it. Just sit down and talk with me."

Susan considered his words … as much as she had avoided this conversation, the truth is she would never do anything to hurt Tom and would die before she let anything happen to Luke.

"Fine!" she said, "But you're buying me another drink."

"Deal" he replied.

He poured her a jack and diet coke, a disgusting drink in his opinion, but it was her favorite, and he knew it.

"Well, I'm listening." She said.

Tom began his speech, one he'd rehearsed over and over in his head, but never was able to get out, because Susan always left after the first sentence.

"Susan, you're too good to be selling yourself. I mean you're as good as family, I love you and you deserve better … you always were better than all of us. I'm sorry about the accident, I know you don't blame me, but I'm still sorry … God damn it, it should have been me … not your brother driving the damn car."
Susan cut him off by gently placing her hand on his and gently said,
"Tom, I love you … it wasn't your fault, and it wasn't your brother's fault … it wasn't even my brother's fault."
Tom looked at her, this was never an easy subject, he poured a shot of whiskey and downed it, otherwise he was going to cry, and damn it, that just wasn't an option for him. "Susan … I … look let's not play the blame game here. We both know whose fault this is … and he can rot in jail for the rest of his life for all I care. I just … look you can work here, the money isn't bad … hell maybe we can turn this place into some sort of Asian themed restaurant, hire Korean Sushi Chef's, clean it up …"
Susan laughed "That's about the dumbest idea I've ever heard. What sort of yuppie trash would want to come to a restaurant like that?"
Tom laughed, "Whatever, you get the idea … just sort of clean it up. I mean it's not as easy as being a prostitute."
"I'm a call girl …" she interrupted.

68

"Fine, call it whatever you want, but I worry about you. I mean, what if something does happen … what am I gonna tell Luke? You know you're the only thing that makes him happy, I mean really happy … like in his soul … I can just feel it. When you're around, he's better; he remembers more … he smiles more. I don't know …"

He stared at Susan who was just staring at him with a blank stare.
"My turn?" she asked.
"Yeah go ahead Susan."
"Thanks Tom. First of all, I appreciate you giving a fuck about what happens to me, but I'm an adult. I make my own decisions. I'll be fine, I still love you and Luke, I don't blame you for my Brother's death, furthermore, I am not a whore, I am a professional, and I have an appointment to keep."
With that she gave tom a kiss on the cheek, finished her drink, and headed out. Tom just stared at her as she walked out.

It was six PM, Susan pulled up to the parking lot of the Come on In Motel. A crappy, and depressing collection of what passed for buildings rising into the sky a mere 3 stories, and having as it's crown jewel, a pool that was just big enough to swim in, if you were brave enough to swim in a greenish sort of sludge that passed for water. The rooms were cheap, dirty, colorless, inconspicuous, and of course for

rent by the hour ... one of the few things
that kept this place from being demolished
and turned into ... well another vacant lot
populated by homeless people and trash.
Although the trash seemed to take up
residence in the parking lot all the same. Of
course the same could be said of the
clientele who rented the rooms.

Susan sat in her car, a 1999 Honda
Prelude with all the trimmings, in her usual
parking space, and stared for a few minutes
... then she started to cry. The truth was that
she was sick of this ... she hated selling
herself. It was great at first ... lots of drugs,
money, and of course all the Pier 1 shit she
could ever want ... but it was like she didn't
feel anything anymore. Not that she
objected, it was a hell of a lot easier than
feeling pain ... but she'd had enough. She
wiped away her tears, took a deep breath,
and decided once and for all that this was it
... her last John. To hell with the agency,
and any physical harm that came to her
afterwards ... this was it.

Susan looked up at Mr. Snuggles, the
stuffed dog that sat on her dashboard as her
car's toy ... Susan believed that every car
should have a toy, it helped keep them from
being bored or lonely while they were
parked for so long by themselves ... and
asked, "What would you do Mr. Snuggles?"
To her surprise, the dog looked back at her
and answered.

"I'd just quit now. Go back to Wigglies and get a steak … you haven't eaten in a while … besides, the guy's probably just some ass hole cheating on his wife anyways, what's he going to do, report the agency to the Better Business Board or the local Chamber of Commerce? Come on, go get a steak … you know you wanna!"

Susan just sat there a little stunned and confused … her car's stuffed animal was talking too her … which meant she was hallucinating … this couldn't be good, she looked down at the radio and blinked her eyes a few times trying to shake it off without staring at the talking dog … the radio just looked at her and said

"Don't look at me … I think you should listen to Mr. Snuggles."

Susan took a deep breath.

"OK Susan … no need to freak out … it's not the first time you've hallucinated … that coke you did earlier must have been laced … plus you are a little hungry, and drunk … just take a deep breath, shake it off and go do your job … quickly."

Susan closed her eyes for a moment, and when she opened them, she stared at Mr. Snuggles, expecting him to say something … he just sat there, cute and lifeless … just the way she liked him.

Susan collected herself, and stepped out of the car … closed the door, and started to walk off, when she heard a muffled voice speak to her from inside the car

"OK Suzie, it's your funeral ..."

Susan didn't answer, she didn't look back, she just went up to room 27 and didn't look back, but she did find it remarkable that Mr. Snuggles sounded like Cheech Marion.

Susan's head was spinning, whether it was the hunger, the booze, the drugs or the fact that she was about to orgasm ... Wait, oh yeah it was the orgasm, not that the other things didn't help, but the reality of it all was that Susan was about to have a huge orgasm ... another sign that something was really wrong ... or right, whatever it was, this guy was taking too long. So after her head stopped spinning from the orgasm, she started to think about dinner. After all, it had been a long night, three clients, all of them wanting a couple hours each, and none of them thoughtful enough to buy her dinner ... drugs and alcohol, yes, but not dinner. Why was that she wondered, I mean they were going to get laid anyways, so why not pay for dinner, I mean it was cheaper than drugs and alcohol, and a lot of nights, more satisfying.

She figured tonight had been a decent enough night, and she wanted a steak, maybe a rib eye at Ruby Tuesday's. Were they open this late ... oh wait, another orgasm ... oh god this was a strong one, she moaned with pleasure. Her head was spinning. Wow that was interesting … man she was hungry, and it felt like the room was starting to twirl every which way, oh god again! Her heart was racing really quickly. Shit, maybe doing all that cocaine along with … she didn't know how many drinks she'd had, was a bad idea. I mean she felt sufficiently numb, and the orgasms may have tipped her to the level of feeling good for the first time in a while, but her heart wouldn't slow down. God damn, it was hot and cold here at the same time. Wow, she was laughing and screaming at the same time!

"Am I fucking dying?" she thought to herself.

"God I want a steak."

And that was Susan's last thought as a sentient being. Susan was now nothing more than a dead hooker.

As she left her body, she looked down to see her client … um, she wanted to say his name was Steve … well whatever it was he looked terrified. She didn't blame him, and for the first time in her life, she really felt sorry for one of her clients. Then she found that feeling suddenly leave her, as he turned over her dead body, and proceeded to finish what he was doing … fucking bastard!

"I hope your dick falls off" she screamed as she prepared to go … wherever it was she was going.

"At least I hope your wife finds out.

The Reckoning

Susan walked into a room, it was like a giant field in a domed stadium, the dome was a beautiful clear crystal with a hole opening up to the heavens, the sky above was magnificent, never had she in her life seen so many stars, and so many colors, well maybe, but drug induced hallucinations didn't count, of course she couldn't be sure that wasn't what this was, but she usually preferred to pretend it wasn't until proven otherwise. The ground was … bouncy, not like a moon bounce, but like the field at the University of Oregon in Portland, the one made of recycled rubber from all those old Nike shoes. Dead center in the field was … a man? So many questions rushed through her head. Was she dead? Was there a God? Would she meet him? More importantly, was that such a good idea considering the life she'd led? Would she ever get that steak she wanted? Do they serve steak in the afterlife? She imagined death would be a little scarier, more … well terrifying fire and brimstone. But she wasn't scared at all. As much as she'd "sinned" in her life, she had no regrets, no problems with the way she'd lived her life. No, it was something else she was feeling in her body … some familiar feeling, she couldn't place … oh wait, she had to go pee.

She approached the man in the field. He was just lying there, in a blue checkered pajama bottom, and a black tee-shirt. Just sort of staring at the sky and, mumbling something to himself … what was it? She couldn't quite make it out, it was a sort of … something, she moved closer, closer, and then finally she was lying next to him, although she didn't quite know how she'd gotten there. Just listening to him … he was counting … "three hundred twenty two zillion seven hundred and three."

"Oh!"

He stopped short and half jumped up.

"Shit I didn't see you there, I was just um counting the stars. I was almost finished. Oh well, I'll come back to it later. You really snuck up on me there, I must be getting slow in my old age … not that I'm old, really I'm just barely middle aged, but to you I must be like a gods age old!"

He chuckled at this for a little bit, maybe a little too long; Susan was definitely getting a little uncomfortable.

He said, "Uh, yeah, ahem … Susan, it's good to see you."

She looked at him for a few moments … he was a young guy, in shape but not a model. He had short cropped hair, blonde, with just a hint of grey … with a little stubble. He was cute … but certainly no one she'd ever met.

"Do I know you?" she asked.

He smiled a little smile, looked at her, and spread his arms wide, a little wider than

he should have been able too, suddenly a
bright golden light illuminated the
background, and seemed to light up the sky
as he floated into the distance, but never
seemed to get too far away, his voice
boomed out from the distance as a heavenly
chorus of thousands of angels rang out from
the distance, and he spoke with a mighty
voice.
"I am the almighty God, creator of the
heavens and Earth, Lord of the Universe as
you know it, the Grand master of the uh …
the … uh, whole big planet Earth."
He looked at Susan in the distance who
looked very confused and was saying
something, but he couldn't hear it because
he was too busy being full of himself, he
hushed the voices in the distance, and turned
around to reveal a cheap, plastic dimmer
switch behind him and he turned it down so
the glowing lights went away, and suddenly
the lighting was as it had been, and he
instantly transported himself back to in front
of her.
     "I'm sorry dear, what was that?" asked
God.
She just looked at him and chuckled a little.
"Am I tripping? Because if I am, I want
more."
God stared at her with a very judgmental
stare, but couldn't hold it very long, and
started to crack up.

"All right, all right, so maybe that was a little overkill, but seriously, I'm God, and you're dead, nice to meet you."
She looked at him quizzically for a moment, and then said
"If this is real then …"
God rolled his eyes, but not in a condescending way.
"Go ahead" he said.
Susan's face lit up like a schoolgirl, and she immediately lunged at him and began mercilessly tickling his stomach, to which God responded by squealing and laughing like a little girl. Susan jumped back and looked at God like her puppy just pooped on the new rug before it was scotchgaurded and said,
"Oh my … oh my …"
God just smiled and pointed at himself to which she simply replied
"yeah, exactly."

"Huh" said Susan as she stood there staring blankly at God's face.
"What is it?" he asked.
"Well, it's just that, I thought your nose would be bigger. I mean, not that I thought you'd have a giant honking Schnozz or anything like that. It's just that … well you are Jewish aren't you? I mean, far be it from me to stereotype here, but I've fucked a lot of Jews, and generally, they have big noses. Yours looks more, well like a roman statue."

77

God rolled his eyes and pulled out a box of cigarettes.

"Smoke?" he asked.

"No" said Susan, "That shit will kill you." God was in the middle of taking his first drag when she finished her statement and laughed so hard that he dropped his cigarette, and milk came out of his nose.

"Yeah, you're probably right, you should look after your health … you'll live longer." God continued to laugh, but stopped when Susan was obviously unable to detect the irony in his statement. God leered at her.

"Susan … you're dead … your health is the last thing you have to worry about. Besides this coming from a woman who eats a peanut butter covered citrus fruit for breakfast, and then proceeds to consume massive quantities of drugs and alcohol all day, while having sex with multiple partners … by the way that last guy was a real douche bag wasn't he." Susan just stared at him, then calmly removed the cigarette from his mouth, threw it on the ground, and extinguished it.

"I don't care" said Susan.

"Alive or not, I don't appreciate it when people smoke around me, and all mighty or not, you won't be smoking around me mister."

God just stared at her in awe for a moment then smiled and said

"Wow … I've been around for a long time, but this really is a first for me. I mean a lot of people disapprove of my nicotine habit, but you're the first person to actually stand up to me about it."

Susan rolled her eyes a little.

"Oh come on, you see a lot of people come and go, someone must have stood up to your smoking before."

God answered, "Actually no … I mean people have either been too scared, or too addicted to a lot of vices themselves to stand up and say something. Even if they do say something, it's usually kind of a weak rebuttal … honestly; everyone else is too scared of me."

Susan looked at her feet for a moment.

"Oh … right … sorry."

"No, no! Please don't apologize! I appreciate that you aren't a candy ass."

Susan looked at him confused, "You know, I've never been real big on the Bible, but for someone so revered in society as morally superior, you sure do talk a lot of smack."

He answered, "Yeah, I know it. Thing is I'm a lot older than the Bible, or any of those other holy books you people seem to have prescribed yourselves to in recent years … really, most of that stuff was made up by a bunch of uptight pessimists and oligarchs to try and scare you in to doing what they tell you is right … it's a pretty good form of mind control, kind of like self help books, but older, and with better sales!"

"Wait a minute" said Susan, "So what you're saying is that religion is crap?" God thought about this for a moment and then said,

"No ... religion isn't crap per se ... it's just the way people choose to practice religion that's crap. People focus on the negative ... they get overzealous about following the instructions as written, as opposed to thinking outside the box and applying it to the world around them in a way that corresponds with the time and the society you live in at the moment."

Susan thought about this as God put his arm around her in a non-threatening, brotherly way and walked her out of the stadium into a city street lined by magnificent Baobao trees and tall buildings made of crystal that stretched well up into the clouds ... they were beautiful, except that you could see into them, and people were doing some rather disgusting things. Finally Susan pushed this all out of her mind, and said the one thing that was on the tip of her tongue, and usually at the forefront of most people when they reach the afterlife.

"Am I going to hell?"

God sighed and looked ahead stoically, "Susan, I'm afraid you are, but walk with me, I'll keep you company along the way. You can ask me anything you want."

Susan looked a little devastated as the meaning of his words began to sink in.

Susan was quiet for a time, but finally said,

"Why? I mean I know I probably shouldn't have done all that prostituting myself out, and I guess getting more stuff from Pier 1 isn't exactly a great cause to dedicate yourself to while living out what little time you have on the planet, but ... I mean in my heart I was always a good person. I cared about a lot of people in my life, and hey I probably could have made something of myself, except that you took away everyone I ever really cared about, well ... almost every one, and then the rest were either damaged beyond all repair, or just ... well there are a lot of people that are seemingly going to live forever that I strongly feel should no longer be living on the planet Earth ... that's all I'm saying."

God looked at her as they were walking together and said,

"Susan ... you are a good person. As far as the drugs and prostitution ... I don't really care about all that. You want to have sex for money then I say more power to you. If you want to do a butt load of coke and then wash it down with LSD and alcohol ... well not something I'd suggest doing, but really, I'm not concerned with that ... it doesn't define whether someone is good or bad. If I took that approach I'd have to bar people with incurable diseases as well … drug addiction is a sickness too. I don't fault you for being sick. I don't care that you had sex that was premarital, or homosexual, or with multiple partners. If I judged people based on those criteria, I'd have to ban most of the human race … and the people that did get in would be fucking miserable and boring as all hell to live with. I mean seriously, the restrictions you people put on yourselves with sex are mind boggling to me. You're one of three species that you know of on the planet that loves to have sex, and you've found ways to make it so that you can do so with very few consequences to yourself and others, but yet you choose to limit the number of partners you have. Do you realize how many people on your little planet are suffering because they're homosexual or more often Bi-sexual and are afraid for their lives to admit it? I'd say that only about 25% of the Earth's population falls into the category of truly straight, or truly gay. The majority of you have been blessed with the capacity to enjoy anyone with a pulse, and yet you beat yourselves up over it on a daily basis, suffering alone in silence along with almost everyone on the planet! Hell, from the first humans, all the way up to almost the end of the Roman Empire in Europe had sex with tons of people, and there some of my best friends! No dear, I'm not taking you to

82

Hell because of all the things you think you did wrong in your life."

"Well then, why am I going to Hell?" Susan asked with tears in her eyes as they approached a large building at the end of the street that was clearly marked with a big sign that said "Hell" on it. Susan was almost hysterical now sensing the inevitable

"Tell me why? Huh? I mean you're such a great and powerful being, and you claim to live and accept people for what they are despite all the things we think of as sins, yet here we are, at the gates of Hell, and you proclaim to love and accept me? Yet you're ready to throw me into the bowels of Hell all the same"

"Susan" interrupted God.

But Susan snapped back "No, ass hole, I'm not finished here, and if you're going to throw me to the mercy of Satan, then you will hear me out!"

"Susan" God tried to interrupt …

"NO! You will not interrupt me! You got that?" she screamed.

God just looked at her with indifference and sat down on a bench that happened to line the streets of wherever they were, and smiled a little.

"OK, fine" he said.

"Speak."

Susan was livid now.

"You!" she said!

She proceeded to walk about in a violent rage, but never hitting anything. She looked like she had something profound on the tip of her tongue, but never once did she utter a coherent word. Just a lot of F bombs and the S word ... Stupid ... and finally after shed paced back and forth enough to wear a hole in any new plush rug, she just collapsed in front of him in tears, and said one word through her angry sobs and sniffles.
"Why?"
God placed a loving hand on her shoulder, got down to her level and said,
"First of all, Satan is my pet dog ... actually his name is Santa."
Susan couldn't help but laugh a little through her tears as god smiled at her and said,
"I know it's OK, laugh ... it's just one of those weird historical inaccuracies that you people write down as scripture and then take at face value ... but if it makes you feel any better, he has been a very bad dog ..."
Susan laughed out loud at this one, still crying through her laughter, still not able to lock eyes with God.
" ... and finally, and this one is the kicker ... Hell is a family style restaurant ... I like to take people I think have suffered the most on Earth there for a nice meal before going on ... really, it looks like a palace inside, and the food is great, and the service is ... well the service isn't so great, but I kind of

84

like that … I mean, who wants some ass hole bugging you about your drinks every five seconds, or asking if the food is good? It's probably great food, but I can't enjoy it because they won't fucking leave you alone and let you eat in peace! You know what I mean?"

Susan looked at God right in the eyes, she was no longer crying, but her face was red and wet still she laughed a little and shrugged off the last of her tears.
"Can I have a steak?"
God embraced Susan and said "Of course you can dear, and they make the best White Russians here … but if I recall you're more of a scotch girl yourself right?"
Susan just nodded with her head buried in God's shoulder.
"Jack and diet coke."
God embraced her as she sobbed a little, calming down now
"That a girl, it's all right."
He looked her right in the eyes and smiled.
"That'll teach you to believe everything you read in the Bible."
She laughed, to which he responded by looking at his watch.
"Oooh! I forgot, it's Wednesday! Wednesday is bingo night in Hell! You should partner up with me. We could win a lot of cash?"

Susan just looked at him a little dumbstruck.
God replied by looking off to the side,
pouting a little, patting her on her shoulder.
"Right ... no bingo,"
Susan and God both got up, and went
through the gates of Hell arm and arm,
smiling. Susan said to him as an
afterthought, "You're paying right?"
God answered "Yes dear, this one's on me."
Susan chuckled a little, "Actually that
wasn't a request."
God patted her on the hand "Of course it
isn't dear ... of course it isn't"
Susan smiled and said "I like you, you learn
quickly."
The inside of hell was a little bit comical ...
imagine if you'd gone to the most upscale
Manhattan hotel, and gone to their roof top
VIP lounge, and it had sweeping views of
Central park, and those people they put in
the bathroom to hand you towels, soaps, and
for a little extra will wipe areas of your body
clean that are usually only exposed in a
bathroom. Imagine all that and more ...
grand marble walls, with frescos painted by
Michelangelo himself hovering above you in
such brilliant detail that it looked like God
himself would reach out from the painting
and hand you a latte ... in fact Michelangelo
himself greeted them at the door, apparently
this place had been kind of run down and in
faded glory until he died and made himself
the King of Hell.

Imagine all that opulence, and grandeur … except imagine that it houses one of those cheap, chain restaurants that you go to when you want sterile, overcooked food in family sized portions for one … the kind you go to when you don't really want to impress your first date, but you don't want to appear too cheap. To make it even stranger, in the parlor across the way was a group of very attractive men and women, naked, sitting on leather chairs, with cheap plastic card tables in front of them … playing Bingo. Imagine all this … and you'll know what hell is like.

Michelangelo greeted them (he was somewhat shorter than she'd imagined, but then he was Italian).

"Hello and welcome to hell! I am Michelangelo, please come this way, I seat you! Your usual table Mr. God?"

God replied, "Yes Mike, that will be fine, but how many times do I have to tell you, it's just God … my father was Mr. God."

Michelangelo smiled as if oblivious to this last comment, looked at Susan.

"And you Miss, this must be your first time here … so, what you think?"

Susan looked around in wonder at the elegance she was surrounded by.

"Wow! This is amazing … it's so beautiful."

Michelangelo suddenly got a little sour with her.

"Of course it looks nice, I decorate it! You ever been to Florence?"

87

She nodded in disbelief.

"Well I decorated that too, and it's beautiful, so of course this place is!"

Susan leaned in to whisper in God's ear "What's he so worked up about?"

God leaned in and said "He means his hair … he's a little bit touchy about it … expects everyone to notice or he gets pissy. He is one of my favorites, but sometimes I just want to smack him."

Susan quickly scanned his hair … it was kind of a reverse Mohawk bouffant style, but dyed purple … she was going to lie and say it was brilliant, but instead she told the truth. "It's hideous. I hate it … not that it isn't creative, it's just that it's … well … overkill." She unconsciously pulled away waiting to get smacked by one of the masters of the Renaissance.

Michelangelo came right for her, and gave her a huge hug and kiss.

"I love this one" he said.

"She is so honest! It is crap … everyone tell me it look good so I keep it like that, but it's crap! I need to just cut it and let it grow out, natural, like when I was a young man. Oh for you tonight I serve the Michelangelo special, on the house, no argument! And for you Mr. God, I get the usual."

God tried to correct him on his name again but, Michelangelo scurried off to the kitchen as giddy as a school boy.

88

God Said, "Wow! You really made an impression on him! Most people get to the hair part, and they tell him it's brilliant and he just sort of fades off after that. See, I told you that you were special."

"Well ..." said Susan.

"... I try. So, what is the Michelangelo special?"

God kind of grimaced, "Um, it's a ... well it's a little like fish and chips, but with baby squid instead ... it's kind of gross, but the chips are great!"

Susan put her hand on God's, "Well it isn't steak ... but I love fried squid almost as much."

God stared at her as if she really were from Venus.

"I guess I should have known that about you, but ewww ..."

Susan just smiled, "Don't worry, I won't make you eat any of it."

God reached out to shake her hand.

"Deal!"

God wasn't kidding when he said the service wasn't as great as the food was ... it took an eternity for the food to come, at least God said it had been an eternity, but at the same time, time was irrelevant up here. In the interim they talked about the meaning of life, why bad things happened to good people, and all the irrelevant things that everyone wants to know, but really don't need to ask. What it all boiled down to was that Susan couldn't know the meaning of life, because to know it would make life pointless … he suggested reading the book catch 22, and bad things happened to everyone because there really weren't, with the exception of seven people in history, any good or bad people, just sort of grey people, which spurred the topic of aliens, which of course were real, but none of them looked like Grays. When the food got to them, Michelangelo waited to see what she thought of the squid and chips, and when he saw how much she liked it, he proposed marriage, but she refused, which he said made him love her even more because he already had four wives and two husbands, and marriage was really just a pain in the ass anyways.

After what was a pleasant meal, and a fairly deep but pointless conversation, Susan asked "So, I'm guessing you didn't just bring me here for squid and chips, and whatever it was you ate, right?"
God smiled, "I had acorn squash and a trogledorf stew … it's, well it tastes a lot like chicken, anyways … no, that isn't why I brought you here. I brought you here to play Bingo, but you said you didn't want too so …"
Susan rolled her eyes, "All right, all right, I'll bite. Let's go play Bingo."

90

They both got up to go play Bingo, but God put his hands on her shoulders and gently pushed her back into her seat.

"Actually, no … I'm going to go play Bingo, you are going to sit here and wait."

"But!" Susan Started.

God replied with, "No buts, Just stay here … trust me; you're exactly where you want to be."

A few minutes passed, Susan played with the remnants trogledorf stew, or as she liked to call it, the chunky brown mush. She even took a bite of it. God was right, it did taste like chicken. Then a man came over to the table, he had on a dark brown trench coat, with a grey pinstripe suit, and a fedora to match. He sat down, took off his jacket, and removed his hat … it took her a moment to recognize him … it had been so long since she'd seen him like this, but after a quick but careful examination, she realized it was Luke.

Susan stammered for a moment, taking in the enormity of it all.

"Wait … what happened? I mean, you aren't dead yet? Are you? How long have I been up here?"

Luke just smiled at her and said "I'm not all the way here. It's sort of a transitional phase. My body still has life in it, but my mind, and with it a lot of my essence, are dead. They have been since the accident."

Susan shot back, "So you knew I was coming here then? I mean you got all dressed up ... you look hot."

Luke Just laughed with a little shy grin like he used to do, what seemed like a lifetime ago.

"I wish that were true ... Oh, but for the love of God I wish it were true, but to be honest ... I wasn't expecting you."

Susan looked at him, a little confused.

"So why are you here?"

Luke blushed and was almost unable to get the next few words out.

"Well, I ... I'm here for ... that is ... I'm here to show you the desert menu. You see Susan, I work here."

Susan was shocked, she didn't know what the bigger surprise was, running into someone who wasn't dead yet in the land of the dead, or the fact that even after you died, you still had to work. Ultimately she didn't care, she did the one thing she'd wanted to do for years, but had always been afraid to do ... she came up next to Luke and gave him a huge kiss on the lips. Only to her surprise, she passed right through him ... as if he were a hologram.

He responded, "Sorry love, my physical body is still on Earth ... I'm just going to have to wait until it fades away ... it's really a waste."

Susan burst into tears, slow at first, but then hysterical after she noticed Luke trying to comfort her … only to have his hand pass awkwardly through her head.

"It isn't fair … it just, isn't fair." said Susan. Luke looked her in the eyes and said "No it's not love, but it isn't forever … and I'm here, even if only partially … and we can talk, for the first time we can talk."

Susan laughed a little through her tears.

"Yeah I guess so … you're not too upset about it."

"Oh believe me love, I'm balling my eyes out right now, and my brother is trying to figure out what's wrong … one of the weird quirks of my situation … I feel everything, but I can't express it … physically anyways, although I can still laugh, and I thank God every time he comes in here for that. But regardless, this isn't forever. Our lives are short, and my body will die … eventually." He smiled, "Hell, with you gone, Tom just might kill me."

It wasn't really all that funny, but Susan found herself laughing because it was all she could do to keep from crying.

Susan found herself ashamed, not that she hadn't felt ashamed over the past few years since he died, all the things she had reduced herself too. But the constant influx of drugs, booze, sex and shopping had pretty much numbed her to really being able to comprehend what she'd done to herself all these years. She threw up … it didn't make things any better that Michelangelo was there when she did. She was sure he'd take it personally and throw her out, but too her surprise, he simply snapped his fingers, and a robot, not unlike the one the Jetsons had came out of the closet and zapped the mess away, then without a word, he came over and hugged, her, gave her a kiss on the cheek.

He said "Don't be sad … those who have suffered the most, deserve to be the happiest. Please, I know it's hard, but try to be happy, at least pull yourself together for your other visitor."

Susan looked at him confused, "What visitor?"

Michelangelo blushed and stammered, "Oh, I guess he no tell you about your other visitor … it's a surprise."

Realizing she was trying to have a private conversation, he quickly extricated himself off to greet another party coming in the door.

"Luke" said Susan, "I'm so sorry … I've … the things I've done. I mean, oh God you probably already know, I mean I told you everything … I just thought."

Luke raised his hands to stop her.

"I know Susan … I know. Look, I don't care about any of that shit. I mean, you were suffering. I guess I just wish you'd gotten over it before now, but I mean … there wasn't a day that I didn't want to just tell you it was OK. So I guess I will now. Susan it's OK, I forgive you. Not that you need forgiveness, but if it makes you feel better ... then I forgive you."

Susan gave a weak smile, "Thanks."

Suddenly someone kicked the chair out from underneath her, she quickly regained her footing and turned around, ready to kick the living shit out of whoever did it ... but just as her fist pulled back about to pounce, she jumped on the man and gave him a huge full body hug. It was her brother, standing in front of her, alive, young, and beautiful.

"Oh my God Bevon ... I can't believe, I mean I believe it, but ..."

Bevon laughed out loud, "I know Suki, I know."

They embraced for what seemed like an eternity ... Susan didn't care; it felt like the first thing that had really gone right in many years. Finally she let go and looked him in the eyes ... he was crying a little and holding her shoulders.

"I'm sorry Suki ... I'm so sorry."

She kissed him again, "It's OK, you were always kicking my chair out from under me, in more ways than one. I used to find it annoying, but ... well nothing could have made me happier."

Bevon started, "Suki, I ..."

Susan shushed him "Shut up, and sit down." He wanted to go on, but instead, he just obeyed and sat next to her.

"It's good to see you Suki."

95

Susan hated this nickname, but as long as it was coming out of Bevon's mouth … it was OK.

Susan took a long hard look at the two of them … it had been so long … too long since she'd seen them … well at least alive AND well. Susan spoke first
"Wow … all we need is Tom to show up and it'd be just like old times!"
She noticed that no one was smiling,
"What?" she asked.
Luke answered, "Love, if Tom were here, he'd be dead."
Susan turned red, "right … I guess that would suck … but it'd still be nice to be together again."
Bevon laughed, "Yeah that would be nice. How is Tommy boy doing these days?"
Susan lied, "He's doing well!"
Bevon frowned and said, "You're lying … I could always tell. His life is shit isn't it?"
Susan kept quiet; Luke spoke up, "Yeah pretty much. These days he pretty much spends most of his time cleaning up after me, and then trying to clean up after a bunch of drunken rednecks."
"And the rest of the time he spends trying to fix me." said Susan.
"That's because he cares about you, he knows you're suffering, and really, you're the only family he has left that can speak in complete sentences, and recuse herself to the

bathroom, before extricating her bowels."
said Luke.
Susan laughed a little too hard at this.
"Sorry Luke, you're right, it isn't funny."
Still she continued to laugh.

Time passed, they all ordered food,
Susan had steak, as she now had room for it,
and they caught up on old times and pretty
much made complete asses out of
themselves. It was marvelous, but as all
conversations you have with people that
have been dead for a while, someone had to
go and blow it, turning the conversation to
an awkward place … namely Bevon.

He got very quiet and looked down at his
mostly empty plate.
"I'm sorry Suki … I really fucked
everything up."
Susan looked at him, confused, "Sorry for
what?"
Bevon answered "I just … I mean … the
accident. I'm sorry I fucked up your lives."
Susan stared at him; Luke looked like he
suddenly had to go pee.
"You fucked up our lives? That's the most
ridiculous thing I've ever heard. You saved
Tom's life, and well, at least part of Luke's,
hell you're a fucking hero … if anything,
I'm the fuck up here. If I remember right,
you didn't want to go, and you were the only
one with a working car, but I pushed you …
I made you go out, thought you needed it.
Fuck if I'd just kept my mouth shut, we'd all

be having this conversation with Tom at some other Bar. Luke and I would be married, Bevon would have settled down … eventually, I'd be a successful Lawyer, Luke would have gotten his editing business off the ground, and Tom … well Tom would have … huh, you know I'm not sure he would have ever amounted to much, but he sure as hell wouldn't be as miserable as he is." "No!" said Luke, "This is my fault … Bevon wanted to go earlier, and I insisted he stick around. I was convinced we could get him laid that night, but instead we all got shitfaced drunk while he sat in the corner sucking down sodas and quietly cursing us." Bevon slammed his fist down, "No! God Dimmit I was the one driving and I should have been more careful, I saw the guy coming, and I had just enough time to pull over but … I didn't."

A familiar voice chimed in, "Once when my son was young, I sent him to Earth to help people out but he got nailed to a cross, and I could probably have stopped it, but I didn't." There was a long silence as God's words sunk in … finally Susan piped up. "Awkward …"

God pulled up a chair that wasn't being used from the table next to them.

"The point is, there is always something else you could have done … but ultimately we are responsible for our own actions, and how they effect everyone around us is not really in our control."

Bevon clearly wasn't satisfied with this answer.

"Bull shit … if you could have stopped him from dying, then why didn't you?"

God was silent, "I begged him to let me, I almost did save him … it would have taught those idiots a lesson … but that wasn't the point. Free will has to prevail, regardless of the consequences. If my son hadn't died, then an entire religion wouldn't have come about."

Susan burst in "A lot of good that religion did; all those idiots who for centuries inflicted pain, war and damaging legislation upon a population that never did anything wrong in the first place."

God didn't have to think about this for very long when he said, "But that isn't my fault … or my son's for that matter. In any case, you don't realize what the alternative would have been."

Everyone just stared at him.

God went on, "Wow … after all these years you still aren't much closer to getting it are you?"

Susan interrupted, "I think I get it … you mean that had we not done all these terrible things to each other, we wouldn't have gotten where we are today."

God lit up a cigarette, rules and company be damned he needed one.

God said, "Susan, Bevon, Luke … let me enlighten you for a moment on the grand plan if you will … I gave you free will, and religion, not so you'd worship me and be good little Christians, Muslims, Jews, Hindu's, and Buddhists … and all the other ones I'm leaving out, but the list is too long. I did it more, oh how do I put it? So you'd worship yourselves. Not in a narcissistic way … the religious order of Wall Street does that quite well, and it doesn't really work. It's more like … you are all responsible for each other. When you each learn to value each other's lives as if they were your own, then you'll get it. Until then, you don't have to create a mythical hell full of fire and damnation … you're already there."

They all nodded in agreement as if they understood, and to some degree each one of them did, but Susan, having lived the life she had for so many years was the only one that really did.

God took a deep drag of his Cig, and as if by magic, when one was done, another was in his mouth and lit.

"The saddest part is that you've almost gotten there so many times, and had so many leaders that were willing to show you the way … Jesus, Siddhartha, Cicero, Aristotle, Muhammad, Moses, Nicheren Daishonin, Gandhi, Martin Luther, and later Martin Luther King Jr., Mother Teresa, hell the list goes on and on, but you either call them crazy, kill them, or make their lives miserable until they die. Many of them choose to come back and help again, even though you choose to make their lives fucking miserable, but hey, whatever. You don't even get that Earth is a beautiful home, but you choose to make it a prison … fuck, the universe is so much bigger than you all think! Don't you people fucking get that!?"

At this point, God was shouting like a lunatic, and it was starting to disturb more than just the people at the table.

"I'm making an ass of myself again, aren't I?" he asked the three of them.

Only Susan had the courage to touch him gently on the hand and say,

"Yes … yes you are."

"Right" said God as he put out his cigarette on the table and stood up.

"I'll fix this …" suddenly he shouted to everyone at the restaurant "everyone's meal is on me! And Mikey, throw in a drink or desert for whoever wants one, will ya?"

Michelangelo smiled came over to God and gave him a big kiss on the lips and said "thank you beautiful."

He walked away to fulfill the orders of many now satisfied customers. Everyone at the table looked at him a little funny until he got nervous and said,

"What? I really love that guy! Really!"

While Bevon and Luke just shook this off, Susan smiled and took God by the arm and said, "Now what big guy?"

God Just smiled at her, "well if you want, I can love the two of you later on in my private quarters."

God winked at her, "But I'm pretty sure you've had enough of that kind of love for a little while."

Susan laughed "Yeah, maybe just for a little while, but um … don't give up on a girl."

It was Susan's turn to wink at God.

"OK, OK" said God, "Say goodbye to these two, we have to talk."

Susan turned and gave a huge hug and kiss to her brother, who preceded to pick her up and squeeze her as hard as he could while laughing.

"Oh Suki you always were a little gullible."

Susan just laughed, "Maybe, but I always got what I wanted from Mom and Dad."

She turned to Luke and said, "Well, I'd give you a big hug and kiss but, well …"

"No worries" he answered, "just take care of yourself, OK?"

She laughed, "Sure baby, but I'll be back for lunch sometime … promise."

He half smiled, yeah … I'd like that, and maybe someday we can hold hands and talk at the same time."

Susan smiled and said, "It's a date."

She left Hell feeling lighter and happier than she ever had. And her and God walked out into the darkness, and past the beautiful crystal city, out into a field that should have been pitch black, but it was lit by so many stars, planets, and other heavenly bodies, that she could see the color on the purple flowers that surrounded the clearing they walked out into.

In the middle of the field was a huge red and white checkered blanket with a little picnic basket sitting in the middle. God held her hand and brought her over to the blanket, and they both lay side by side, eating exotic cheeses, and drinking a sweet desert wine, just staring into the stars.

"It's really beautiful … thank you." said Susan.

God just grinned, "Well you deserve it after all, it's been too long since someone has taken you out and treated you like a human being for a change."

She pondered this and wanted to cry, but just answered, "Yeah, I'd almost forgotten what that felt like … thanks."

She started to chuckle "and thank you for not smiting me oh mighty smiter!"

They both laughed hysterically at this.

Finally God broke in "No problem … thank you for understanding me … it's rare that someone does, which makes me sad to say what I have to say next."

"What's that?" asked Susan.

"You have to go back."

Susan spat out the chunk of cheese she was eating, and it landed on God's PJ pants. "Wait, what? You want me to go back? To that? But … but"

Susan stammered on, but at the same time she kind of wanted to go back.

"Don't worry about Bevon, or Luke, I promise I'll take care of them, I wanted you to see them so that you knew they were OK. I have an important task for you … take care of Tom, and what's left of Luke. They need you, but I really need you to be there for them, understand?"

Susan looked up into the sky almost lost in the magnificence of the sky above her. "Yeah, I get it."

Susan was sad, she wanted to talk more, she wanted to eat at Hell again, she wanted to cry, but she didn't. She just looked off into the cosmos, and watched as the universe flew around her like a perfectly tuned watch … flying hither and thither, putting her into a trance like state, until she passed out. God sat up, kissed her on the forehead and held her hand, and gently said "Susan … Susan, Suzie, please wake up, please. I just, I don't know what I'd do without you. Truth is, I think I love you, but I guess that just wouldn't be right." There was a long silence, followed by the sound of pinging, and the sound of air being pressed into … into her lungs. Susan suddenly felt very uncomfortable, and even a little bit in pain.

Her eyes opened, all she saw was light …
and it hurt, a lot! Everything was blurry, she
couldn't quite make anything out. Then as
things started to clear up, she saw what was
a sort of greenish, cream colored room, a
hospital room, she was hooked into some
sort of machine, an IV tube was stuck into
her arm. She tried to speak, but she had a
tube shoved down her throat, which made
speaking impossible. Instead she called forth
an enormous amount of strength, and
squeezed the hand that was grasping hers,
the man who was holding it suddenly sat up
and nearly jumped all the way to the ceiling,
before bursting into tears and coming in
close to her and said,
"Suzie, oh Suzie!"
He kissed her on the forehead, it was Tom.
"Oh thank God" he said, "We thought it was
all over for you, they wanted to disconnect
you last night, said the chances of you
waking up were slim to none … but I
wouldn't let them … oh it's so good to see
you again. Luke, Luke! Wake up! Suzie's
up!"
She looked to her left, and out of the corner
of her eyes she saw Luke, or at least the
crippled version she had become
accustomed to. His eyes burst open, and he
clapped and laughed at the same time, his
hands and legs flailing about so much that
Susan thought he'd fall off of the chair.

Tom calmed Luke down a little and walked
him over to Susan
"You hold her hand for a minute; I'm gonna
go get the Doctor."
Luke held her hand, smiling, with that semi-
vacant look in his eyes.
"Crap, I overdosed" she thought to herself.
"So this was all just a weird trip … oh well."
In response to her thought, Luke suddenly
looked completely in control of himself
again. He stood up straight, leaned over and
kissed her gently on the cheek, then
whispered in her ear.
"Trust me love, it was more real than what
you're experiencing right now."
A tear rolled down Susan's cheek, she
wanted to tell him how much she loved him,
but she couldn't, he just sat down, squeezed
her hand, smiled.
"I know" he said.
Then, as quick as it had come, his eyes were
vacant again, and he had that stupid grin on
his face he so often got when Susan was
around, but he never let go of her hand.

The Doctor ran in with Tom, and a
Nurse, he ran a few tests, started to ask her
questions, unhooked her from the machine,
and well a whole bunch of other stuff, she
couldn't really remember it … all she
remembered was Luke Holding her hand the
whole time. Tom took her home, and took
care of her and Luke at her place … partly
because he wanted her to be comfortable,

and partly because her place was a whole lot bigger, and cleaner.

As soon as Susan had recovered, she took the advice of Mr. Snuggles, and gave up the whole prostitution gig. It wasn't easy, the agency threatened her a few times, but she'd been prepared for this, she leaked a little information out to the press and the media about a few of their medium profile clients, and threatened to let out the real juicy stuff if they wouldn't let her go. She wasn't sure if this would have the desired result of them letting her go, or them killing her, but it really was a moot point, as the agency owner had a heart attack and died right after she had released the information. After that, they pretty much left her alone.

Susan never stopped loving Luke … even if he was only half alive, he was still the love of her life … not that Susan believed in such nonsense … but if it were true, then Luke was the proof. Pretty soon Luke and Tom moved in with her. She had always found it hard to be around Luke before, but now, since her near death experience, it actually comforted her. There were many nights that she would sit with Luke and talk about her day, talk about the new Hardware store that she and Tom had opened up together. Talked about how much she missed him, and read stories to him, sometimes kids books, Luke had always liked Dr. Seuss, even before the accident. They used to read them together and act out the books together, and then make love. It was weird … but it was something uniquely theirs.

After a year, Luke died from complications related to the accident. Apparently there was a tiny piece of metal that had lodged into his body, and over the year it travelled through his system, eventually travelling to his heart, and killing him … or at least his body.

At Luke's funeral, Susan thought she would be sad, and indeed she would miss Luke's company, but she found her tears were tears of joy. She knew that somewhere Luke was whole again, maybe he had even gotten a better job than at Michelangelo's restaurant … "Not that there's anything wrong with your restaurant" she mumbled, seemingly to no one.
She knew he'd be happy, and hopefully he'd be able to move on. As time went on, something else started to happen … something she didn't expect. She started to fall in love with Tom. This brought her even greater pain than Luke's passing, but as far as Tom knew, she was still mourning Luke's death, so he gave her space.
One day Susan was in her car … well her new car (actually it was her old car but she'd had it painted and detailed with flames on the side … she knew it was silly, but it was always something she'd wanted as a kid), the hardware business wasn't too bad for

them, especially since they'd distinguished themselves by decorating the place like it was Halloween all the time, and playing heavy metal all the time. It became known as the Hard-Core Hardware Store ... but officially it was Tom's Hardware.

She was sitting in her car, and contemplating leaving it all behind ... Tom, the business, her whole life as she knew it. She was planning it all out in her head. She'd leave a nice note, and take a suitcase full of stuff, and move to Montana, where she could just disappear. Live out the rest of her little life, away from it all. But then she heard a familiar voice call out.
"Susan ... you're being stupid, and more than that, you're being selfish."
"God?" Susan cried out!
But it was just Mr. Snuggles ...
"Holy crap" Susan thought, "I'm relapsing."
"No Susan, you're not relapsing, and this is God. I like to speak through Mr. Snuggles, we go back a long way, which is actually a story for another time ... the point is, I gave you back your life so that you could take care of Tom and Luke. Tom has done nothing to warrant your disapproval. Why would you leave?"
Susan was in tears now "Because I love him ... I can't love him, I love Luke. What the fuck is wrong with me?"

Mr. Snuggles was quiet. Susan picked up
Mr. Snuggles and started screaming at him,
"Talk to me Damnit!"
Another voice suddenly came into her ears,
this time from the teller window of the drive
through at Mr. McBurger Barn.
"Ma'am, your number 7 with a large drink?"
The teller handed her the bag with the meal
while staring at her like she was some sort
of pariah … it was her favorite … not that
she ate fast food much, but when she was
really upset, this was the thing she loved …
Luke had introduced her to it. She wasn't
sure how she'd gotten here, but she wiped
away her tears, and took the meal from the
scared teller, and thanked her, then realized
after a long pause that she had to move
along … there was a line after all.
Susan pulled into the parking lot; she picked
up Mr. Snuggles and tried numerous times
to get him to talk, unsuccessfully. But the
words rang in her ears … she had been
given her life back … and then some. But
she still wanted to leave. She started to eat
the meal, and calmed down some. Her hands
were greasy, and she reached for the
obligatory giant stack of napkins they
always gave you, even if you did only use
one or two. She noticed that one of them had
writing on it. It was a note from Luke.
It Read:
Susan,

First, I love you. There has been no greater joy in my life than my relationship with you, both before the accident, and after. Your love and companionship have made my life complete. Second, move on with your life. I'm not just asking you too, I'm telling you too. I won't love you any less, nor will I begrudge you for loving my brother like you loved me. I want you to be happy, and I promise you I will do the same. Remember, love is eternal; we will be back together, someday. For now though, my brother needs you, and you need him.

God explained this to me, and helped me write this letter, he explained that there is more than one person out there for everyone, in fact there are about 1000 people that would make great matches for any one person, and this is by genetic design. If there was only one person out there for every other person, people would just die and be miserable, and since they accomplish that quite well on their own, this is one less excuse they have to be miserable. At the same time, there is such a thing as a soul-mate, and yours and Tom's Soul-mates have both passed on ... you're both waiting for someone, but it's important you live out your lives, together. Be happy, we will be together again.

Love always,

Luke

Susan considered the implications of this letter for a long time then looked at Mr. Snuggles.
"Thanks." She said.
She then proceeded to wipe her face with the letter and stuff it with all the other trash into her McBurger Barn Bag.

She went home that night to find a fairly distraught Tom who was watching TV and rocking back and forth. Susan checked that he wasn't watching the news and an arsenal of nuclear weapons or anthrax was heading their way. When she was sure of their immediate safety, she sat down to look at Tom. She wasn't sure what to say to him.
"I love you, marry me and let's have 2.5 kids together!?"
It sounded cheesy and sudden. She sat there for a long time trying to come up with the right words … but nothing sounded right to her.

He just eyed her suspiciously while she stared at him … seemingly waiting for him to say something, finally he blurted out, as if it were all one word.
"Yesterday I drove your car and … and the stuffed dog, I mean Mr. Snuggles said I should ask you about what you thought of the napkin at McBurger Barn please don't send me to the hospital I swear it really did."

Tom then squished himself up, preparing for Susan to take him to a place where they had white walls and a nice staff that smiled nervously around you all day long. Instead, she sidled up close to him, looked him in the eyes for a moment, and proceeded to kiss him, and for the first time she'd kissed someone since Luke's accident, it felt amazing.

Ben Jacoby and God

Ben Jacoby Strolled into O'Grady's bar promptly at 5:30 PM. Just like he had yesterday, the day before, and ... well just about every day since he could remember, except for weekends, he worked half days then, and came in early. In fact he worked just about every weekend to make up for the work he wasn't doing after work. But as long as he made up for this extra, unpaid work ... no one cared much.

O'Grady's was an Irish "themed" bar. It had once been owned by Gracie O'Grady in the 1880's, and passed down to 3 more generations of O'Grady's ... surviving wars, depression, downturns in the economy, hippies, coke addicted yuppies, and punk rockers only to be bought out by a Korean family, the Kim's, and since making it an Japanese Sushi restaurant didn't play well in this part of the Midwest, and changing the name to Mr. Kim's Irish Pub, or O'Kim's was just plain silly ... they just kept everything the same. Yep, same bar, same seats, same pictures, same floor, same light bulbs, and same dirt that had started to accumulate since the day they bought it. In fact, the combination of the last two factors was extremely helpful, as the lack of adequate lighting, combined with the evenly distributed layer of dirt gave it the illusion that it was cleaned from time to time.

114

Ben took a moment, strolled up to his usual place at the bar, right next to the TV, and the electronic gaming machine, the one he considered a complete waste of money, but used every night all the same. A nice young lady strolled up to him, she was Korean, and a little younger than him, she had brilliant almond eyes, and her hair was short and cropped into a pony tail. She was wearing one of those silly shirts with a clover over it to make sure you remembered that this was an Irish "themed" restaurant, he didn't mind too much because she had a nice rack on her, and the shirt hugged it enough to make him forget his day even before he started drinking. It made him think for a second that "maybe the clover on her shirt was lucky. Not that it mattered anyway, much as he might love Korean culture, and adore Korean women, he'd learned a long time ago from the Kim's that unless his name originated from a province in Korea, and "Lee" didn't count … he didn't have a chance.

She tossed down a paper coaster with a popular Irish beer logo on it and said in a very American accent, "What can I get you cutie?"
He smiled and chuckled a little, "You're new aren't you dear?"
She answered, "Yeah, this is my uncle's place and he said if I did really well at taking care of the place, he'd look at letting

me buy the place. Although honestly, I'm not sure who else he'd sell it to, his kids are all degenerates."

He pondered this for a second and asked, "From one generation to the next, but still an Irish Pub?"

"Eye laddie!" she shot back with an accent that sounded more like a bad mix of Scottish and English than Irish.

She went on, "I know it's weird, and I'd love to try making some changes around here without upsetting the locals too much, maybe paint, clean, and change up the décor a bit. But for now, what can I get you cutie?"

He chuckled again, she was cute.

"I'll have a vodka tonic with a lot of lime wedges, followed by a few of those popular Irish "themed" beers. Just keep them coming until I need a cab, or someone can set up a cot out front."

She hesitated for a minute and said "Oh … OK."

He answered her somewhat startled look with, "I'm a regular here sweetheart, you work here long enough and you won't even have to ask me anymore … I always have the same thing."

She didn't say anything, just looked at him for a moment, maybe too long of a moment, sighed, and then went to make his drink.

    The night progressed a little, he watched some TV, long enough to know that the world was still depressing, and that in some far off land that he'd always wanted to visit, but was too busy to go to … someone hated him and was doing their damndest to make sure the world knew it. Eventually sports came on, which was interesting for a short time, then his team started to loose, as usual, then they turned on Golf, or Tennis, or some other God forsaken second rate non-sport(even if soccer was the #1 sport in the world it didn't interest him any). Which by 8:30 PM led him to the game machine for ½ an hour, then he got to talking … it didn't particularly matter who it was (mostly because, while it was a different person every night, it was the same person on the same nights). Tonight was John Bacon's night. John was a tax lawyer at a local firm, and on a regular day he would be the most boring individual on the face of the planet, but after hours of drinking, to Ben Jacoby, he was one of the most interesting people on the planet.

"Tell me again, about uh the compound interest thing. Why is it (pause) is it so interesting, I mean why is it … so interesting, wait … that's not what I meant."

John would then go into a rant that is entirely too boring, and entirely out of the realm of understanding of the author of this story, needless to say, you could drink twelve Latte's, do five lines of coke, take some speed, and smoke crack for a solid hour, and it would still put you to sleep. But for Ben it was contact with another human being, something that was sorely lacking in his life, outside of any lifeless business conversations he had in the office. So for him, it was both fascinating and fulfilling. But tonight it wouldn't last, because tonight John Bacon (no relation to the historical John Bacon, the English Carmelite and theologian, born towards the end of the thirteenth century, but not to worry because in this part of the Midwest, the only history that was brought to mind at the mention of his name was a great barbecue from last weekend featuring, you guessed it, bacon) had to call it an early night.

Ben Pleaded with John, "Come on man … man on come!"
Ben laughed a little too long at how witty he thought he was being.
He continued, "I wanna, to hear about the shelter in the tax of people on the compound thing."
John sighed, he wanted desperately to correct Ben, but honestly, no one else listened to what he had to say with such intensity, in fact his wife encouraged him to come here every week, because she said he came home relaxed and was eerily better in bed after someone actually listened to him. Sadly though, he had an audit to attend tomorrow, at 5:30 AM … why it was so early completely escaped John's

comprehension, but he did what he was told, and got paid well for it.

"I'm sorry buddy, I gotta go. Duty calls" …

Ben burst out laughing.

"Duty calls, ha ha ha! That's funny man."

John stared at Ben, a little concerned for his mental well being, and a little appaled at how juvenile that last joke was.

Finally he said, "Right … see you next week."

And just like that, he was off. Suddenly, Ben was all alone.

This was strange, the bar never emptied out this early, even on a weeknight, it was usually 10:30 PM before it even started to clear, and here it was, 9:30 PM, and empty, except for him and the amazing looking Korean girl, Jenny was her name. He knew this not because he'd been hitting on her all night, or because he'd been involved in any sort of Semi-coherent conversation with her at any point. In fact, unlike most men, Ben became incredibly shy around most people after a few drinks. More so than he normally was, in fact no one really knew much about Ben, the only reason so many people talked to him, is because he listened so intently, even when he didn't understand or speak back much, he listened, and was even genuinely interested in what you said, even if it was a chemically induced interest.

Ben knew her name because at some point someone was hitting on her, and as much as he wanted to knock them out of their seat … he just listened. In fact he was fascinated from what he'd heard. Her name was Jenny, she was well read, and had a degree in business administration from Wellesley, but as she put it, the guy who was hitting on her wouldn't know Dostoyevsky from Dr. Seuss. Being an avid reader, this only fascinated him more, especially since he loved to draw parallels between the two authors. As much as he could be, he was in … well not love, but he was most certainly infatuated with this woman. Sadly he knew it would never work out, he was white, and she probably wasn't interested. So even though she was the only other person in the bar, and he was so drunk that he could have tried to pee on the floor, and all would have been forgiven, as long as he attempted to flush … he said nothing, and the dust continued to amass it's unchallenged army in the relative silence of something utterly disinteresting on the TV.

The silence continued, painfully so for what must have been hours, but in actuality it was 15 minutes. Finally the door opened, and someone came in. He wondered who it was, eagerly trying to see across the … well it would have been smoky bar a year ago, but with the ban on smoking, it was more of a cloud of dust. With all the nicotine the dust had picked up over the years, he was pretty sure it had the same effect when inhaled.

The stranger was a large, and hairy man, he had a scruff that could almost be called a beard, but was more like an unkempt soldier, just come back from the desert where he had been isolated for a couple weeks. He wore a long Tan Duster that nearly hit the ground as he walked, with what must have at one point been a nice dress shirt underneath. But now it was faded and worn, but not torn … just old, and to top it off, he had a pair of tight fitting jeans that looked like they had been taken right out of the late 50's. He was tall, lean, and a bit imposing.

Ben was scared for a moment, but when he came in and looked up at Ben, he no longer looked menacing, just peaceful, actually if you screwed up your eyes a little and forgave the short cropped hair-cut, he looked a lot like Willie Nelson. He walked straight over to Ben, pulled up a seat and smiled at him. Ben smiled back, and introduced himself. "Hi, I'm Ben Jacoby!" The man just looked back for a moment finally answering, "I know who you are …" There was an awkward silence as Ben just looked at this man he'd never seen before, but felt so close to … it was a little like his Mom had just come into the bar, except, this was most likely a man. Then the man realized something suddenly and said, "Hi, I'm God, good to meet you."

Ben just stared at him for a moment …
still smiling back at him … he wanted to
laugh, but he was a listener, and instead of
cutting off what would inevitably be an
interesting conversation, he just did what he
did best, accepted the world for what it was,
reached out and shook his hand, and
listened. God shook his hand and laughed a
little. "You see I know you too well, and I
knew you'd listen to me. That's why you're
one of my favorites. Still, I feel bad for what
I came here to tell you, so let me take care of
your tab tonight, and let's see … Jenny, my
friend here will have another Vodka Tonic,
top shelf Vodka please, and I'll have a …"
God seemed to suddenly be lost in thought,
as if he were pondering some great cosmic
mystery. Finally his thoughts coalesced, and
he came to a conclusion, "I'll have a White
Russian."
Ben just smiled for a moment, and then
spoke, "So should I call you God, or would
that be taking thy name in vain?"
God laughed at this for a while then said
"Ben, you can call me Larry."
Ben shot back with "And Larry when you
call me, you can call me Al! You can call
me Al! Na na na na …"
They both laughed out loud.
God continued, "Oh Ben, dear Ben you
always were funny without really trying to
be funny, and I want to talk more with you,
but time is short, so I'll get right too it. Ben,

I'm sorry to say this but, you're going to die tomorrow."

Ben was silent for a moment, then downed his Vodka tonic … though for a while.

Finally he said "In that case, Jenny, I'm going to need another one of these!"

She mumbled to herself so he couldn't hear "Why not, you've pretty much drank all the alcohol in the bar anyways."

God Started, "So, Ben … I know this is really weird news and all, and I'm pretty sure you don't believe me so go ahead ask me anything."

Ben thought for a second and said, "Well … Larry, assuming you are God …"

"I am" interjected Larry.

"OK sure why not" Ben answered, continuing, "My uncle was a transvestite that married a Vietnamese hooker and had a wonderful family and life in France, so I guess anything is possible."

God Chuckled for a moment and answered, "I liked your Uncle Shelly … although he/she and your Aunt were always a little disappointed that you never called him, her … I mean while Shelly was a Tranny, he really always thought of herself as … well a lesbian. I mean I know that's sounds weird and all, but trust me, there are a lot weirder, and more important things to worry about in the universe, and certainly on this planet. So … yeah, anyways, go ahead, ask me anything."

Ben absorbed this new information for a little while, this guy must be someone he knew, but from where? The fact that he knew about his Uncle … er … Aunt Shelly was too personal; he had to be either a family friend, or a French spy.

Finally Ben asked "OK, so you're god, and you said there are things that are much more important in the grand scheme of things … like what?"

God, pulled out a ciggie and it lit itself … Jenny either didn't notice, or didn't mind.

God took a while on this one and finally said "Cheeseburgers Ben … fucking cheeseburgers."

Ben stared at him for a moment and said, "What? I mean … what the fuck is that supposed to mean?"

God sighed and took a deep enough drag to finish of his ciggie.

"I know it doesn't make any sense to you now, but you people, or, my people I guess is a more appropriate term, have managed to create a perfect killing machine!"

Ben thought for a moment and then chuckled, "You mean because of all the cholesterol from the combination? Is it Mad Cow disease, or bovine Spongiform Encephalopathy … the Variant form of Creutzfeldt-Jakob disease?"

God smirked "No, no that isn't is … that's just to do with beef in general, and yes that one will cause more damage to my people in

124

your future than you know about, but that isn't it … you see, it has to do with CERN, and what they discover because of their particle accelerator … well that data along with the unique chemical compound of seasoned, cooked ground beef with homogenized cheese on it, creates one of the most devastating weapons known to mankind … or it will if you guys figure it out … which really you probably won't, but you never know, cheeseburgers could cause the downfall of this planet! Which would suck for me, because then I'd have to start all over again." Ben looked at him carefully for a moment, and suddenly the whole Willie Nelson resemblance was starting to make more sense as he wondered just what Larry was smoking … and where he could get some.

After some contemplation, all Ben could say back was "Huh … who knew! Can I have one of those Cig's?"

God thought about it and said "Sure, what the hell."

Ben took one of "God's Finest" in between his lips, and they began to tingle a little, and as he took his first drag, he felt elated, and well … sadly sober … but more relaxed than he had in a long time … possibly in his whole life!

Ben blurted out, "Wow, these are good!"

"Ben?" asked God

"Yeah Larry?" said Ben.

God replied, "Ask me another question … I don't think … well really I know you aren't convinced."

"OK, well this one is a big question … you ready?" asked Ben

"Is that the question?" asked God, "Because if it is, yes is the answer, but I don't think you're quite convinced yet."

"No, no" Ben chuckled, "What is your … I mean God's favorite baseball team?"

God Smiled "Wow, baseball is in my opinion the second greatest sport you guys ever created, next to soccer that is".

With this comment Ben started to doubt that this was indeed God.

God went on, "My favorite team is … the Toronto Blue Jays."

Ben stared at him in disbelief.

"The Blue Jays? You like the Blue Jays? What the … I mean seriously, what the fuck dude? Next to Kansas City they have to be the worst team in the history of the league!"

God shot back in disbelief, "What!? Are you Trippin? Look maybe I like the underdog? I mean, I still think that the Cubbies have a shot this year, but catching a game at the Rogers Centre is the best!"

"The what centre?" asked Ben.

"The Rogers Centre! Only one of the coolest ballparks out there! That's right you've never been. Man you don't know what you're missing!" said God.

"Sure Larry, whatever you say." said Ben.

126

An awkward pause passed between them. How could this be God? I mean … the Blue Jays were horrible. After a few swigs of his drink, Ben felt more sober than he had in a while.

"Huh … this drink must not be very strong." he said.

God replied "yeah."

The silence got more strained.

Finally Ben said "So um … tell me about Satan! I'm sure that's an interesting story."

"Oh you mean my dog Santa! That's a great story."

But God could see from the look on Ben's face that he wasn't buying it.

Suddenly Jenny interrupted them with, "so you want another sweetie?"

While the interruption was a welcome one, suddenly the sobering reality of Ben's current state of mind got the better of him, and he felt … what was this feeling … embarrassed, he was actually embarrassed to talk to someone.

He stammered, "I um I'll take another one of you … I mean I'll um … yeah sure, drink … good times."

Suddenly Ben wanted to shrink down as small as he felt. She stared at him for a moment then smiled.

"Be happy to get you one of those."

Ben being the pathetic dreamer, and completely inattentive to "Signals" from women just looked at her strangely, and said

"Thanks."

"Boy you really are an idiot" said God.
"Wow! That's the first thing you've said all
night that makes sense." Ben replied.
God looked at his watch a little concerned
and said "OK, I can see we aren't getting
anywhere, and since I wasn't kidding about
the whole dying tomorrow thing, why don't
I just tell you what you want to hear."
Ben stared at God a little dumbfounded and
slightly annoyed with this short haired
Willie Nelson Wanna-Be.
"Fine" said Ben, "Tell me what I want to
hear you hairy hippie reject."
God smiled and said sarcastically, "ouch
that hurts, but don't worry, I'll get you back
for that one. Let's start with second grade …
you peed in your pants at that after school
program one day while wearing those
ridiculous 80's super short shorts, you know
the shiny red ones with the stripe on the side
because you were too nice to bother the
recreation center manager, you know the
one, Russell with the afro/Jerry curl look
that even back then looked ridiculous. But
instead of admitting it, you cut your pee
stream off and ran to the bathroom before
anyone noticed. In 7th grade you had a thing
for that Indian girl Ellen, but you were so
afraid to talk to her that you sent her an
anonymous love letter that was so passionate
that you avoided her at all costs after you
wrote it, and when Henry Miller took credit

128

for it, you were so afraid of what she would say, that you let it go. They got married and had three beautiful children, and he isn't half the lover that you are but don't know you are. Then in high school you had such a crush on that Dominican girl Leela that you bought her expensive gifts for her birthday and Christmas, and were always there for her all the way through 12th grade, even though she dated that ass hole boyfriend Marcus, and obviously adored you, and was just waiting for you to stand up to him … but you never did. Finally in College you fell in love with a Korean exchange student and became great friends with her, even made out with her a few times when the two of you were drunk, but immediately folded when you found out from her family that they would never approve of the two of you together even though she was madly in love with you … but you just wanted to spare her feelings, and those of her family. Did I miss anything you stuffed suit, G-man wanna-be?"

Ben sat in stunned silence … every word of it was true, even if he had never really admitted it all to himself. When the ciggie ran out, God snapped his finger and produced another one, put it in Ben's unmoving and now very dry lips, and it lit itself.
Finally he spoke, "I get it now … it all makes sense … you're some sort of private

129

eye magician whose been following my every move for years and then psychoanalyzing me, who somehow hypnotized me to think I've been drinking alcohol, even though it was water so I'd sober up! It's the only explanation that makes sense!"

God just put his forehead down into his hand and shook his head.

"Oh for my sake's, you are the most skeptical, blind son of a bitch I've ever met. I don't suppose if I turned water into wine you'd believe me?"

Ben chuckled "of course not … it's all hypnotism Larry! Hypnotism and psycho babble!"

God thought about this for a long time and then came to the conclusion that in Ben he'd made someone who was both too smart, and too skeptical for his own good. "All right Ben, fine … don't believe I'm God … we'll get to that part later. For right now, we have an understanding that you know that I am very insightful into the events of your life, right?"

Ben pondered for a bit "yeah I guess so."

God went on, "Also, I haven't done anything to hurt you right?"

Ben answered, "Well starting off the conversation with "You're going to die tomorrow" felt a little threatening, but I guess on the whole you seem pretty harmless."

"OK" said God "Let's just go with the premise that I understand you, and that I'm here to help you, and forget the whole dying tomorrow thing … let's just say I care an awful lot about you Ben … and I want you to understand, that your life has followed a pattern that, well is self-destructive. Why not live like there's no tomorrow? What if there isn't? What then? When you meet the real God, what are you going to say to him or her, although I like the term it? I was going to live my life tomorrow, but I just had some drinking and work to do first? Fuck that Ben, time is short … you guys are lucky if you get 70 years of life, and even then not all of it is viable."

"soooo …" said Ben.

"Sooo …" said God, "Get off your overworked, drunk arse, and go live your life! Do the thing you have wanted to do all your life and stop waiting!"

Ben thought about what he'd said for a long time, boy these were good cigs.

"You know what Larry, you have a point!"

"That's the spirit" God replied!

"I'm gonna do it! I'm gonna go join the circus so I can learn to juggle."

God rolled his eyes.

"Ben, for once you're not listening … so I'll do you a favor and spell it out for you." Ben sat in confused silence; he'd always wanted to be a juggling carnie.

131

God took a deep breath and started "You are a passionate and caring man, who has never found love in this world because you're so good that you choose to cut yourself off from it, hence my earlier examples. You have a great heart, and deserve love at least once in your life. Do you think it's a coincidence that long after closing Jenny continues to serve you drinks, laughs at your … well quite frankly pathetic jokes, and just now when you slipped up and asked for "another one of her", she just smiled and took it …"

There was a pause as God tried to let this soak into Ben's head.

"So what your saying is I should go out and find a girl like Jenny, except more my type?" God banged his head on the table, then leaned in really close and talked directly to Ben in a way that no one had ever spoken to him, it was as if he suddenly became clearheaded, and understood every word this man was saying with complete clarity.

"Ben, Jenny is in love with you, she doesn't just like you, she isn't putting up with you, and she doesn't just find you somewhat amusing. She, in the span of a few hours, has met someone that inexplicably, she is head over heels in love with, and if you asked her to get married tonight, while she'd probably say no because that's just a little weird and sudden, she'd still go out with you because in her heart the answer to that question is yes I want to marry you and spend lots of time with you, and if you want, make lots of baby clones of the two of you. This is a rare gift, one which most people never get, or get once in their lives, but you … you stupid git! You continually get these chances, and ignore them, or cut yourself off … now get up, and go ask Jenny out."

For the first time Ben wasn't so sure this guy wasn't God … because he knew that everything he'd just said was not only factually true, but emotionally true as well … so like a man possessed, he nodded, put the ciggie out after a long drag, straightened out his shirt, and stood up to go walk over to Jenny, determined to ask her out. The only problem was that he was really dizzy, and only then did it occur to him, that despite all his clear-headedness, that he was in fact, hammered. But he was just sober enough to keep focused on his plan … to ask Jenny out, but just as soon as he went to the head and took a leak, and as if on cue, God reached out his hand to stop him.
"No Ben, Jenny first, then use the potty."
Ben was too drunk to argue with an old hippie who'd just used the word "potty" in a sentence, so he floated awkwardly over to Jenny and sat down at the stool right next to where she was standing. Suddenly his head cleared up a little, but the urge to urinate did not go away. So concentrating on not

repeating his second grade mistake over again, he looked right into Jenny's beautiful almond eyes, and she stared back at him eagerly expecting him to order another drink.

Ben started off "Jenny …" and she came back with "yes love?"
Suddenly it was too much for him to bear … he just blanked out, and suddenly wanted to just bolt for the little boy's room. He stammered a little, and then the right thing to say finally came to him … he said nothing; he just leaned over the counter, pulled her towards him and kissed her passionately on the lips. He'd kissed a few girls before, even had sex once or twice, but this was better than any kiss, or really anything he'd ever experienced. He felt suddenly calm, and coolheaded, but like he was floating, and his whole body just tingled with an electric current that vibrated between the two of them. And after what seemed like an entire lifetime, the kiss ended, but the connection didn't … they were both floating, and Ben asked her to marry him. She looked awkwardly at him for a moment, as if seriously considering the offer.
She simply smiled and said "not yet … but I will go out on a date with you."

Suddenly, and without booze, or despite it, Ben was happier than he'd ever been in his entire life.

"OK" he said, "It's a date!"

"Where are we going?" she asked.

Ben thought for a second about this and said, "I'll tell you when I get out of the Lou." This sounded more gentile than "potty" and less vulgar than "head."

"Hurry back Benji." she replied.

Quicker than he'd ever gone before while this drunk, he ran to the bathroom. But he stopped briefly and looked at Larry and said, "Thanks God … you're the best stalker, private eye, hypnotist, Supreme Being, hippie in the world. I'd say more, but I have a date with the head, and then with the lady, so see ya soon!"

With that he ran off.

Without Ben hearing it God frowned and said "Sooner than you think."

Ben rushed awkwardly to the bathroom, and looked at his 2 choices, the urinal that went all the way to the ground, or the one that was just slightly too high for his happy wiggler to spray down upon. As usual he chose the low rider. He took a look at his watch; it was 2 minutes past midnight, better hurry. In a mad fit he pulled down his pants, afraid that he was too drunk to trust that he'd have the time or coordination to pull his worm out of the hole before the little hoser spouted off its yellow stream of wisdom. When he was finished draining the lizard, he felt more exhilarated than he had in his entire life. As he bent down to pull his pants up, he lost his balance, and being that he was standing just far enough from the toilet, his head managed to come down hard against the toilet handle, which knocked him unconscious, and flushed the toilet at the same time. In fact he hit the handle so hard that he broke it so it was stuck in a position where it wouldn't stop flushing, an unfortunate circumstance, as he passed out face first into the urinal, and drowned in the very water that was meant to do good, and clean out the pisser for the next customer, and at 12:10 AM the following day, as Larry had promised, Ben Jacoby was dead, face down in a flushing urinal, his pants still not pulled up.

The only thing he could think before he completely blacked out was, "I wonder if this is how Jimmy Hoffa died."

Sadly the world will never know.

Ben opened his eyes to see … well nothing at first.

"Holy shit … am I blind?" he wondered?

He answered this thought by saying, "Damn, if I'd known I was going to go blind after an accident Like that, I'd have masturbated a lot more."

Then suddenly he heard a familiar voice cry out, "Ben?"

Ben paused for a long while, and then he said "Mom? Please tell me you didn't hear all that stuff about masturbation."

Suddenly her face started to come into focus a little, just a little, she looked more like a fuzzy round blur than his mother.

Timidly she said, "Sorry dear, but I did."

There was a long pause as Ben thought over the implications of his Mom, who incidentally had been dead for almost 7 years now, having some firsthand knowledge of his personal "Sexy time", and just when he thought things couldn't get any worse she had to speak up.

"Well there's nothing to be ashamed of, everyone does it! I did it all the time …"

"Mom, please stop." He shot back.

She politely answered him, "Well it's true! It's a natural thing, and your father god bless him wasn't great in the sack."

Ben tried desperately to stop her, "OK, well if I wasn't sure if I were dead before, that just killed me!"

"Sorry Benji, I forgot how sensitive you get sometimes." She answered.

He pleaded, "Mom, please don't call me Benji, it's so demeaning."

She shot back "Well I always thought it was cute."

He stopped her again, "Mom! Can we just have a serious conversation for once!"

As Ben said this he sat up, and his vision returned to normal, although he wasn't sure for a second as he jumped back in a bit of a shock as he saw a very young, and scantily clad version of his mom sitting on a bench.

It wasn't really the scantily clad, youthful, and oddly arousing nature of her appearance which gave him a start (although this was quite disturbing to him), no ... it was the shocking fact that she was wearing a planet of the apes mask on her face, and not the kind you get from a corny drug store with a plastic smock painted like it was some sort of outfit they couldn't replicate cheap enough in China to mass produce it ... but the kind you saw in the movies. Which was arguably just as cheesy, but scarier because its lips moved.

"Mom What the fuck!" said Ben.

To which she replied, "Give your mom a kiss!"

After declining a kiss several times, both because of the hideous ape mask, and the fact that the younger version of his mom, was giving him a hard on, Ben was finally able to fully grasp the fact that; A. He was dead; B. he had died by tripping and falling into a urinal ... not even a toilet, but a urinal; and C. he was pretty sure he was in Hell. He pulled up on an old bench which seemed to be made out of an old, milk chocolate brown, milk crate. It even said in big red letters on the side "ilk" with the "M" scratched out. "Mom ... why am I here?" asked Ben.

"Because Ben, you fell in a urinal and drowned." his Mom replied.

Ben rolled his eyes and answered, "Yeah …
OK, thank you captain obvious, but I mean
on a sort of spiritual level … what was the
point of it all?"
She answered, "Well, I never really figured
that one out while I was alive either, but
having been up here for a while, I think it
was to be as happy as possible and to help
others do the same."
Ben just stared at her for a long while.
"Wow, pretty good insight for someone who
was drunk most of the time."
She shot back, "Yeah, I guess we have that
in common … Drunky McDrunkdrunk!"
As bewildered as he was, what happened
next made him freak out even more. His
Mom started to laugh uncontrollably, and
her head started to expand like a balloon,
filling the room, and shoving Ben against
the walls of the room. Suddenly her head
exploded in a deafening roar, although he
could still hear her laughter.

Then the heavens opened up, and he was
surrounded by one of his worst childhood
nightmares. He was in heaven, floating atop
clouds, which stretched into hilltops, and
mountains, and it was filled with people
from the planet of the apes, and even as he
started to cry out, the next part of his
nightmare came true … in unison, they all
started singing ala a Sondheim musical in a
chorus of "Apes, apes, apes, apes …"

Over and over, while in the distance a lone baritone sang "We're apes, we're gaudy apes! Capable, of many apelike things! We came to this world, and the people we enslaved, yes we're apes! We're MANLY apes!"

For the first time in Ben's existence that he could recall, he was truly terrified. He realized that his earlier intuition was in fact a reality.

He screamed out "OH MY GOD I'VE DIED AND GONE TO HELL!"

Then suddenly he was snatched up and transported … by some sort of sticky rubber hand that came out of the sky, stretching seemingly from a kid's hand off into the heavens, it suctioned on to him, and then recoiled, flinging him into space faster than he had ever experienced … and he looked down, and saw a sight more beautiful than anything he had ever imagined … he was floating through the cosmos … there were stars and galaxies, entire universes being created and destroyed before his very eyes … it was fantastic, until the end of the ride, when he found himself flung into the window of a room, in what looked like an old English castle, or at least what he imagined one would look like since he'd never gone to England.

He flew through the open window and landed with a thud on the ground, it was hard, marble, and cold … and for a dead

140

guy, it hurt like hell. Ben Slowly got up and looked around; he was in a library, one of the biggest ones he'd ever seen. The stacks went up almost 50 feet high and seemed to stretch on forever … in fact as far as he knew … it did. There, sitting in the middle of the room … in a big comfy, velvet lined, mahogany easy chair, was the man he had seen in the bar … God. He was smoking a pipe, and looking through a book labeled "The Economics of Flangdorfs." By Eeker Smith. He started to approach God, but found it extremely difficult, as the bottoms of his shoes, which had been the point of contact for the big sticky hand were, well, sticky. After trudging over to God, and finally crossing what was a really big room to get to him, Ben sat down exhausted in another chair … the chair proceeded to massage him, and all was good. "You mean all was God right?" said God.

"What?" said Ben?

"Nothing" said God … "I was just fucking with the narrator."

Ben stared at him confused for a moment "Huh?"

"Never mind, just … um, here, have a new pair of shoes."

And just like that, Ben had a nice pair of New Balance shoes … although not a brand he was familiar with.

"What is this place?" he asked.

"This is"

Suddenly the rest of God's words were loud and echoed, like in an unnamed bad movie where God is telling Charlton Heston to write the Ten Commandments.
"The Great Hall of Wonderful Knowledge and Fun Filled Facts of the Universe!"
Then the echoing stopped, "But you can just call it the library for short."

Before Ben could ask his next question, God, like a Johnny on the Spot, handed him a book called, "The Meaning of Life for Dummies, The Human Edition."
"Wow" said Ben, "it's like you read my mind!"
He studied the book for some time; it was as he imagined such a book would look like. It was a hardback, leather-bound book, with gold lettering, and a weathered look, as if it had been around since the 1800's, although he imagined it was much older, unless this was a later printing of a much older book.
"Wow, can I really look at this?" he asked.
"Well I gave it to you so I guess that means you can look at it right?" God replied.
Ben went to open it, it was heavy and thick, and his hand trembled as he pried open the cover. A thick cloud of pleasant smelling dust materialized before him as it opened. As the dust parted he saw the contents of The Meaning of Life, and it greatly confused him ... it was ... a coloring book. What's more, as he thumbed through the pages he

noticed that all the pictures were of people performing various sexual acts.

"Is this some sort of joke?" he asked.

God replied "While I'm fond of jokes … this is not one of them."

"So … the meaning of life is to have sex?" asked Ben, utterly confused, and once again aroused.

"No!" cried God, "Not just to have sex, but to color, and have fun!"

Ben sat and thought about this long and hard for a while … he wanted to argue, but really when he broke it down, he really didn't have a way to counter the argument logically, even taking into account the advice given to him by the ape version of his Mom.

"What was that by the way, the whole Planet of the Apes thing?" Ben asked.

"Oh right, sorry, that's why I don't like to go to Earth much, things get all mixed up in heaven and Earth when I'm away. I just was a little distracted, and you got off course for a bit, ended up in a cross between one of your nightmares, and someone else's fantasy, sorry about that. But I sent Nich as soon as I realized what had happened to get you." "Wait, you mean that giant sticky hand thing has a name?" asked Ben.

God just looked at him and shrugged. "Why shouldn't he?"

Ben changed the subject, "Wait you said heaven and Earth … what happened on Earth?" "Oh right." He replied, "Well let's just say that a butterfly in Florida is going to flap its wings, which will lead to the writing of a certain book, which will ultimately spell the end of the current government of Burma."

"You mean Myanmar?" countered Ben.

"Um ... not when the whole thing is over with, but for now, yes Myanmar." said God.

"Wow!" Ben replied, "How anti-climactic is that."

"Yeah" answered God, "nobody really cares all that much right now, but I think in the end it will do some good in the world."

Trying to change the subject again, Ben asked "So what's with the book? What's a Flangdorf?" God replied, "Oh that, yeah it's nothing, just sort of a pet project I'm working on with a friend on another plane of existence ... they're kind of like a cross between a Giraffe and a spider, but with the intelligence of a ... well you wouldn't know what one of those is either, but let's just say they're very smart."

"Wait so you don't create everything intelligent in your own image?" asked Ben. God sighed, "Actually ... no, I create the material for you to create yourselves in your own image, you just see me the way you see yourselves ... if you knew what I really looked like ... well I'm not entirely sure anymore what I really look like. I kind of just let myself look like whatever you people want me to look like, because your

144

heads would probably explode if you did see me the way I am … at least in this stage of your development."

Ben's head hurt and he just stared at God … finally god just patted him on the head, and said "here, have a cigarette."

After sucking down one of God's fags, Ben reflected for a moment.
"So what happens now?"
God looked at his watch, "Well its tea time according to my watch, so let's go have some tea."
Ben hated tea, but who was he to argue with God?
Ben asked, "Wait, you know I hate tea, so why are we going to have tea?"
"Because" said God, "You called me a hairy hippie, and now I'm going to make you appreciate tea."
Just as Ben was thinking this wasn't such a bad punishment, God added "While watching this year's Country Music Awards Ceremony."
Ben shuddered, but God just smiled at him.
"You see I can be a wrathful God from time to time."
Ben just slumped over and followed him out of the room, knowing full well from years of hearing other people talk about religion, because he was never one for Church that it was no use arguing with God. Just as he was about to ask if not going to Church was

going to count against him God looked at him and smiled, and with a single look Ben knew that it wouldn't.

"I am not a person who appreciates people worshipping me, and then using me as an excuse to kill each other."

All Ben could do now was appreciate the fact that his new shoes were really frickin' comfortable.

Where they went next was probably the strangest place Ben had ever been to ... it was an elaborate tearoom (he knew this because the sign out front said "An Elaborate Tearoom"), but it was painted in all sorts of bright, tropical colors. In addition, it had little vignettes on the walls, where someone had taken toys from his childhood and glued them onto the wall somehow, and they were all reenacting scenes of different sorts, strange ones, like two Transformers, one Autobot, and one Decpticon, being married in a big chapel by what appeared to be some sort of dinosaur in a tuxedo and bowler hat.

"It reflects all your childhood dreams" God said.

"I don't understand" said Ben.

"Whatever it is you ever imagined, or dreamt of as a kid, is reflected on these walls, one wall for each stage of your life." God answered.

Ben stared at a wall that consisted almost entirely of naked women and men molesting him and each other.

"I'm guessing that one is my teenage years." God laughed, "Yeah around here we call it the orgy wall. Pretty much everyone who comes in here sees a different variation on the same theme."

Ben blushed a little.

"Don't worry, whatever it is, I can't see it, it's personal to you and you alone … well except for the one Michelangelo saw when he was up here … he painted it in a chapel. But then on the other hand, knowing you people, I can pretty much paint my own picture, and it's nothing to be embarrassed about, it's all just meaning of life stuff. In fact it's interesting, the meaning of life is one of the things that humans tend to spend most of their lives shunning in the name of morality, and they throw my name in there to boot … maybe that's why so many people look for it, but never find it."

Finally they sat down at a tiny round metal based table, with a clear glass top, with a swirling light in the middle, they each sat at odd sized chairs, one large, wooden, and throne like, with a red velvet covering held in place by gold buttons, the other one being a tiny wooden stool with a pillow top, and lime green tassels hanging from it. Ben of course got the stool, but as he sat in it …

147

it was the most comfy thing he'd ever had
the pleasure of settling his rump into.

The waitress came along, or at least Ben
assumed it was a she … as the name tag said
Flo on it. She or, it as Ben assumed looked
like a six legged creature with a head and a
small torso. What was odd to Ben was the
skin. Her skin looked as if she were made up
entirely of multicolored rubber bands, which
had all been conglomerated into this strange
shape he saw before him.
It spoke "Hey Lucci sweetheart, haven't
seen you here in a while, what'll it be? The
usual I assume."
"The usual sweetie, and make it two for my
friend Ben here." God said.
"Oh hey!" said Flo, "I didn't see your little
friend there, say he's pretty cute, you're
pretty cute sweetie, you can come around
and sit in my seat anytime, if you know what
I mean!"
Ben had never felt what he was feeling now
… it was a combination of repugnance, fear,
exhilaration, and oddly enough … he was
turned on by the idea.
"I … uh, maybe later." he stammered.
She just nonchalantly answered, "Suit
yourself honey, but the offer still stands."
Ben wasn't sure, but he thought she winked
at him, assuming that was its eye.
"Wow" said God "she really likes you, and
Flo doesn't just go after anybody, trust me, I

know, I'm God and I've been trying for ages
to get her in the sack."
Ben just stared at God, not sure what to
think of him, although at this juncture, very
little surprised him.

As Ben looked around, at the clientele,
all sitting in similarly themed, mismatching,
and worn furniture, he was reminded of the
cantina scene in the original Star Wars,
except that instead of being bloodthirsty
pirate types, everyone here seemed to be
very proper looking, all sipping tea, and
enjoying polite conversation. Flo came back
to the table with two neon orange,
translucent crazy straws, like the ones Ben
loved as a kid, placed them down on top of
carefully placed napkins.
"Enjoy cutie!"
She rubbed one of her extremities along his
head as she walked away. Oddly, her skin
didn't feel like it looked. It was very
smooth, and smelled, well sexy.
Ben suddenly looked at God and said, "Why
does she turn me on so much? She's … well
… ick is the best word to describe her."
God answered while he picked up the straw
and stretched the end out until it reached the
glowing light in the center of the table, and
stuck it in, like it was a milkshake.
"Actually, she's very closely related to
humans, more than most species, just a little
more advanced. Her pheromones are 1000
times stronger than yours are, and are mostly

149

compatible with your species … plus on her planet, she's quite a hottie!"
Ben sort of contemplated this with quiet disgust, but just accepted it as truth, then pulled out his straw and hesitantly put it into the glowing light. He took a sip, what he drank warmed his entire body instantly, and tasted perfect … not like anything he'd ever had, not too sweet, or bitter, just … delicious, in a non-threatening sort of way.

Ben was about to ask another deeply philosophical, but pointless question, when the room went dark, all of a sudden, and a hush fell over the patrons; Ben took this as his cue to shut up. The silence lasted for a long time, but Ben amused himself as he looked around, and saw all the slightly illuminated faces of the patrons, their faces lit up by the soft glow of the delicious wells in the center of the tables … well that and one of the creatures was glowing slightly (like a glow stick would on Halloween), this stopped suddenly as the, well he guessed she was a woman, sitting next to … it … smacked him on his side and blurted out. "Harold!"
The creature quickly apologized and quickly de-illuminated himself. Suddenly an area bigger than the largest movie screen he'd ever seen lit up to show a stage, with thousands of people filling it to the Brim, and an announcer's voice came booming out of the screen.

"Ladies and gentlemen, welcome to this year's CME Country Music Awards, live from Nashville, with your host …"
What came after that was sort of a dull blur. While Ben had a rudimentary appreciation for, and understanding of country music … for the most part he could care less.

Ben looked up at God and noticed that he was nodding off a bit himself.
"Larry, er I mean God … why are you doing this?"
God snapped to for a moment and said, "Well to punish you for the offhanded remark you made about me being a dirty hippie wannabe earlier."
Ben just stared at him with an eyebrow cocked, "so you're going to sit here and watch the whole thing with me?"
God looked a little uncomfortable at this question.
"Well, umh … I suppose I am. I mean, I can't have you sneaking off and you know going somewhere."
Ben smirked a little, "So what if I were to just say I was really sorry I said that?"
God started in a fatherly way, "Well Ben, while I appreciate the sentiment, the point of a punishment is …"
At that moment, they introduced a surprise guest, Billy Ray Cyrus, who was to come out and perform his old standby, "Achy Breaky Heart."

God appeared to leap out of his seat and blurted out, "apology accepted, let's go." Ben wanted to be a little devious and try and talk God into staying a little longer, but the idea of having to listen to another second of this ridiculous awards ceremony was more than a little unappealing. That and it appeared that if he stayed any longer, Flo was going to try and jump him. God pulled out a handful of coins, 30 pieces of silver to be exact, and threw them onto the table, and the pair exited quickly.

As they walked along a narrow purple brick path that led through a field with a small grove of what Ben could only describe as upside down trees, he started thinking about the whole scene he just witnessed. "God" Ben started "Now I'm no scholar when it comes to the Bible. In fact, other than some rudimentary facts hammered into me through pop culture, I barely remember the bible. It occurs to me that the little episode we had back there was punishment for something I did to upset you. Now, knowing what I know about you, you aren't really lenient on the punishment of man … I mean I do remember there was a lot of smiting going on in the Bible, a lot of … well people dying in horrible ways. Now I'm not asking for a harsher punishment, but that was well not to sound mean … but that was a really weak."

God stopped in his track, looking somewhere between annoyed and confused, with a hint of anger thrown in … Ben wondered if maybe he'd crossed a line.

"Ben, sit down!" God said abruptly with a force behind his voice that needed not to have been shouted.

Ben stopped right where he was and immediately plopped down on the ground a few feet in front of God, not even looking at him.

God took a deep breath, and seemed to calm himself before he said "No Ben, sit on the park bench."

Ben turned his head to the left and not even a foot away from him off to the side of the path was a Green metal park bench, with ornately carved, pointy birds for handles, and wooden slats connecting them. Ben quietly obeyed, and even though the wooden slats seemed to be made out of some type of wood that was soft and plushy like a giant couch from some upscale furniture store that only rich people could afford to shop at, Ben felt really uncomfortable.

That changed quickly as God seemed to calm himself completely, took a seat next to Ben, and put his hand on his knee.

"Ben I want to get one thing straight in your head … I have never willfully, or spitefully killed any one of my creations. The reality is that you do it to yourselves. As far as the Bible is concerned, well … most of it is

153

gross exaggerations. Take Moses for example, he was a very smart man. He knew a lot about nature and its cycles, and he very much wanted to end the slavery of his people, so seeing his cause as a grand and just one, I came down to help him out. I gave him a little fore knowledge about some natural events that were about to occur, events I might add that were a result of the Egyptians mismanagement of the land. I said he might want to use them as a scare tactic to convince him that he was some sort of wizard and convince him to let his people go."

"Now that was sort of a mistake on my part, as I should probably have let things progress naturally … looking back the Egyptians may have just freed the slaves in a few years anyway, as they were starting to get to a point where they didn't really need them as slaves anymore, but Moses just had such passion for his cause, plus he was kind of cute … so I interfered. Well some floods and plagues later, although the scope of them is grossly over exaggerated, hell that whole taking the first born son of all the Egyptians thing … really what happened is one noble kid dies, and all the parents of the other kids get freaked out because of this whole plague thing that Moses "predicted" and they started a rumor that all their first born were going to die, which freaked everyone out just enough to let them decide

to banish the Israelites. Banish, not free …
and that whole story about the parting of the
Red sea and drowning all those chariot
riders was exaggerated as well. What
happened is they provided an escort for the
Israelites to make sure they left Egypt for
good. Now after they had crossed a bridge
over a minor, un-named river, NOT THE
RED SEA, these military geniuses decided
to follow behind as closely packed together
as possible on heavy, metal chariots, god the
Egyptians overdid everything, anyways, so
they all pack on to this old rickety bridge,
and try to cross together. Well surprise,
surprise the thing collapsed, and everyone in
their heavy metal chariots, with heavy metal
armor on, drowned."

"Later on when the Israelites had all
settled down in some horrible rock of a land,
and Moses started claiming it was the
promised land, which most people doubted,
and that I had led them there, and I put him
in charge, and all other sorts of nonsense, I
decided to have a little talk with him on Mt.
Sinai, you know just to ask him to tone it
down a bit … well he proceeds to see this as
some sort of sign that he was right, he lets
his perceived good fortune and power go to
his head, and just sort of started ranting
about being a great leader, and even came
up with those silly 10 commandments …
some of them are interesting, and I rather
agree with the subtext behind them, but then

155

he claims I will destroy them if they don't listen to him, etc, etc … Well eventually people caught on that while he meant well, Moses had a bit of a screw loose, so they decided to form a more democratic government, and pretty much stopped listening to Moses. That was fine for a while until one day there was an earthquake, and some of the Israelite leaders died, and they decided that maybe a less democratic government was needed for earthquake recovery efforts. After that … well they say absolute power corrupts absolutely, and this was no different. People started using my name, and twisting my stories to their liking, even saying I had appointed them ruler of the land. I thought people would be smart enough to see through all this, but I guess I was wrong, but hey, I decided I had interfered enough up to that point."

Ben just sat dumbfounded, and a little amused at all this new information … in fact he found himself completely speechless. Finally God said "I know, it's a lot considering what you people believe, Ciggie?"
God pulled out one of God's finest, Gold Edition, and offered it to Ben who gleefully accepted.
Finally Ben spoke "So all those stories … all that speculation was …"
God interrupted, "it was just that, speculation."

"So none of its true?" asked Ben?

"Well ... there is truth in every story. People make up stories to cope with realities they can't quite comprehend and call them truths, and once it becomes obvious to a group of people that a truth is made up, then it becomes a story. Take conspiracy theorists for instance. There are people that believe that the Pyramids were made by aliens, and the like, or that the US government has aliens held hostage in a top secret facility as the only explanation for leaps in technology, when in reality it's all you. It had nothing to do with the aliens your Government has stashed away at area 51. I find it interesting how little credit you people give yourselves. Is it so hard to believe that human ingenuity and spirit isn't enough on its own to create such wonderful and horrible things?"

Ben chuckled a bit and agreed that it wasn't that hard to believe.

After a long silence, Ben started to cry a little.

"What's wrong Ben?" He calmed down a little and then sniffled out.

"It's just that, well, I want to go back ... I want to try again ... to finish the life I started." God contemplated this for a while then smiled.

"Come on Ben let's go."

"Where?" asked Ben.

God answered, "We're going to go watch a football game."

While this wasn't exactly the answer he was looking for, it did seem like a lot of fun.

After a long walk through what appeared to be a strawberry patch tended by gnomes down a path lined with stones that seemed to change color at random, but never when you were paying attention, they came to a stadium on the outskirts of an old and not particularly clean city. It was one of the largest stadiums he had ever seen before; it was painted pink with brown polka dots, and had a sign that read "Corporate Sponsorship Stadium." Underneath the sign was an electrical sign that seemed to change every few seconds, briefly displaying the name of a company, and then changing. What was odder was a sign at the gates (which were called the pearly gates but actually were made of milky quartz and painted to look like pearl) that said:

> This is a football stadium, it is meant for entertainment purposes only. Any attempt to construe, whether actually or artificially this stadium as anything else, i.e. an arena or an elephant, is strictly forbidden by law. Anyone attempting to use this stadium for any other purpose is punishable by lima bean based meals for up to a period of five Earth years ... and so on.

Ben looked at God quizzically.

God just rolled his eyes and said, "We have lawyers up here too."

Ben asked "Do people in heaven sue each other as well?"

God replied, "Well yeah, if they're smart they do."

Ben couldn't remember the last time he actually went to a football game, let alone the last time he watched one. Not because he never watched one, in fact he was constantly bombarded by games from all sports at the bar every night. More because he was usually too drunk to remember watching it the next day, but despite this he always agreed with everyone at work that "last night's game was" ... fill in the blank ... and that "he couldn't wait for next week's game against" ... fill in the blank. The inside was immaculate, giving a stark contrast to the city he saw all around it. The columns that lined the entry way were tall and painted pink with more polka dots like the outside of the stadium. But that didn't really interest him as much as the fact that everyone who worked there was Asian, and by Asian he meant Chinese, and by Chinese he of course meant panda bears. The entire stadium was staffed with giant panda's. Not that he found this sort of thing odd considering the rest of his day, but it was still a bit unnerving as Ben thought they all smelled funny, like a wet dog, but more intense.

"You want a beer?" God asked Ben.

"I thought you'd never ask."

God went up to a lean shaggy looking panda-vendor, and asked him for 2 beers and 2 hot dogs, one with everything, and one with ketchup, and relish.

"That'll be $30.00" said the vendor.

God kind of grunted a little and said "Fine." He pulled out $30.00.

Ben leaned over and whispered "They use American money in Heaven?"

God chuckled a little and said, "Yeah, but only in Panda Town … no one knows why, but it makes them happy, so … what the hell."

They marched down a long narrow hall, with really high ceilings, if Ben were to guess it'd be around 400 feet tall, but then, Ben was very bad with spatial distinctions in architecture. At the end of the corridor was an embankment of elevators, every ticket holder stood in line and put their tickets into a machine which verified they were real, and then got into an individual elevator that took them … well he guessed to their seats. The line was really long, and at one point he saw someone put their ticket into the machine and an alarm went off, with a big flashing light overhead that said "SCALPER" in flashing letters. Suddenly a big claw attached to a metal cable came flying down

160

and grabbed the offender loosely by the pants and hauled him up and over to a drain hole that apparently led somewhere, but where Ben couldn't say. Unfortunately (or fortunately depending on whose perspective you're referring to) the claw wasn't holding on quite tight enough, and the scalper fell to the ground (which for legal reasons was padded with some sort of material, which looked and felt like hardwood flooring, but became softer the harder you hit it) bounced a couple of times and then casually walk-ran away out the exit.

"Well that was thoroughly amusing and highly ineffective." said Ben.
"Yeah, nothing really works the way it should here. Even if he had gotten put down the drain, generally they can get out with a bribe, which sadly is usually done with counterfeit bills that are accepted all over town."

Finally it was their turn. God placed the tickets into the machine to be scanned, and a pleasant, but thoroughly sickeningly sweet woman's voice said "Thank you, proceed." Their elevator opened up, and right next to a sign declaring in legal-speak that it was illegal to smoke in the elevator was a very sad looking clown with entirely too much makeup on … even for a clown. He was smoking a cigarette, and looked at them with dead eyes
"Step forward please."

Then as the door closed he shouted, but at no one in particular "Stand clear of the closing doors."

As the elevator started to move he looked straight ahead at the wall and began to recite from memory a speech in a monotonous and miserable voice "Welcome to Corporate Sponsorship Stadium, the hap, hap, happiest stadium in all of this section of Panda Town. My name is Bo-bo and I'll be your clown elevator operator for the evening. While on the elevator it's important to observe a few rules, first of all there is no smoking on the elevators …"

He hacked up a lung after he said this, and Ben pretty much stopped listening to anything else he said. Apparently as long as you knew the rules, it was OK to break them, just as long as you didn't get in trouble for it.

They got off the elevator on, well he wasn't sure what level it was, as their clown elevator guide had simply pulled a lever and taken them where they wanted to go. As they got off, Bo-bo was still rambling on about the rules, barely aware that they had even left the elevator.

God remarked, "Wow, in all the time I've been coming here, that has to have been the most upbeat elevator clown I've ever had."

Ben just looked at him a little cross eyed and kept his mouth shut as he tried to imagine someone even more morose than Bo-bo the depressed clown operating the elevator.

"You know, it's funny" said Ben, "There's a small part of me that always imagined that you looked like some sort of sad clown." God chuckled a little and said, "Very interesting."

As they rounded the stadium to get to their seats, he noticed that the field was completely dark, to the point where he couldn't see anything.

Ben remarked, "Considering this stadium's track record on safety from a legal standpoint, don't you think that the field is a little dark?"

God just said, "What happens on the field and what happens off the field are two completely different things."

"Huh … well I guess that everything else in this stadium is a contradiction in terms, so I'll just go with this one being a contradiction as well." said Ben.

At least the beer and hot dog looked and tasted like a beer and hot dog … but then what the two of them contained was a mystery to him both in heaven and on Earth.

Right before the match started an announcer's voice boomed over the PA, with brilliant clarity "Ladies and gentlemen, welcome to the three hundred trillionth annual soul bowl! Today's game will be played for the soul of the lucky ticket holder in section Loge 6-G!"

163

Suddenly a blinding spotlight appeared out of the heavens and shone down upon Ben directly, and everyone cheered!

"Holy crap!" God remarked, "This never happens to me!"

Ben shouted as if he were trying to talk over the light "It's still not happening to you! What the hell is this anyway?"

God looked at Ben in awe and said "You've been chosen! I always thought these things were rigged, but I guess not! If the visiting team wins the match, you get to go back to Earth and live out the rest of your life!"

Ben was a little flabbergasted at his luck. "What if they lose?"

"You usually get a free subscription to digital cable for eternity."

Ben wasn't sure which one was better, but when he thought about Jenny, he thought that the grand prize might be the better one.

Suddenly a little tiny man with a giant head floated over to Ben on a little stand and started to interview him.

"So son, what's your name?"

He replied "It's uh … uh … Ben."

"And where are you from uh … uh Ben?" the announcer continued.

"Earth …" answered Ben.

Everyone in the audience started to laugh including the interviewer who went on,

"Well of course you are! Is there anyone you want to say hi to out there on Earth?"

Ben couldn't think of anyone and just sat there with sort of a blank look on his face … the interviewer seeing that this wasn't going anywhere just turned to the little floating camera that had joined them at some point. "Well good luck today!"
As quickly as it had come, he and the spotlight were gone.

Suddenly the lights came up, and that's when the real disappointment started … it was a soccer game. The only sport outside of golf that Ben refused to watch on TV, and even golf was fun to play.
"Whoa, whoa … you said this was a football game, when did it become a soccer game?"
God just looked at him with that "you idiot" look his mother used to give him all the time as a kid when something wasn't all that obvious to him, but it was to the rest of the world. This was appropriate as suddenly Ben felt like he was 10 years old again, and he'd hidden his Dad's porno under his pillow before his Mom walked in … only he'd forgotten to put the pillow on top of the magazine.
God just grinned at him devilishly (as much as God could) and said "Soccer is an American word … for Football, my favorite sport."
Ben just sat back and cringed a little, "I wish we were watching the Country Music Awards."
"No you don't" said God.

Even though Ben was trying to be stubborn about the whole thing, God was right, but then everything he'd ever been taught told him to expect that from God.

The match started with the announcement of all the teams … apparently it was the home team, the "Trans-Galactic Bone Crushers", a team of gigantic hairy … well they looked like big Yeti's but with yak fur, and about 25 feet tall. The opposing team was … Brazil

"Wait, Brazil plays in heaven?" Ben asked.

"Of course they do" said God "They won the Worlds Cup, and whoever wins that game gets to come play here didn't you know that? It's televised?"

Ben was about to argue with him, claiming that they never aired any soccer games that took place in heaven verses large … well … yak people, but instead he kept his mouth shut. For all he paid attention to soccer, they could have been doing this for a very long time, and he would never have noticed. Of course, as he thought about it, that would explain why so many people in Latin American countries where they played soccer were so religious … of course, it all made sense now … I mean why else would you watch soccer.

As if he read Ben's mind, God looked at him and said, "Don't knock it, it's my favorite sport."

"Well" said Ben "I guess it'll make it a little
more interesting watching 25 foot beasts
trampling on Brazilians."
God rolled his eyes, "Just watch."

What transpired next was somewhat of a
blur to Ben ... apparently the game was only
90 minutes long, but to him it seemed like
an eternity. Not only didn't the 25 foot yak
people provide any extra entertainment by
accidentally smashing one of the opposing
team's players ... but in fact they seemed a
little dainty on the field. If anything it was
the Brazilians that were overly aggressive,
and in several instances where a fight could
have broken out, the opposing team just ran
like little girls afraid that, people who in
their perspective must have been
Lilliputians, were going to clobber them. He
also remembered something about a red card
being given to one of the players, but what
cards had to do with soccer was beyond him.

He started imagining that the cards they
handed out were Monopoly cards, and that
someone had just won a beauty contest, or
had to pay income tax. It provided brief
moments of entertainment, but in the end ...
complete boredom. Afterwards God looked
at Ben like a kid who was just brought into a
toy store and told he had 20 minutes to grab
as much stuff as he could, and that
everything he got would be his to keep.
He said, "Wasn't that a great game!? I mean
did you see the way that Brazil handled the

ball? It was like they were in possession of some sort of dark magic! The other guys never stood a chance!"

Ben answered "Don't you frown upon dark magic … witchcraft and all that?"

God rolled his eyes and said, "No of course not … you're getting me confused with the puritans. But what do you think of soccer now?"

Ben just stared at him blankly, not wanting to disappoint a very eager and happy God.

Ben said, "Well, I mean it certainly was … um … what was the final score?"

God just looked a little dejected and kind of looked down at his lap and played with his fingers a little.

Finally he said "1-0 …"

Seeing the look on Ben's face, he reluctantly added "Brazil won."

"Oh, cool" said Ben.

"Wait … that means I won right? I mean I can get my soul back and go home?"

God looked at him a little upset that he didn't like soccer a little more, but understanding "Yes it means you can go home … but to clarify, you always had your soul. The only people who don't have one are people who choose not to."

"You mean politicians?" asked Ben.

"Exactly" replied God.

Suddenly a huge hole opened up in the middle of the field, Ben and God were swept away in their seats and carried down to the field amongst uproarious applause.

An announcer's voice boomed out of nowhere and said "Ladies and Gentlemen, let's give a warm round of applause to our winner of this year's annual soul reclamation contest, sponsored by the Take a Guess Foundation, making dreams come true for countless lower beings for eons. Here he is, Uh, Uh Ben!"

Suddenly the noise from the crowd was overwhelming. Ben couldn't even hear himself think, let alone say goodbye, but as a swirling vortex sucked him down into a dark hole of whatever it was that seemed to be both pulling him and making him feel like jell-o all at the same time, Ben tried to ask a few more questions.

"God, I have so much more to ask you."

God cut him off and shouted all the answers he wanted to hear.

"32, there was no 9-11 government sponsored conspiracy, I don't like pizza from large chains, yes there is hope for a man with a small penis to do well in bed, and Jenny loves Baseball!"

With those last words, Ben was completely engulfed into oblivion.

Ben woke up to a flushing sound and dirty water lapping quickly against his face. His head was a mess, and he felt as if his chest had been broken, and glued back together with kid safe paste. Yep there was no denying the feeling he was having … he was sober, and probably all the way sober for the first time in several years. It felt good. He stumbled over to the mirror, his wits barely about him, every movement felt like he was moving each joint, each muscle for the first time ever. They were stiff, creaky, and needed to warm up before he could get them to do what he wanted. By the time he had gotten to the mirror and sink basin, he was already feeling a lot better … at least until he looked in the mirror.

"Is this really what I look like?" he said aloud to himself, as if someone was in the shitter patiently listening to him.

Ben continued his rant, "Fuck! I look like a damn train hit me. I smell like it too."

Ben took a few moments to freshen up, fixing his hair, washing his face and hands a little, and throwing out his jacket, which was probably older than he was, and probably hadn't been washed since he was a kid. This seemed to get rid of a lot of the smell, but not his armpits. So he took off his shirt, took a moment to observe the difference between when he sucked in his small, and only somewhat noticeable gut, and when it hung out. He washed his armpits with the soap from the dispenser, which must have been made from some sort of chemical that in its downtime likes to melt steel, then attempted to do the same to his shirt's underarms. When he had finished toweling it all off with the brown, eco-friendly paper towels, which doubtless would be put into some recycling bin that would then be emptied into a dumpster by someone, and put directly into a landfill. All while wrapped up in a nice, eco friendly plastic bag, so that it will decompose in about 200 years. When those ran out he used the hand dryer, which also claimed to be more Eco-friendly than using paper towels, which filled up landfills.

"So why the fuck would you have both in every bathroom?" Of course as he used the melting power of heat to dry off his shirt, he imagined some coal plant out there burning 10 cubic feet of coal to dry his shirt, and laughed.

"I'm such a fucking cynic when I'm sober."

After cleaning up as nicely as he could, straightening his shirt and pants, and even sucking on a breath mint, Ben walked out to the bar feeling like a new man. He strode up to the bar to a waiting Jenny, and before he could say anything she looked him up and down, laughed, and said … your fly's down. Overcoming some brief embarrassment at this new revelation, he simply looked her right in the eye.

"I know, I left it open so you could close it up for me."

Jenny just rolled her eyes, the embarrassment returned, and he quickly restored order to his pants, and apologized for his poor judgment in the humor department. She quickly forgave him noting that she thought his awkward sense of humor was charming.

"Oh hey" said Ben, "What happened to Larry?"

She looked at him with a great deal of confusion, and then said "Oh, you mean the hippie wannabe?"

Ben laughed at the irony, maybe a little too long, then recovered and said "yeah that guy. He left almost as soon as you went to the bathroom. He told me to tell you something, but it doesn't make sense."

"What did he say?" asked Ben.

"He said to tell you that the answer to my question was in your left pocket … and something about seeing you at a soccer game … I don't know that's all I got."

"Huh" said Ben as he fumbled around his left pocket where, there was in fact a large envelope that had not been there before. As he pulled it out Jenny asked him "So have you thought about where we're going for our first date?"

Unfortunately Ben was distracted by the envelope and missed the question, but was quickly sucked back into it as he pulled out another envelope containing tickets marked as baseball tickets. Suddenly Jenny's eyes got big.

"Are those what I think they are!?"

Ben just answered a little confused, "I dunno … what do you think they are?"

Before he could get an answer, she had ripped open the skinny envelope and pulled out two tickets … to see a baseball game at Wrigley Field, behind home plate! They were both ecstatic … God knew how much he loved Baseball, and apparently the feeling with Jenny was mutual.

"How did you know?" she asked.

"Well" Ben swaggered a little "I had a little help, from a higher power."

She laughed, "You must have, because I've never told anyone how much I love the Blue Jays!"

Ben quickly looked at the tickets; they were in fact for a Cubs game vs. the Blue Jays. Ben looked up and chuckled a little, somewhere he knew God was laughing at him. "Yeah" he said, "although I've never actually been to the Rogers Centre before." The idea of dating someone who was a big Blue Jays fan suddenly didn't appeal to him all that much, but all that doubt evaporated as she grabbed him tight, and gave him a big kiss on the lips … no, no … this was going to work out just fine.

"Well" said Jenny, "I've kind of gotta close up the bar … but um, I'll see you Tuesday?" He was a bit confused, but then looked down at the tickets; they were indeed for a Tuesday game.

Ben said, "Oh, yeah … right! So should I pick you up at say five? Here?"

She winked at him and turned as she replied, "See you then lover."

Ben couldn't remember leaving the bar … he was so high on the pheromone induced rush that he actually couldn't remember how he got out of the bar, and apparently back home .

"Wait am I still drunk?" he mused aloud. Then he gave himself a half assed sobriety test, finally giving up when he decided that no one could recite the alphabet backwards no matter how sober or drunk they were. "Who gives a fuck?" he finally said, and wandered into his apartment satisfied with the day's events.

While he was getting ready for bed (which essentially consisted of stripping down to his undergarments and crawling in bed) Ben pulled out the envelope God had apparently left for him. In it was yet another envelope, this one was sealed, and had a little note written on it. "Do not open for ten years." Ben put it aside, deciding it was best to just trust that God had some grand plan in mind for him. But after lying in bed for only five minutes, his curiosity got the best of him and he opened the envelope. Inside it was a handwritten note, and another smaller envelope. He read the letter:

HA! I knew you couldn't resist opening this! Haven't you ever heard of the story of

174

Adam and Eve? Do you know what I'm going to do to the Earth now? To you? YOU'VE NEVER SEEN FURY BEFORE YOU'VE SEEN MY WRATH! Ha ha, just fucking with you. Besides, that story was made up by a pissed off nobleman who'd been turned down by a hooker, and nothing I could do to the planet is half as bad as what you guys do to it everyday. Anywho, I put what I really didn't want you to see in the other envelope, along with an explanation. There are tickets to another game in here, one that won't happen for another ten years, and involves teams you have either never heard of, or don't care about. What I want you to do is open the envelope in ten years to the day you open this (assuming you opened it five minutes after you went to bed the night you got it). Don't worry, it's on a timer, it'll beep when the time is right. Just keep it with you.

Yours,

Larry, A.K.A. God

Ben rolled his eyes and went to open the envelope, inside was another envelope and a hand written note stating, "Seriously, I have this thing rigged so you could do this all day and night forever and it won't show you what's inside, until the timer goes off." Ben tried a few more times with the same result and finally gave up. He went to sleep, and dreamt of Jenny.

The next ten years went by like a pleasant dream. He had two beautiful children, he gained the respect of his Korean family, mostly because he had children that they loved, and he took care of, but also because they thought he was a good face for business at the bar, especially since he had stopped drinking so much. He and Jenny turned what was a lackluster Irish themed bar into an Asian-Euro fusion restaurant, specializing in the best of the East and the West, or so the ad claimed. Really all they did was clean it up, put a few new decorations with an "Asian Flare" whatever that meant, and served some sort of homogenous Asian food (or at least what Americans expected Asian food to look like) adding a few spices to make it "original", and sushi to make it "trendy". This drew a

whole new clientele, rich, stupid, yuppies …
who liked to think that what they were doing
was hip! Whatever, it didn't matter, because
for the first time in his life, Ben knew what
it was to be truly happy and miserable at the
same time. Sometimes, he realized, the two
things were one and the same.

Ten year anniversary

It was a week night like any other. Ben got home from the restaurant, it had been a slow night, but Monday's usually were. He came in a little early (11 PM) and was immediately assaulted by his kids, who should have been in bed, but inevitably came up with any excuse they could to stay up late … usually this would not go over well with Ben or Jenny, and they'd go off mad that both of their parents hated them and "never let them have any fun!" but such was the unfairness of being a child. But tonight was not a school night, it was summer vacation, so sometimes they let them stay up late, but not usually on a Monday night … it was after all one of the slowest nights and they generally liked to have some time together while the kids were asleep. The fact that they were up either meant something cool was on TV tonight, which, since they had a DVR cut one more excuse from the kid's repertoire of excuses for staying up late.

What was more likely was that he was in trouble … and if Jenny hadn't even bothered to put the kids to sleep so she could yell at him … well then it was something big. Ben's first reaction was to try and get some information out of the kids … they always knew what was up … even when he and Jenny didn't.

"Hey guys, you're up late … so, um … something on TV tonight?"

His six year old, Jack just got a big grin on his face and said "Nope!"

So, no help there, next he went to his oldest, Daniel, the eight year old, taking the more direct approach … eight year old boys were after all, a lot more mature than six year old boys … really.

"So Dan-o, did Mom ask you to go to bed yet? Are you giving her a hard time?"

Daniel looked at him; a little puzzled and said "Nope!"

Ben shook his head and put them in his hand for a moment, then just decided to stop beating around the bush.

"OK guys, its way past your bed time and I'm sure your mother has told you to go to bed, why are you still up?"

The six year old continued to smile and hit himself over the head with a fire truck, and complain that it hurt, but then continued doing it. Finally Daniel spoke up.

"It's a little weird. She hasn't really said anything to us. She's just sort of been sitting in the kitchen drinking tea, and occasionally mumbling your name … she looks mad, so we just stayed out here and played for a while."

Yep, Ben was in trouble for something. He quickly snatched the fire truck from Jack who looked confused by the whole idea of

179

the disappearing fire truck before he actually did some sort of permanent damage.

"Well guys, I'm home now, and you're going to go upstairs, wash up, put on your PJ's, and go to bed, and tonight if you don't there will be no TV, video games, or even toys for a month."

They both looked at him in disbelief … he was not usually the disciplinarian of the family, but they knew from his tone, that he really meant it, and they both skulked off quietly, Daniel dragging a confused looking Jack off to get ready for bed. Jack was a nice kid, and good looking too, which was great because he wasn't the brightest bulb on the tree.

Ben sat in the entryway to his house on the nice looking storage bench they'd gotten from Pier 1 a while back … Ben loved it … Jenny hated it. But in the end he'd let her have that God awful looking baker's rack she wanted so much. What the hell could she be so mad at him about? He really hadn't done anything wrong. He put the lid down on the toilet for the last week; he was helping around the house more … something Jenny was constantly on him for. He'd even made dinner a few times this week … not a great dinner, but it was something right? After ten minutes of thinking, and coming up with nothing, he finally decided that the only rational thing to do was get a hotel room for the night, and hope she didn't notice he was gone. But sadly, this was a marriage, and he did love her so … he went into the kitchen.

One look at her told him that this was going to be a long night, and an even longer time that he'd be in the doghouse … he meant doghouse figuratively, but she might mean it literally judging by the look on her face. She was just sitting there, dressed really nicely, like they were supposed to go somewhere … sipping on tea, and judging from the looks of things this was far from her first cup. He walked over slowly and kissed her on the neck … she liked that … but not tonight she didn't. She just looked straight ahead, as if he weren't even there. Ben was petrified, not even a slap to push him away. Finally he sat down across the table from her and stared lovingly into her eyes.

"Hon, I'm not going to lie to you, but … I'm really not sure what it is I did … so if you could just tell me, I mean I'm sure it's big, and I'm sure that I'm really sorry … and we can work it out … right?"

She continued to stare at him, but not at him … through him actually piercing him and staring straight on, into the universe. Ben felt violated, even a little mad, but he knew that getting mad only made things worse, so he kept his mouth shut. Ten minutes passed, then twenty, and finally an hour had gone by, and she was still staring through him, occasionally taking a sip of tea. Ben had of course tried to interject a few times, even tried to hold her hand … but it was as if he weren't even there. Finally she refocused on reality, and on him, and quietly, while a little tear went down her cheek said "Ben, go pack an overnight bag, and stay somewhere else tonight. When you figure out what today is … you can come back and we'll talk." Ben tried to protest, but before a sound even came out of his mouth … he thought better of it and just went upstairs, pulled together a few things, and before he left his bedroom, he heard it, a beeping sound, like a watch alarm.

Ben was curious, so he walked over to the closet, and there in the back was an old chest, full of things that Jenny had allowed him to keep from his bachelor days, but was never allowed to take out. He went through an assortment of useless objects, an award he got for winning 2nd place in intramural basketball at the recreational center in Wakefield when he was in Eighth grade, an old transistor radio from the fifties, that was still in the original box; some old Coke cans commemorating events that had long since passed and many of them, like Woodstock 1994, long since forgotten; finally he came across a big yellow hat, an ugly one he had gotten when he was in the Caribbean on vacation after high school … he still thought it was cool. In the hat was the envelope, the one he'd managed to stuff away and forget about … it was time to open the envelope from God.

Inside it were printed out directions to a Lenny's Pub and a set of tickets from TicketBastard, to see … what was it? "Ha!" Ben laughed! They were tickets to see a soccer match, Italy vs. Brazil, in Italy … there were first class tickets on his favorite airline as well. As much as Ben had hated soccer ten years ago, he'd learned to … appreciate it more since the last game God took him too. You see it turns out Jenny was a huge soccer fan, and of course, her favorite team was Brazil. So while Ben couldn't claim to be a soccer fan … he at least understood what was going on, and had even gotten to the point where he kind of liked it … kind of. Along with the tickets there was also a hand written note that said:

Ben,

I know you're still too dense to understand the significance of these items, so please follow the directions to Lenny's Pub for more information.

Love,
Larry a.k.a. God

So without another word, he grabbed his bag and went out the door, making sure to stop and tell an immobile Jenny that he loved her … Still no response.

He followed the directions to Lenny's Pub, down several familiar streets, and pulled up to what looked like an office building … in fact, that's exactly what it was … the one with the ATM from his bank he always used. There was no pub here … at least not that he knew of. He did have a tendency to ignore little details like, his surroundings. So he walked into the lobby, a large sterile looking place, with fancy looking marble floors and a homogenous looking fountain in the middle, with plants that probably wouldn't survive in this climate on their own, but hey they fit right into an office lobby.

He approached the lobby rent-a-guard, who just stared at him with coal black eyes, angry, Ben figured, for one of three reasons; either his uniform was a size too small, his heart was a size too big, or he was mad because Ben had apparently interrupted his game on a hand held video game device of some sort, forcing him to actually work for a little while.

"What?" he stated in a professional manner befitting a disgruntled, homicidal employee.

"Uh … I was looking for Lenny's Pub." Ben squeaked out.

The guard stared at him for a few moments
with that "are you mentally retarded" look
on his face, then lifted his arm slowly, as if
it weighed a thousand pounds and pointed
right behind him.
"You mean that Lenny's Pub?"
Ben looked just to the right, and there, right
in front of him was a restaurant, out in the
open taking up the entire right hand side of
the back lobby, with a big lit sign that said
"Lenny's Pub" on it.
"Oops" he squeaked out sheepishly.
"How did I miss that right? Ha ha, I mean
wow right? Thank you so much sir, you
have a great night."
     The guard responded by staring at him
for a few more excruciating moments,
apparently deciding whether to punch him,
or go back to his game. Luckily the latter
urge finally took hold, and he went back to
the strenuous task of playing video games
while on the clock. At least he was smiling
again.
     Ben walked into Lenny's Pub, and what
he saw inside made his jaw almost drop to
the floor … it was an exact replica of his
restaurant … only from ten years ago, when
it was O'Grady's Irish "themed" restaurant
and bar. He recognized it right down to the
last spec of self aware dust. It was quiet …
in fact; there was no one there, except for a
bar tender. So Ben strolled up to the bar,
walking carefully, as if not to disturb the

dust as much as possible, perhaps because he felt guilty for evicting it so many years ago. He strolled up to his usual seat, it even had the original stains and tears, with that faded red vinyl covering. The bartender said nothing, just made a drink, turned around and handed Ben a vodka tonic with an insane number of lime wedges crammed into it.

"Thanks" he said.

The bartender winked at him and said, "You're welcome cutie."

This took Ben off guard a little, this guy was fresh. Who did he think he was with his Jeans, faded dress shirt and tan duster … it took Ben a moment to register all this … oh right, it was God.

Ben took a sip of his vodka tonic … it had been a while since he'd had one, but damn, the taste never got old.

"Wow" said Ben, "It's been a while since I saw you last … you haven't aged a day!"

"Yeah," said God "I'd say it's been ten years, wouldn't you."

Ben pondered this for a bit.

"Yeah, as I recall you did say that envelope would go off in ten years, didn't you?"

"Yeah, actually it's been ten years and one week … think about that for a while."

Ben did, he remembered all the crazy shit that had happened to him all those years ago with a sort of fondness. God stared at him

186

blankly, apparently expecting him to make some sort of a connection.

God spoke "Yep ten years and one week … pretty crazy all that stuff we did, but well worth it when you think about the resulting relationship."

Ben chuckled while reminiscing, "Oh yeah … life was so worth it after that, you really opened my eyes that night … man if it hadn't of been for you, I probably would never have asked Jenny out, and I certainly wouldn't have taken her to that game a week later."

Ben sat reminiscing in blissful ignorance while God stared at him in disbelief .

"Yes Ben, that was ten years ago today … that game … the one you took Jenny too." He paused for a second while Ben just smiled and agreed with him, remembering all the great things in life he'd experienced since that moment. God just rolled his eyes, he was obviously not getting through to Ben. He said, "Yeah exactly ten years ago … this calls for some sort of celebration … doesn't it?"

Ben stared at god because he was suddenly talking really loudly and close to his face. So Ben playing along got in his face a little and belted out, "Yes a celebration would be nice, maybe we could open up the good vodka and go crazy eh?"

God just leaned back and shook his head in disbelief.

"Ben" he said "I love you like I love all my children … but you sir, are an idiot."
Ben just looked at him confused.
"What did I do?"
God blurted out uncontrollably, "Oh come on! Ten years to the day have passed since the first time you went out with Jenny, so what does that make today?"
Ben just looked at him horrified, as if he had just been hit with a ton of bricks.
"It's Monday?"
God slammed his fist against the bar and said, "No … Ben it's your ten year anniversary with Jenny."

     Suddenly Ben's sarcastic reaction to God's earlier comments became real genuine horror.
"Holy crap you're right!" said Ben.
God replied, "Of course I'm right, why do you think I called you in here tonight? More importantly, what's with that phrase "holy crap"? I mean I do number two just like all of you, and do you think I really prize my waste that much?"
Ben looked confused.
God said, "Never mind, just go home and give her the tickets. Oh and this too."
God reached under the bar and pulled out a black flat stone, it was smooth, and dull, with white streaks running across it, and had been attached to a white gold chain. Ben's eyes got big as he looked at the jewelry.
"You had this the whole time?"

188

God answered, "No Ben, as far as she knows, you've been holding on to it since you dismantled the old bar ... just for this occasion. Say it just like that."

"Thanks!" said Ben.

God added "And give her the tickets ... tell her that you wanted to take her to another special game, you were just waiting for another Tuesday to give them to her, like the game you guys went to originally."

"Wow ... that's really thoughtful!" Ben answered.

"Well go on! Don't waste time! You may even get laid tonight if you hurry!"

Ben was out the door faster than the dust bunnies could catch him.

Ben ran out the door and past the security guard, who was diligently ignoring him, hopped in his car and sped off home. It was a little past 1 AM when Ben got in, Jenny was sitting on the couch watching TV, apparently she had been crying.

He ran into the living room and enthusiastically said "Hey Babe!"

To which she enthusiastically threw the remote at him, hitting him right between the eyes.

Ben staggered a bit and said, "Wow, you should have been a marksman ... I guess I deserved that."

He pulled out the tickets, "look I was going to save these for later, I wanted to take her to another special game, you were just

189

waiting for another Tuesday to give them to
her, like the game you guys went to
originally."
Jenny looked at him with a blank stare and
said, "Why are you referring to me as "her"
and you as "you"?"
Ben smiled and just said "Because God told
me too?"
For some reason that was exactly what she
needed to hear … she started laughing
hysterically. Then she looked at the tickets
and the airline tickets, and smiled.
"That's why you wanted us to be off work
tomorrow, so we could go see the game!
You even had my Mom coming to get the
kids … that's so sweet … I, I'm so sorry
Ben."
In reality Ben had gotten off work and had
his Mother in law come get the kids because
he wanted to go drinking with a few of his
buddies, and didn't want Jenny to think he'd
just left her with the kids … but this worked.
"Oh … and one more thing, I got you this!"
Ben pulled out the necklace with the stone
and handed it to her.
"Oh my God! Where did you find this?"
asked Jenny.
"Well I've been holding on to it since we
dismantled the old bar … just for this
occasion."
It was a stone her grandmother had given
her when she was a child, called it her lucky
stone and said she had to give it to her

grandchild … that was the only way it'd be good luck anymore.

What ensued was a lot of crying and well, eventually sex. They had an incredible anniversary in Italy … Brazil won and they were the only two happy people in the audience. I'd say they lived happily ever after … until their twentieth anniversary rolled around, and that my friends, was a nightmare.

The Enforcer

Sister Mary Elizabeth O'Hurley was a kind and compassionate sister of the order of the Sacred Heart Church in Los Angeles. Sister O'Hurley had nothing but compassion for the poor and unfortunate souls that came often for a meal and a place to sleep, and more often to urinate and defecate in the pews, having mistaken them for the restroom in a drunken stupor. They were polite enough about it, usually when she pointed it out, they'd get embarrassed, stop what they were doing, and go into the confessional booths to finish. All she could do was hope they were flushing … or at least trying to, she supposed God would know.

Sister O'Hurley did her best to comfort and love all of God's creatures. Unfortunately, most of God's creatures had developed a perverse idea of what love was. In fact sister O'Hurley was so repulsed by the goings on of some of these heathen bastards while sleeping in God's house, and under, the Lord's charity, and even just under the sky which the lord had blanketed their wretched souls with, that often times she found it necessary to carry out God's will with her own hand … and of course a paddle fashioned from one of The Lord's lesser, wooden creations, which she had hand fashioned into her own implement, with the inscription "The hand of God is merciful" scrawled into the wood with a buck knife. She just called it Bertha.

This particular evening she happened to walk in on two women while in the act of defiling each other within the Lord's house. Perhaps walk in on wasn't the right word, more like "kept a hawk-like gaze upon each room via a special closed circuit security monitoring system she had installed using the Lord's donations." was more appropriate. Yes the lord was working through her to watch over its flock, and come hell or high water, she was not going to let this disgusting debauchery continue while she had something to say about it.

The two culprits in question were a younger Mexican couple, neither one of them could have been much older than 19 years of age, she knew, them well and watched them often. They claimed to be in love, IN LOVE! Oh how far they had strayed from God's teachings. The very thought of two women, flailing about, caressing each other, kissing and stroking each other in a way god had not intended. The thought alone made her shiver with … with what she could only describe as incredible distaste, but then she was a nun, and such things were beyond her, and she was glad for it. Still she would have to say ten Hail Mary's to make up for the images the devil had placed in her head via closed circuit television.

Now Sister O'Hurley was not an unreasonable sort, she did see the value in training others to carry out the lord's work … delegating was the secular term she had heard a young businessman by the name of Marcus Walters call it. But then Marcus was a heathen bastard who only came out to the lord's house because he had been cursed by the devil with an affliction of sorts. You see he was attracted to Nuns, lord bless him, in particular, Sister O'Hurley. At first she used Bertha to propagate God's will, but this only seemed to encourage him and bring the devil closer to the lord's house … but then that also led to impure thoughts for which she would ultimately have to have him say so many Hail Mary's and Our Father's, that she'd barely get any sleep, and she was a cranky Nun to be sure when she didn't get her eight hours.

Sister O'Hurley rushed into the quarters of Sister Carla Lopez; a Spanish speaking Nun from Mexico, Sister O'Hurley figured Sister Lopez was the right person for this particular job. Unfortunately when she got to Sister Lopez's room, she found her in no state to enforce God's will. You see Sister Lopez was highly inebriated, and could barely stand up straight when Sister O'Hurley came in. Sister O'Hurley stood staring at her in utter disgust.
"Why you ungrateful little …"

194

She wanted to use the word bitch, but sadly alcoholism was all too common in the sisterhood, and the most she could do was yell at her for her incompetence. Not that she had been drinking, but that she was drunk. You see Sister O'Hurley herself drank heavily, she felt it helped her get closer to the lord and at times allowed her to push back the evil thoughts that permeated the minds of people like herself who dealt with such horrible atrocities on a daily basis whilst in the service of our lord. What angered her was when people of the clergy, in any sense, allowed themselves to get so inebriated that they were outwardly affected. This was using God's gift for the sake of pleasurable and therefore sinful pursuits, as opposed to a tool to help enforce the Lord's will.

Sister O'Hurley wanted to say something that would stick to Sister Lopez's conscious, but all she had time to say to her as she stood there slack-jawed and practically drooling, having God knows what thoughts was "Say Hail Mary's and Our Father's until you sober up!"
To which Sister Lopez just nodded and started mumbling to herself "Hail Father Mary" over and over again. Sister O'Hurley would have to deal with this later. For now, she had more important matters to attend to, lesbians!

Sister O'Hurley grabbed Bertha from her room, where she had it gingerly mounted on the wall, and stormed in on the two of them passionately defiling each other … Sister O'Hurley just stood there, her mouth agape, her eyes wide … it was so … disgusting to her. Even if she had seen it over and over again on CCTV, it never seemed so real until she saw it in person. They both let out a little squeal, they knew they were caught and that there would be punishment for such disgraceful behavior, and they recoiled in terror.

As Sister O'Hurley Raised Bertha into the air ready to reign down with the force of the lord onto these two lovely creatures who had gone astray, her hands trembled. There was always a mix of fear and excitement when she had to dole out such a punishment … it was a feeling she disliked, not for a moral reason, but because it made her heart race so quickly that it made her a little bit nervous even a little dizzy, but she wouldn't let a little discomfort stop her. Not tonight! For tonight she was going to reign enforce God's wisdom and compassion until they knew the Lord loved them. Nothing was going to stop Sister O'Hurley from her mission of mercy tonight … NOTHING!

That night Sister Mary Elizabeth O'Hurley died suddenly while carrying out God's will … Perhaps it was the excitement mixed with the constant anguish and strain of spreading God's love that had led her to an early grave. At least that's what she thought, and what the sisters at her funeral would say. But in reality it was the words of the coroner that were most revealing.

"Sister Mary Elizabeth O'Hurley died at 11:35 PM from complications brought about from an acute myocardial infarction, or AMI for short … more commonly known as a heart attack."

You see with the combined stress of constantly carrying out God's will, along with the constant influx of alcohol, and the occasional cigarette she snuck in once or forty-eight times a day, and her love of honey glazed ham and bacon, a meal she had regularly to calm her nerves. Sister Mary Elizabeth O'Hurley's arteries looked like a squeeze tube full of frosting.

Lightning followed by thunder was the first thing Sister O'Hurley saw in the afterlife. At first she thought it was a continuation of the blinding pain she had experienced while caring for those two poor misguided souls … but no … it was something else, something less profound but equally as mystic, it was lightning and thunder, viewed through the window of a lonely tavern overlooking a beautiful, hilly, green countryside, with grey clouds floating above, pouring rain upon the ground as if on a short deadline. The wind swept across the barrage of falling water, creating waves in the air. Sister O'Hurley sat in long pants and a T-shirt with a picture of Bono on the front at a rickety table with a proper pint of Lager. She could smell the oppressive air clearing up, as the rain often did in this part of the world. She was back in Loughrea, a town a little ways east of Galway.

Sister O'Hurley could only assume one thing, that she was dead and this was her heavenly reward for her years of service to her lord, just to be sure she took a sip of her Lager. A slight tingling feeling went up and down her spine as she sipped the frothy brew, and she did something she hadn't done since before she left Ireland all those years ago, she smiled.

After a long time she started to wonder if this was heaven. It was the most beautiful place she'd ever been in her life, but it just seemed to be replaying itself … except different, everything felt so much more real to her. It felt, well it felt great. Maybe this was her life flashing before her eyes, maybe it was because she was still sober … it didn't matter, what happened next made her freeze so still that she almost felt time move past her before coming to a stop. In walked Lisa McMurray … suddenly Mary wasn't so sure she was in heaven, purgatory, or anywhere in between anymore. She was in hell.

Maybe this was her chance to set things right, maybe this was her opportunity to atone for her sins. Mary took a final swig of her drink, turned around, and walked right out the front door of the tavern. For a second it worked, she was free, overlooking the little village of Loughrea, green hills in the distance as the cool rain fell upon her brow, but as she took a step forward, she found herself walking right into the middle of the tavern, drink in hand, right into Lisa McMurray, spilling her beer all over her meathead of a boyfriend … whatever his name had been, Mary couldn't recall. She blushed horribly as she looked at the mess she'd made.

"Look where you're going you fucking whore" said the man with Lisa McMurray. Mary was so flustered, and embarrassed that she didn't know what to say or do … she just used her hands and tried to wipe it off him like she had a magic napkin folded into her hand. The man pushed her away so hard she hit the wall and her head against the support beam that ran up from the ground. "Get your fucking hands off me bitch, I'm not one of your customers."

Apparently the liberty this man took was one too many, and everyone in the Tavern knew it. Without a word Lisa McMurray kicked him so hard in the balls that he didn't even get to scream, he just fell to the ground and cried silently to himself, quietly wondering if he'd ever father the little bastard children he'd hoped to father someday. The taverns keeper, Seamus came around the bar with a bat of some sort, picked the tall, but obviously overweight man up with one hand, and proceeded to throw him out the front door, screaming at him.

"The next time you come around here, expect to have this shoved up your arse, after I bash your head in with it!"

Mary just sat there dumbfounded as Lisa came over and put her arm around Mary's shoulders and gently led her over to the bar, where she sat her down and took an ice pack from Seamus who had magically produced one from the bar somewhere. Lisa placed the pack on the back of her head, and held her hand, Mary was simultaneously feeling better and sick to her stomach at the same time. It was too late, she was going to have to relive this whether she liked it or not. She took the shot of whiskey that Seamus had placed before her, and then a second one. She felt delirious as the barkeep apologized for the man's behavior, and Lisa proceeded to start her introductions, but Mary didn't hear it … this was one of the most vivid memories in her life, the day she met Lisa McMurray, the day she wished she could take back.

Lisa was the Village wild child. She had dated everyone in town, and slept with most of them twice, in Seamus the barkeep's case … several times. She had dark red hair, straight with a pale complexion, but just a hint of olive in her skin, and those eyes … those eyes would haunt Mary for the rest of her life, and apparently in her afterlife as well. They were the lightest green eyes she'd ever seen on another human being, she remembered the way they sparkled in life, and how they would flicker out as Mary watched Lisa die later.

"No, God forgive me, but I can't do this again" Mary thought aloud to Lisa as she attempted to get up and walk out of the bar. Lisa looked extremely confused as Mary walked out. Only to find herself once again in the seat she had been placed in, Lisa staring lovingly with those beautiful Irish eyes of hers at her, introducing herself again, apologizing for her boyfriend's abhorrent behavior, as if she had anything to apologize for.
"I'm Lisa McMurray, and that was Peter … my … ex-boyfriend. Please let me make this up to you."

Mary wanted to refuse, to run away, to go anywhere but here, but as much as she wanted to leave, she couldn't, and as Lisa stroked Mary's hair to console her, Mary felt that feeling she had long sought to push away, that feeling which had pushed Mary into a thankless life of servitude to the Lord, Mary was in love. More than that, Mary was desperately attracted to this woman. It was as if fate had brought them together. Even though she knew it was wrong, she couldn't help feeling what she felt for this woman.

The Rain eventually let up, and Lisa asked Mary if she felt up to going to her favorite spot in Loughrea, the old castle outside town, without any hesitation, Mary said yes. She was once again under the spell of this beautiful woman. At once she was transported to the old keep, the empty tower was altogether creepy, and dank, but the light of the sun peeking through the clouds between storms combined with Lisa's magical touch, and bewitching voice, was enough to coax Mary on, and see these old ruins, as a magical castle. The two sat atop the abandoned tower looking over the hills, as a rainbow appeared in the horizon.

Mary may have been young and naïve, but Lisa was far from it. Experienced in the ways of love, loss, and lust … she took Mary on the ride of her life, and while the rainbow peeked out from the distance, Lisa suddenly pulled her close, and kissed Mary passionately on the lips. A fire flew through Mary, she knew this was wrong, it went against everything her Catholic upbringing had taught her … she liked men … it was what women were supposed to like. God frowned upon people who committed such atrocities of nature. And yet, here she was … nothing in her life felt as right as it did to her today, and after this evening, nothing ever would feel right again.

Again time jumped. She was in Lisa's house in the village, her parents were on holiday, and had left her in charge, alone. Mary found herself in Lisa's embrace, both of them completely naked. She followed Lisa's lead as she taught her how to make love to another woman, as making love, in whatever sense, is always a bit awkward for someone the first time.

Following their lovemaking session, Mary found herself engulfed in darkness. The next moment she found herself in bed with Lisa, it was the middle of the night, and it was too late. Mary remembered this moment as being both the happiest, and most terrifying one of her life. There was a loud knocking on the door, it woke Lisa up, the unmistakable voice of Peter piped up he was obviously very drunk, and very angry. "Open this door you slut … you whore, or I swear to fuck I'll break the God damn thing down!"

Not in the least bit deterred, Lisa got out of bed, stark naked, grabbed a large wood plank with an old rusty nail sticking out of it and walked right up to the front door.
Lisa said to Mary, "This will only take a minute love, hold tight."
Mary wanted to scream out, tell her to stop, she was so beautiful, the moonlight streaming in through the window, illuminating her body.

Mary wanted to cry out, get her to stop, maybe if she never opened the door, they could escape together out the back, run away from this place, and live a life together. But Mary was frozen, unable to speak, something was keeping her from changing events, something was making her relive this.

Lisa opened the door, and standing there was Peter, huge, sweaty, ugly, and drunk as a skunk. Before Mary even had a chance to swing, he'd overpowered her, not so much because of his superior size, Lisa had shown herself quite adept at defending herself against oafish boyfriends. No Lisa was overpowered by Peter, and three of his immensely large, and equally as drunk, idiot friends. Before Mary could move again, three more of them were upon her, holding her back, making her watch as they brutalized Lisa, called her far worse insults than the lowliest of individuals deserved, and then took turns beating and raping both women as the other was forced to watch.

In the end, they heaped their two bodies together in the middle of the living room, doused the home with gasoline, and set it ablaze. Mary pulling together the last of her strength, tried to wake Lisa, tried to pull her out of the fire, but it was too late. Lisa McMurray was dead.

In the past Mary had pulled herself out of the fire, managing to wrap herself in a blanket before leaving, not that she remembered it, everything after Lisa's death had been a blank for Mary, but she watched now from outside her body as she watched her young, and severely battered self drag herself to the back door, absent mindedly pulling a blanket out the door with her, wrapping herself as she escaped the burning structure that just seconds after her departure was engulfed in flames. Never once looking back, she walked to town, laid down in an alleyway, and fell asleep sobbing.

Time leapt forward again. Mary was in a confessional booth. She stank, her hair was matted with blood and mud, and her blanket was wet from sleeping in the alley. She stared into the void of the confessional booth, knowing there was another man there, knowing that she eventually confessed to this man what had happened. But instead of alerting the authorities, instead of getting her medical help, food, shelter, clean clothes, and some much needed counseling. This man of the cloth told her to beg God to forgive her sins. He convinced her that Lisa's death was the direct result of their homosexual escapades. He made her believe that what she had done amounted to blasphemy and murder, and that she would burn in a much hotter fire than the one that had engulfed the McMurray's home that evening if she didn't commit the rest of her life to God. He went so far as to say that he would go to the authorities and let them know that she had confessed to the arson and murder of Lisa McMurray if she didn't dedicate the remainder of her life to the service of the lord.

Mary wept, vulnerable, she was confused and cornered, though illogical, what this man was offering seemed like the only way out for her. So rather than standing up to defend the life of the woman she loved, and fighting the injustices wrought down upon her, she submitted to this man's will and became a Nun.

What she didn't know was that Peter McMillan, the man who along with his immensely oversized and undereducated brothers had committed the real atrocity, were this priest's nephews. She didn't know that the man she was talking to, Michael McMillan was more corrupt than any politician. That Michael was in fact less of a holy man, and more of a shyster. He used his calm demeanor and gift for gab, and hid behind those priestly robes in order to extort money, power, and even sexual favors from men, women, and children alike. All Michael had been concerned with was keeping this quiet. Which he did after he bustled her off to a Convent in Los Angeles, to get her as far away as possible, he then convinced the whole town that the brutal act against the McMurray's daughter had been perpetrated by one of his enemies. A man who took care of his mentally retarded brother, a man who saw right through Michael and his deviant ways and was very close to revealing it to the town, this man for his troubles and valiance, was doled out what amounted to mob justice. The townspeople beat him and his brother senseless, and burned their house to the ground, with the two of them in it, never even having had a trial.

Still knowing how everything turned out for her, and always having a feeling as to how things turned out in Loughrea, Sister Mary O'Hurley had always felt a debt of gratitude to this perverted man, for having saved her life.

So now, as she had all those years ago, she crossed herself slowly and said, "Forgive me father for I have sinned."

She then proceeded to recant her story as she had all those years ago, through tears of anger and confusion.

But instead of the lecture she was waiting to hear from behind the privacy screen, all she got was silence. A long, and unnerving silence. Finally, a cloud of cigarette smoke came through the screen followed by a woman's voice.

"Really? After all that, you still want things to turn out how they did? What a fucking candy ass. I really thought after all those years you were going to really let that asshole Michael McMillan have it. I even

have him tied up back here just for you to
yell at, Jesus!"
 Suddenly another man's voice came out
from behind the privacy screen.
"Yeah what's up?"
The female voice shot back, "Look, just
because I say your name doesn't mean I
need you to come."
There was a small pause and then, "Sorry!"
Then the voice was never heard from again.
   Mary, getting a little antsy and annoyed
at all this suddenly blurted out, "What the
fuck is going on here for God's sake!"
Suddenly the privacy screen dropped, along
with the booth itself. Mary found herself
inside of the Basilica di Santa Maria del
Fiore. It was completely empty, save for a
two chairs, one she was seated in, across
from a stunning looking Italian woman who
was smoking a cigarette while her legs were
crossed. She wore a yellow sun dress with
blue flowers on it, that was … very
revealing. Behind her was a very pissed off
looking father McMillan, hog-tied, and
gagged, laying on his stomach behind the
beautiful woman.
   The woman spoke, "God is way too
formal, you can call me Francesca."
Mary was too stunned to speak,
instinctively, she knelt before the woman,
and bowed her head, starting to say an Our
Father, Francesca stood up and pulled her up

by the arms so that Mary was facing her dead on.

"Oh stop it, all of you religious people get so uppity and pious, you think I like it, but really … you're just embarrassing yourself. Stand up!"

Mary instinctively obeyed.

"Isn't that much better eh?" said Francesca as she gently slapped Mary on the face with her hands, as if framing it.

"You have pretty eyes" Mary suddenly blurted out backing off suddenly and covering her mouth, ashamed at what she was saying, and even more so at the lustful things she was now thinking.

God just rolled her eyes and said "you see there? That's what I'm talking about, you pay me a compliment, you think nice things about me, but you're ashamed. It's like you live in some backwards world where up is down and down is forbidden … Madonna Mia, have a seat."

Behind her suddenly appeared a big comfortable chair, and Mary sank down into it. The chair was so soft and comfortable, Mary felt like she could stay there for eternity, and everything would be just fine.

"Oh, I almost forgot" said God.

She suddenly clapped her hands, and Mary found herself completely clean, and clothed in a clean pair of jeans, and a T-shirt that said, "Kiss me I'm Irish" on it.

She went on "Now what to do with this one … hmmm … should we burn him alive? Make him work for the entertainment company represented by the big ugly mouse who shall not be named? Oh! I know, we'll turn him into a Pomeranian and make him live with Paris Hilton!"

Sister Mary just stared at this female image of God standing before her, completely baffled by what she was saying. Suddenly Francesca blushed a little. "Well … um … despite all the horrible things you've written about me in your holy books, I'm actually not that good at thinking up suitable punishments. Mary couldn't help herself, she started chuckling a little, and then started laughing outright. This was all too much for her to handle.

"HA!" said God, "I knew there was a human being in there somewhere." There was a prolonged silence as Mary finally spoke up, "God … er … Francesca, why do you have father McMillan tied up in the middle of the Duomo in Firenze?" God answered, "Well he is the one who is responsible for your poor excuse for a life, in fact he is responsible for so many lost lives, but none so tragic as yours, I thought it would be fitting to punish him."

"As for the Duomo … I don't know, believe it or not, you picked the place, although I do enjoy bowling here on Wednesday's with Brunelleschi."

210

"I picked the place?" asked Mary.

"Yes" answered God "I think you once said when you were visiting here that if you had to imagine what heaven would look like, it would be here."

Mary thought about this, and suddenly remembered very clearly saying something along those lines, she wasn't sure, she might have been a wee bit drunk at the time.

"Please don't punish father McMillan, if it weren't for him, I'd have never dedicated my life to your service." said Mary.

God just stared at Mary for a long while, then, took a drag off her cigarette.

She finally said, "Fine, you will punish him, it is your life he ruined after all."

"I will do no such thing!" said Mary, suddenly standing up with anger in her eyes.

God just smiled at her, and said "How can I refuse a beauty like you, fine, we break even, eh? I will take you through this man's life so you can see exactly what he has done to you, and then you can decide what to do. Whatever it is, I will respect it."

"Fine." Said Mary, "but you're wrong … I'm not a lesbian, just because I was cursed with this diseased mind full of sin, does not make me such a horrible excuse for a human being."

God rolled her eyes and said "Whatever kitten. You're so cute when you're self righteous, let's start from the ending."

211

Suddenly Mary found herself sitting at a small bistro table; there was a pot of Earl Grey tea, and some shortbread cookies sitting in front of her. Mary was alone, until someone came up from behind her, gently placed her hand on Mary's shoulder, startling Mary so much that she nearly knocked over the table as she leapt out of her seat. Suddenly she stopped cold, as she saw for the first time outside of her wicked reenactment Lisa McMurray, dressed simply in tight jeans and a form fitting t-shirt, and bright colored sandals.
She said "Hi Mary."

As the shock wore off, the two of them sat down and had tea.
"So …" said Mary.
"Um … how's the afterlife?"
Lisa chuckled a little; "yeah" said Lisa "I'm not sure what to say either. You look good."
Mary Blushed some, "Look … I … I'm sorry about what happened."
Lisa looked shocked, "You're sorry? Dear, what in shit and sh'gorin would you be sorry about?"
Mary cleared her throat a little, I'm sorry about killing you. I think about what I did every day, and I pray to God to forgive me … but nothing I ever do is enough."

Lisa looked Mary dead in the eye, "Dear, nothing you did was ever your fault, if anything I should be the one apologizing. I was the one who dated the jerk off who killed me, and brutalized you. I was so sick of his shit, I was so sick of men in general. It's not that I'd never been with a woman before, but there was something about you. Something … I don't know … when I first met you, it was like I'd known you my whole life. The Earth seemed to stop, and when he pushed you like that, I just lost it. I've never lost it like that before in my life. I … I don't know how things would have turned out between the two of us if we'd been able to stay together, but I'm pretty sure it would have been fantastic. Mary, I never got to say this to another person before and mean it, I love you."

Mary stared at her half way to a sip of tea, then gently placed down the glass, looked her right in the eye, and said, "My dear sweet Lisa, I love you too … but you're confused. I'm not a lesbian, and as much as I love all God's creatures, I love you too … but it's not natural what you and I experienced."

Lisa interrupted, "Yes it is we just …"

"NO!" said Mary abruptly, "I must finish. We were punished by God for what we did that night, and I was to spend the rest of my life repenting for both of us. I think I've done that quite nicely, please don't screw things up in the bottom of the ninth inning." With that Mary got up and turned away from Lisa.

"And still you are in denial" came God's voice.

"DENIAL!" Raged Mary as she turned around, angry as hell at God ... Lisa was gone, sadly so was the tea.

"I don't know who you are, but the God I know doesn't sanction this sort of behavior. The God I know deals swift retribution on to sinners like Lisa and myself, The God I know doesn't tie up devout people like father McMillan, and accuse them of heresy. In fact, the only person I know who would do such a thing is Satan himself! And it doesn't surprise me that Satan would come in the form of such a vile temptress. But don't try me she-devil, for my faith is strong, and though God has seen fit to banish me into hell I will not relent my faith even now!"

With that Mary got on her knees and started praying.

God just stood there smoking a cigarette, observing this strange behavior, waiting patiently, until Mary was all prayed out. Finally Mary stood and faced God who said, "You done?"

Stoically, Mary didn't answer, "Such a drama queen" continued God. Mary said nothing, "Let's look at the stoic and devout life of Father McMillan."

With that God transported them from place to place, going over various indiscretions of Father McMillan's from accepting bribes, to abusing his privileges with the Church to cover up everything from petty larceny, to sexual assault, to outright murder, by him, and by others. Taking them full circle back to the Duomo where father McMillan sat hogtied once again in the floor, but this time un-gagged.

"You don't believe me" said God, "ask him yourself."

Mary was dumbfounded, she wanted to believe it was all a lie, she wanted to believe it because it meant her whole life had been a lie. But she couldn't deny the proof that was right in front of her. More than that, in her heart, she'd always known he was a monster, but she rarely trusted her heart, and in the end, it had betrayed her to her grave.

"Father McMillan, tell me it's all a lie" she said.

He just stared at her, anger in his eyes, and said "Fuck off you cunt rag. You always were a prissy little bitch. I sent you off to LA to keep you from turning in Peter, I had great political aspirations for my brother's idiot son, and I wasn't going to let you screw that up! It worked too, Peter became the Mayor, and then eventually a regional representative, we took those poor country sops for every fucking dime we could."

Mary wanted to puke, instead she took the cigarette that God handed her, and took a drag from the self-lighting cancer stick. She thought about the implications of his words, getting angrier by the second at them.

Then she asked him, "Now that you've been dead a while, are you at least remorseful for your sins?"

He smiled like the devil himself and said, "Fuck no. If I had it to do over again, I'd take every last one of those idiot sheep for all their money again and again."

Mary was angered to the point of violence … she picked up a two by four with a rusty nail on the end that just happened to be handy all of a sudden, ran up to Father McMillan, and held it over his head ready to strike. As her hand swept down upon a cowering Father McMillan in a fashion Mary was all too familiar with, the board disappeared. Before Mary could regain her balance to strike again, this time with her feet and fists, a voice shouted out from every direction, "STOP!"

The voice was neither male or female, but the sound it made was so intense that anyone who heard it would have been powerless to disobey. Mary, and Father McMillan Froze.

God walked over with the greatest of confidence in her walk, put her hand on Mary's shoulder, and said gently this time, "stop."

Mary broke down into tears as she hugged God with every ounce of strength she had left, slowly letting the anger dissipate.

"I know child, I know. But before we cast this monster aside, I want you to see something."

God waved her hand, and two chairs appeared. One had Father McMillan in it. He was no longer tied up, but at the same time, he found it impossible to leave the chair, or move it. "Please sit." said God. Mary obeyed, though she was still uneasy about being in Father McMillan's Presence.

The room in front of them became a sort of three dimensional movie screen, and God seemed to disappear as the show was starting. It was a kitchen, a young boy, no more than six years old was in it sitting down, eating cookies. Father McMillan who had been protesting his immobility and cursing under his breath froze, as if a truck were headed for him in the interstate, and he was powerless to avoid it.

The boy continued to eat the cookies, Father McMillan became increasingly alarmed, and mouthed under his breath, "No … Don't … please."

What happened next would burn in Mary's memory for as long as she had one. A woman, the boy's mother came in and stared at the child who went about eating his cookies, smiling. The woman stared at him, and said in an undertone so sharp, yet so quiet, that it would chill even the most hardened of individuals.

"Michael … what do you think you are doing."

The child, having been well aware of his mother's presence since her entry seemed to jump a little, but froze out of fear. He seemed confused by the question, but holding a cookie in mid bite.

He finally stammered, "Eating the cookie you gave me."

His mother looked unconvinced.

"I gave you the cookies, but did I tell you to eat them?"

The boy still frozen, but more and more terrified finally stammered, "I … I thought I could have them."

Mary thought she was hearing stereo, instead she looked over and saw father McMillan, absolutely wide eyed with terror, frozen, and speaking quietly along with the little boy, word for word.

The woman continued, "I told you, you could have them, but I never told you that you could eat them."

The boy seemed absolutely flabbergasted at the information. He began to cry a little, so did Father McMillan.

"Michael" the woman started, snatching all the cookies, save for the one in his hand away from Michael.

"You've been a bad boy. You must be punished."

The child stammered, still trying to understand, "But, you said … I thought."

218

The woman smiled a vicious smile, and said, "You thought wrong, and now you're going to be punished until it hurts more than you've ever felt pain in your worthless little life." The child was absolutely balling now, "I'm sorry Mommy, here, you can have the other cookie, I promise I won't do it again." The child handed back the cookie to his mother, who snatched it from his hand, stared at him and ate it right in front of him. "It's too bad" said the woman, "I might have spared you punishment if you had kept the cookie and eaten it for yourself. You see then you would have been a real man. Real men don't let themselves get pushed around Michael … you, are, a pushover, and now you'll have to be punished doubly."
As she said this she pulled out a wooden plank, a two by four much like the one Mary had tried to use a minute ago. The woman began beating the child senseless with it, as the scene disappeared from in front of them.

Mary turned to see father McMillan sobbing uncontrollably, muttering "I'm sorry mommy, I'm sorry …"
Over and over again. Francesca reappeared, and said to him, "It didn't stop there did it?" Father McMillan shook his head no between uncontrollable sobs.
"She just went on punishing you more and more, to where you were within an inch of your life. All the way until you were 17, and you just took it, didn't you?"

Father McMillan just slumped over, tears still streaming down his face, but unable to sob anymore from exhaustion.

"Yes" he mumbled.

God spoke to Mary "It got worse, much worse, by the time he was ten she was sexually molesting him, by the time he was 13, she'd already become pregnant with the boy that she convinced everyone was his brother. She blamed that on Michael too. Said he was to be ashamed of what he'd done, and that if he didn't keep everything they'd done a secret, she'd do the same to the new child, and tell everyone just how filthy he was. Should I go on?"

Mary was numb with all this new information. It was too much for one person to bear. She looked over at Michael, who by now was beyond tears, he was curled up in a ball on the floor, free from the chair that had held him earlier, convulsing. God went over to him, and stroked his head, kissing him on the cheek, he immediately relaxed, falling into a blissful sleep.

The bistro table with the tea and cookies reappeared they both sat, sipping tea silently for a while. Finally God broke the silence. "I'm sorry to put you through all that, but you have to understand, you are no more guilty of being who you are than he is of being who he is. I don't need to punish any of you. You punish yourselves. Father McMillan twisted his life into an endless

220

cycle of exploitation, constantly looking for happiness by getting back at his mother, and all women, by abusing them in as many twisted ways as possible. And you, you bury yourself so deep that you punish yourself, and others who are like you, all in my name. Really you just punish yourselves. What if you had stood up to father McMillan, exposed him for what he was. He may not have appreciated it, but you would have been showing the greatest compassion you could have, just as he would have been showing great compassion by standing up to his mother. But you were all so young, all so innocent, and you let the world corrupt and twist you until you are barely recognizable as human beings. Let go of all this pain. I give you permission to be Mary O'Hurley, woman of God, and a lesbian. I give you permission to love Lisa McMurray, now please give yourself permission to live your life as yourself, please, and for my sake … have a shot of Whiskey!" Mary looked down at the table to see a shot glass with an amber liquid in it she instantly recognized and said, "Now that's the first thing you've said to me that makes sense!"

After taking a moment to savor what may have been the best damn shot of whiskey she'd ever had Mary asked, "What happens to Father McMillan now?"
God laughed, "You see, for all your anger and hatred, you still care what happens to

others. What happens to Father McMillan is up to Father McMillan. I'll send him back to Earth, to start over again, hopefully this time his parents won't be so cruel, but I can't say for sure … sometimes we play in the gardens of hell so long, we begin to think we're in heaven."

Mary took another shot of Whiskey, as it seemed to just re-appear, every time she put down the glass. It had a strange effect on her, it didn't get her drunk … just relaxed her, but unlike the drunk who claims he's fine to drive as he trips and falls against the wall in front of him, Mary could honestly say her head was completely clear. She was just loose.

"I'm not sure I understand" said Mary. "We create our own reality, even from birth?" God answered, "Father McMillan has chosen to have a shitty life, lifetime after lifetime. He thinks that he's a victim of circumstance, but in reality, he's become so self-delusional that he doesn't even understand that his life can be any different."

"Poor bastard" said Mary.

"Yes" said God, "Poor indeed. But he's not the only one who's disillusioned themselves."

Mary Retorted, "Well of course not said Mary, feeling quite relaxed now, there must be billions of poor fuckers down there who are constantly living lies, angry at themselves for no reason."

God, who was now easily on her 10th shot, looked directly at Mary, her eyes piercing right to her soul and said, "Yeah … sucks to be in denial."

Mary stared at her cockeyed and responded "What are you staring at me with those beautiful brown eyes for Francesca?"

God just rolled her eyes, leaned in close to Mary and ever so gently, kissed her on the lips.

Time seemed to stand still for Mary, she felt as if she was on fire, as if every cell in her body were vibrating.

"Well?" asked God "How do you feel?"

Mary just sat there, frozen, eyes closed, soaking in everything.

God sat back, pulled out another cigarette and said, "That's OK, take a moment … I'll just have a smoke."

Finally Mary snapped back into reality. When she opened her eyes, as wide as she'd ever had them open, and said "Holy Mary, mother of God, I am a lesbian!"

God laughed a little and said, "Welcome to reality, and my mother's name is not Mary, its Bella … but never mind that."

"Wow that felt good!" said Mary.

"What the kiss?" asked God.

"Well I mean yes that was great! But actually I was referring to what I just said …

I'm a lesbian, and … and I'm damn proud of it!"

Mary got up and started doing a little jig singing a chorus of "I'm a lesbian, I'm a lesbian, I'm a lesbian!"

Over and over until finally God stood up and put a hand on her shoulder saying "Yes, yes, we're all very proud of you dear, but really, singing and dancing were never really your strong suits."

Mary stopped and chuckled a little, embarrassed, and said, "Ooops, guess I just got a little carried away."

God laughed out loud and said "No no dear, it's OK, I just have a thing with Lenin in a little while and I'd like to give you your present."

"My present?" asked Mary.

"Yes dear, your "coming out" present. I'm very proud of you, I know how hard that was."

Mary was confused but went along with it, suddenly the scenery changed, and she was in a castle keep, the same keep she'd been to all those years ago, and Lisa was there waiting for her. Mary looked a little stunned.

"You mean to tell me that as a present, you're going to make me relive all that over again?"

"NO!" said God, "Never again … just the good parts, and this time, you both get to do whatever you want. But the catch is, you

only get one day together, then you move on." Mary looked at Lisa, sitting on the edge of the ledge in that silhouetted window … framed so perfectly, then turned to ask God "What do you mean, move on?"
But it was too late, God was gone, and she was alone with the only woman she'd ever loved. She went to her, and they had the most wonderful evening of their lives, all over again.

As the sun was setting, and the two of them were holding each other in bed, Lisa looked at Mary and said, "I love you, and if it takes an eternity, I'll wait for you."
"Where am I going?" asked Mary.
Lisa just leaned into Mary and kissed her on the lips gently, and Mary fell asleep. When she woke up, she found herself in the hospital, all wired and tubed up. She was a bit delirious, and her voice was weak, but she managed to call out to the woman in the corner … the same Mexican woman that earlier the previous evening she'd attempted to beat to death. She was lightly sleeping, and at the Sound of Sister Mary's voice, she jolted awake.
"You're alive!" exclaimed the girl. "I'll go get the doctor she said, as she started to run out.
"Wait!" Mary managed to eek out before the girl left the room.
"Come here." she continued.

The girl hesitantly obeyed, walking over to the old woman as if she were going to rise from her bed and finish the job she'd started earlier. Instead Sister Mary said as she weakly held the girl's hand.

"I'm sorry my dear … for everything."

The girl still wasn't making eye contact, but she had a tear coming down her cheek.

"I'm sorry." she managed to whisper, "I know I'm a sinner, and … and I'm sorry."

Sister Mary just looked at her, "Do you love this young woman you were with last night?"

The girl blushed, "I'm not sure … I just know I've never felt so strongly for anyone like I do for Rosa. But I know she has a boyfriend, and I know that her parents would murder me if they found out."

Mary looked at her through eyes that were clearing up, she really was a lovely young woman, she reminded her a little of herself when she was younger … except for the whole Mexican thing.

"Then be with her child. Be with her, and know that you have God's blessing, and my permission."

The girl had tears streaming down her face now. She muttered something inaudible, but leaned over to Sister Mary, and hugged her, with a face soaked in tears. She then ran off to get the doctor.

The doctor came in. She was in scrubs, with a long white coat that said Francesca

226

De La Rossi, MD in sown on letters. Sister Mary squinted a bit to make sure she was reading her coat correctly, then said "God?" Francesca looked at her and said "Well I'm good, but not that good."

Sister Mary looked disappointed, "It was all a dream then?"

Francesca answered, "Well no one is exactly sure what happens when you die, come back, and lapse into a coma, but I'm pretty sure it might have included some pretty wicked hallucinations."

This made Sister Mary very unhappy she frowned visibly.

Francesca added, "Although I would say that after a traumatic episode like you had, perhaps your mind was trying to tell you something, maybe you should listen."

"Oh" said Sister Mary, "So what happened?"

"Well to put it simply, you had a major heart attack, then died, then came back, only to be comatose for the past three days ... then, you woke up."

"Oh." Said Sister Mary, as the good doctor took her vitals.

"Well" said Dr. De La Rossi, "I'll have to run more tests to make sure you're OK, but you seem to be in remarkably good shape upon first glance. The fact that you survived ... well you might say that was a small miracle in and of itself, a chance at a second life." Still Sister Mary thought about everything that had happened, about Lisa, and about this new reality she was facing, or at least what she thought was a reality … right now Sister Mary wasn't sure what was real. All she knew was that she didn't want to go back to life the way it had been before. Even if it meant going against God's supposed will, or at least the will she'd read about in the Bible.

Dr. De La Rossi went about fiddling with machines and marking her chart, making small talk that Mary didn't really listen to. Finally she walked to the door and said, "Well, I don't really see a reason to keep you here too much longer, I want you to stay overnight for observation just in case, but should be able to get thee back to the nunnery in no time!"
Dr. De La Rossi laughed at her supposed cleverness.
Sister Mary just sulked a little and mumbled "Thank you Doctor."

As Dr. De La Rossi was about to leave, she paused, walked over to Sister Mary, stroked her head a little, and kissed her on the forehead.
"Don't worry, you'll see Lisa again someday … you just have to promise me to live the rest of your life true to who you are dear. You have an important mission to carry out; I'm not so cruel as to yank you back to this life for no good reason."

Sister Mary looked at Dr. De La Rossi wide eyed with wonder as a tear rolled down her cheek.

God just smiled and winked at her, kissing her one more time on the cheek, "We'll meet again my dear, have faith." With that, Dr. Francesca De La Rossi left.

When Sister Mary checked out, she inquired after the good doctor ... no one there had ever heard of her ... in fact she never actually met her real Doctor, although if you were to take him to court, he'd swear under oath that he'd seen her, and all his other patients, just like he was supposed to have. He was so high off of prescription drugs most of the time, he probably would have believed it too.

Sister Mary, true to her word, lived her life as she felt God would have wanted her to. She might have been a lesbian, but dammit all, she was still a Nun, and she was still in the service of the lord as far as she was concerned. She came out privately to the Catholic Church at first. Trying to affect change from within, privately encouraging other Nuns and Priests who were so in the closet that they allowed their lives to be eaten up from the inside. She found that like her, most of them had a very strong connection to God, and wanted desperately to serve ... they just hadn't been able to come to terms with their sexuality, and the contradictions this caused with their employer. What surprised her even more, were the number of straight clergy who while they felt it prudent not to speak out, for fear of retribution, agreed strongly with Sister Mary ... in fact many of them wished to marry themselves some day.

Finally when Sister Mary O'Hurley had a strong following, the Catholic Church did the only sensible and rational thing it could think to do ... it told her, and her band of crusaders to either shut the hell up, or face excommunication. So Sister Mary again did what she felt God would have wanted her to do ... she refused, and announced publicly to the media that she, and a large group of clergy were against Church doctrine regarding marriage and sexuality. In fact she claimed, as she had to many of her cohorts that God herself had spoken to her about this issue.

As a result of her bold actions, Sister Mary was excommunicated, along with three other clergy, two priests, and a Nun. None of her other supporters had the guile to stand up directly to the Church ... they were still too scared.

With the help of several charity organizations, Mary set up a small congregation of reformed Catholics, the congregation was small, and barely recognized by the US government, which despite all its claims of spiritual independence, found subtle ways to make their lives a living hell. It was in service to this new Church of the True Catholic Faith, that Sister Mary O'Hurley died, peacefully in her sleep one night many years later. Her death was mourned by many people … most of them in secret … but the loss that was felt was great for this bold woman.

Mary woke from her final slumber, refreshed, and as with her last trip here, she was 19 again, and in that ridiculous shirt that said "Kiss me I'm Irish". God was sitting in the middle of the Duomo, sipping Earl Grey Tea, with those little shortbread cookies Mary loved so much. Mary took a deep breath and approached God, refusing to sit, or look her in the eye.

God looked at Mary calmly as she sipped her tea, finally saying "Why don't you sit down, enjoy some tea?"
Mary answered, "I don't deserve to … I've failed in my mission."
God just rolled her eyes and said, "For all your good traits, you are soooo ridiculous. You have not failed me … far from it in fact. You've made far more progress for humanity than you know. And yes, while you may not receive the public recognition that someone like Mother Teresa received, your efforts are no less important, and effective."
Mary sat down, partially out of confusion, but mostly because the smell of that tea and

cookie combo was driving her mad with hunger.

"My dear, what you have done has sparked a revolution in religion. People will see what you have done, and build upon it. This combined with the efforts of a few religious groups who, believe it or not, are already accepting of people, regardless of dogma, or their supposed faults, will help lead humanity out of a darkness that has encompassed them for far too long." said God.

Mary let this information sink in, and for the first time in her existence as she had known it, she felt proud of herself. She ate her cookies with a vigor she'd never eaten cookies before!

"Wait", asked Mary, "is pride still a sin?" God laughed, "Not when you're proud of something you've accomplished that truly helps the world … even when it seems like a small thing."

Mary never went back to Earth … unlike many souls, this leg of her journey was over. She was able to spend the rest of her existence with Lisa, as they danced about the universe, living lifetime after lifetime scattered throughout the cosmos … sometimes male, sometimes female, in many species though, gender was sort of an undefined concept. Regardless, their souls never again left each other … and they

danced through the universe, creating
happiness wherever they went.

The Man Who Felt He Never Was

Mark Smith sat in his Mother's living room. It was late, and the lights were out, but the soft light of suburbia illuminated the quiet night. The silence was only broken by the sound of the old grandfather clock, ticking away in the background. Mark listened intently, slowly counting away the seconds as he sat there. In the moonlight he could just make out a picture of him and his Great Grandmother. She was sitting in a chair much like the one he was sitting in, wearing a flowered dress, smiling while he stood under her with a blank face staring off into the distance. Mark looked into the boy's eyes gazing back at himself … looking off in the distance. He was empty then, and he was empty now. The only difference was that he had gone on the terrestrial merry-go-round of life fifty or so times.

He poured himself a drink, finishing off the bottle of whiskey. He took a swig, the alcohol dulled the pain less and less the longer he lived. The clock continued to tick … it was enough to drive someone mad, but for Mark, it was another distraction, and as he felt the pain of the clock burn into his head, he took it in … he deserved it. "What the fuck am I doing?" he thought to himself. He thought about his daughter upstairs in his old room. Sleeping quietly … what the hell

234

kind of life was this for a child? Mark was a failure in life … or so he figured. Fifty-two years old, and what did he have to show for it? Nothing. He was on disability, couldn't get a job, and now … he was homeless, living with his mother, not even divorced hell his daughter's mother hadn't even had the common decency to marry him, let alone stick around long after she was born. Not that this was his fault, but as far as he was concerned … everything was his fault. Even the economy crashing, making it impossible for him to find a job was his fault … at least partially, and as far as Mark Smith was concerned, if a man didn't work, if he didn't take care of his family … he wasn't worth the ground he walked on.

He took a deep breath, that smell brought back memories … the house filled with family, his father before he'd died, his Mom running around after the three of them, one brother and one sadly tortured little sister. Things were so much simpler back then, you knew what you wanted to do, what you wanted to be. Whether it was an astronaut, a policeman, a cowboy, or a Space cowboy sheriff, it didn't matter, that's what you wanted and that's what you were going to be someday. You never counted on being a delivery man for a local grocery store chain. No one ever wanted to be that.
No one ever said "I want to get hit by a car while walking across the street carrying a

235

cranky old woman's grocery delivery, go to the hospital, and have to sue your employer to get them to pay you a miserable sum of money that barely covered half of your living expenses, an amount so small that you had to find a job while in constant pain, which required you to be on your feet anyways."

All the while you received sub-standard medical care from a health care system that cared more about saving money than saving lives, all while raising a child who worshipped the ground you walked on, even if that ground was poisoned.

A normal person would have gotten mad at the system, written their congressman, protested, joined a militia and held a federal building hostage, found religion, anything … but not Mark Smith. Mark blamed himself. Worse than that, his little girl was getting older now, and oh God how she reminded him of her mother. More importantly, she'd start to understand what a looser her father was. She'd see through him and leave eventually … sooner or later; just like her mother … everyone saw Mark for what he was and left.

Mark took the last sip of his drink, and put his head down on the table, where through a steady stream of tears he fell into bliss-less, troubling sleep. The next thing Mark felt was a hand, and a head on his shoulder. He opened his bleary eyes, and saw his daughter sitting next to him, her eyes closed, and her blanket draped over him. Sometime in the night she had come down to sleep with him. He looked at his watch, Five AM. He sighed, and picked her up, returning her to his old room, where he covered her with the blanket, and sat there watching her sleep, watching her chest heave up and down rhythmically. It reminded him of the clock ticking, but it somehow had the opposite effect. It calmed him, and for a small moment, life was OK.

He had to straighten up his life. She couldn't see him like this again. First things first though, he had to eat breakfast, and take a shower ... usually people wouldn't hire you without having done those two things first. He went down into the kitchen, it was like so many other houses in suburban Fairfax, VA ... early 80's chic, with chestnut brown cabinets, that had the cheap handles you could buy in bulk from any hardware store, along with the classic linoleum floor, cleverly designed to simulate a real 1950's tiled floor in someone's imagination of what a kitchen floor should have looked like. There were the new appliances of course ... because none of the original ones had bothered to last much past the mid 90's, except for that damn trash compactor ... the thing just sat there, staring at you, daring you to use it. Mark had often had nightmares where he found himself trapped in the damn thing as it attempted to crush him. To top it off you had the compressed particle board countertops with a thin layer of light yellow ... some sort of coating.

The best part was, you could walk into just about any house in the neighborhood, and find some variation of the same theme. Mark remembered one time waking up in a friend's house in the neighborhood that lived in an identical model to his and walking around groggily, wondering who had switched all the furniture around in his house.

An hour later he sat at the kitchen table again, eating burnt eggs, burnt toast, and burnt bacon ... all cold. He imagined later he'd go to Starbucks and top it off with some burnt coffee, but hopefully warmer. As he sat there playing with his food, his mother came down. Alyssa was an older black woman, with straight, but slightly nappy gray hair, with streaks of black still in it. She was wearing her purple robe with matching slippers. Were it not for a little extra weight, and the gray hair, she would have looked like she was in her early thirties. Maybe even younger had it not been for raising kids, and losing a husband. She looked at him, he looked so much like her husband, Marcus, especially in the eyes, he'd always had the most beautiful light brown eyes.

She said "You could have waited
sweetheart, I would have made you
breakfast."
Mark smiled, "That's OK Mom, I didn't
want to trouble you with it."
She came over and kissed him on the
forehead, "That's your problem son, it isn't
a bother at all, just ask."

He knew she was right, and he knew she
was just trying to encourage him, but still it
made him feel guilty for not having asked
for help all these years past.
"Thanks Mom. You're the best."
She chuckled a little, "I know it. Now
you've just got to believe the same thing
about yourself."
He grumbled a little, "Now come on Mom,
please don't start this."
She started to make coffee, "OK, OK, don't
get all upset with me. All I'm saying is that
if you want something, you know all you
have to do is go out there and get it. I have
faith in you."
Mark just sat there quietly eating his burnt
breakfast, he hated it when people
complimented him … but when they praised
him, especially someone as accomplished as
his mother, it burned a hole right in his soul.
He wasn't good enough, he knew it, and he
knew everyone else knew it, they were just
patronizing him.

He didn't appreciate it, but it was his Mother, and he managed to push out a convincing sounding "thanks Mom."

After eating half of his breakfast, Mark went and showered, got dressed, and almost made it out the door before his little girl, Lisa, came out in her pink nightgown, hair messed up, blanket in tow, came over and latched on to him.

"I love you Daddy. Have a good day."

Mark bent over and gave her a kiss on her forehead and said, "I love you too sweetie. I'll be back tonight in time for dinner."

"OK daddy" she replied, "You'll do good, I know it, you're the best."

He hugged her tight and kissed her as he left. Her words burned him like a snowman being attacked with a hair-dryer. He quickly got into his Powder blue 1989 Honda Accord, and drove off as quickly as possible. He knew she was looking at him waving with a big smile on her face, so he kept his eyes straight ahead, it was too painful to look at.

Mark was a man without a plan. Mark had always been good with numbers. He'd always wanted to be an engineer. It was a strange dream he knew that. Most people had wanted to be an Astronaut or a big shot actor. Not Mark though, Mark loved numbers. He was a number junkie. Even today he loved doing complex math problems … it calmed him down; it brought

him hope, made his dreams more intense …
but not recently. Some nights he sat there
with a pen and paper looking at the complex
problems he'd written down, and he
couldn't do them anymore. The music was
gone … he used to hear music when he did
math problems. But the music was gone,
now the only thing that seemed to make him
feel better now was whiskey, and other
assorted spirits.

Mark drove aimlessly around the empty
streets of Northern VA. Not that they were
literally empty, just that they seemed empty
to him. The hope he'd had as a kid was
gone. He felt alone, all he saw when he
looked around was people who were better
than him, people who deserved happiness,
but not him. Mark was the worst excuse for
a human being one could possibly imagine.
A monster who'd ruined his life, and the
lives of everyone around him. Now he was
doing it to his daughter, the only person that
truly loved him, that didn't judge him. She
would one day if he didn't get his act
together. He went into Starbucks, ordered a
Latte, and sat down. He didn't care what
anyone said, he liked the coffee here, and he
liked the fact that wherever he went, any
Starbucks looked like any other Starbucks. It
was relaxing to him. There was a calm sort
of order to it, an order that seemed to be
lacking sorely in his life these days. Maybe I

could work here he thought to himself …
Why not?

Mark went to the kid behind the counter, though he could have been pushing thirty, to Mark they were all kids.

"Are you hiring?" he asked. The kid looked at him confused and a little scared.

"I don't know" he said, "I'll have to ask my manager."

The kid stood there as if he were waiting for a reply from Mark.

Finally mark said, "I'll wait."

From the reaction he got from the kid, he might have just told him he had to go to Vietnam. The kid begrudgingly tromped off to the back room, the young lady next to him rolled her eyes and snickered a bit.
Apparently he had interrupted their conversation with work.

The manager came out with what appeared to be a giant plastic clown smile plastered on her face. Mark was sure that if he had a conversation with her about drowning kittens, her face would have been the same as it was now.

"How can I help you sir?" she asked.
Apparently the kid who went back hadn't bothered to tell her what it was he wanted … too much work he figured, either that or she didn't care.

"I'd like to know if you're hiring?" he asked a little sheepishly, having second thoughts about whether or not this was really a place he wanted to work.

Keeping the same fake smile, she said "Well sir, we are always accepting applications."

Mark hated this new age corporate crap. It was a canned answer and he knew it.

"So, are you hiring or are you just accepting applications?" he asked.

She seemed to stumble for a hot second, "We're … We're always accepting applications here at Starbucks."

Mark was starting to get annoyed, "So you aren't going to tell me whether or not you're hiring, you're just going to keep on towing the company line."

She continued to smile, but he could tell by the way her eyes had crinkled a little that he had thrown her way out of her comfort zone. She was getting lost … the corporate training had derailed her train of thought.

"I … I … we can certainly take and review an application."

Mark just sighed a little, took the application that she had pulled out from under the counter and was holding out, and quietly thanked her.

Mark sat back down, he looked over the mass produced application and sighed, he didn't know what was worse, having to fill out this garbage, or the fact that he had to go back and ask for a pen. He'd forgotten to bring his with him. After thoroughly inconveniencing one of the other employees

who seemed to be in an important
conversation with another co-worker about
how he boyfriend was a complete ass
because he only took her out to a so-so
restaurant for their one month anniversary,
and she just had to tell everyone in earshot,
whether they were listening or not. The girl
finally found a pen stuck in her ear and
handed it to him, by tossing it on the counter
without looking so it rolled onto the floor,
and proceeded with her diarrhea of the
mouth. That was the problem with kids
today, they all seemed to have the inability
to keep their private lives private, and
separate from their work lives ... everything
for them just sort of seemed to bleed over
into one.

   Mark stared at the application, after
filling out the basics, name, Social, and
address, he got to the work history part.
How embarrassing this was for him. He was
50 and he'd barely been able to hold down a
real job. He was just some grocery store
delivery man ... not that he hadn't taken
pride in what he did, but it was embarrassing
to him to look at his 50 odd years of life and
realize that that's all he'd accomplished.
Hell why would these people hire him.
There wasn't anything worthwhile about
him. He doubted he could even do this job
right.

   It was sad, a man of his age and
intelligence, a man with a family, and as far

244

as he was concerned, he wasn't even qualified to serve coffee to people. The demons of depression began to grip him hard again. What the hell was he doing here? What was he expecting? That they'd hire someone like him? He was old, pathetic, and he probably couldn't keep up with these kids anyways. In a way they were better than he was. They probably had futures, happy ones. Suddenly he felt very small, and very embarrassed. People were judging him. He knew it; all those kids were quietly talking about the old man that wanted to work at a Starbucks, it probably creeped them out, knowing that some old disgusting man wanted to work with them. Suddenly he didn't even want the job. He stopped filling out the application, grabbed the application and walked out.

As he was heading to his car in a blind fury, he heard the voice of the perky manager from behind him.
She had run out into the parking lot screaming oh so politely, "Sir! Sir!!"
Did he forget something? What the hell did she want? He turned to her and said nothing, just stared coldly. This must have frightened her because for the first time since meeting her, she stopped smiling. In fact all the color seemed to have drained from her face, and she looked downright scared of him.

Sheepishly she got the words out, "Sir, you can't leave with that application, it's against the law for us to let it out of the store."
All Mark could think of was, "Of all the stupid things to say."
Who the hell was she anyways? She was just some stupid kid who probably didn't care whether the store burned down or got an award, just as long as she got her paycheck. He just looked at her, and for a brief moment feeling superior to her and said, "Then why don't you do something about it, why don't you have me arrested bitch?" She just stood there dumbfounded … apparently no one had ever had the balls to challenge her on anything before. He got into the car and drove off, making it a point not to look at her as he drove off. He may not have much left, but at least he could leave with his dignity.

Mark drove around aimlessly some more, tried filling out some more applications at a few more retail stores, only to get similar treatment, and eventually have a similar reaction to each place. Finally he got up to Old Town Alexandria, his favorite place on earth to be. Even though it was only 1:30 PM, as far as he was concerned, he was done for the day. He'd had enough humiliation to last him a lifetime. Mark wandered down King Street after parking at the metered lot at the King Street Metro … at 25 cents an hour for 10 hours, and it was free after 6 PM, it was the best deal in town. Plus he loved to walk down King Street when he was depressed. There was something about King Street that was calming to him. It was unchanging, or at least in the context of the area, which had changed so much since he was a kid that he scarcely recognized anything anymore. Farms and forests had been replaced by endless rows of strip malls and cookie cutter housing, many of them named after the families that had been forced off of their land to build, or after the battles that had been fought to form, and re-form this nation. It was depressing to know that places where people had given their lives so that the United States could exist and people with his particular melanin levels could walk around free, now all had a parking lot and a Wal-mart.

Not Old Town … there was an air of respectability here. You could walk down some of the streets that were still lined in cobblestones and imagine what life was like here at the birth of the nation, and during the civil war. You could lose yourself in that history, and eventually you would get down to the waterfront by the Potomac. This is where Mark would wander down to Waterfront Park, and sit on one of the hitches, and dream for hours as the planes flew overhead into Washington National Airport. It was all he could do to keep sane.

After a long time sitting on the waterfront, maybe an hour or two, just lost in his thoughts, Mark began to stare at the brown water. It was peaceful looking, the waves lapped gently against the concrete barrier that had been placed there so that ships would have a place to dock, and apparently so that the town wouldn't flood, but that wasn't usually very successful. The waves seemed to be talking to him, calling him into the water. It was a promising idea. Besides he really didn't have much of a future. Who would miss him anyways? Maybe his daughter … still she'd be better off if he wasn't around.

"Bull shit." a little voice of reason spoke up. "She needs you."

"No" he answered back, "She needs a father, not me."

He'd contemplated suicide for a long time, how long he wasn't sure of; all he knew was that the sun was going down. Ultimately he decided it wasn't worth it. Not because his daughter needed him, or the will to live had suddenly struck him. It was just that the water was dirty, and cold … and that Mark was deathly afraid of being in the water, so much so that he doubted any suicidal urges could drown out his fear of sticking his head into the water. Instead, he went home, defeated, and tired.

That night was pot roast night. His Mom always made the best pot roast. Mark was really looking forward to a good meal.

"So how did the job hunt go today?" his Mom asked.

The moment was over, this could be the best pot roast in history, but Mark wasn't going to enjoy it.

"It was OK Mom … you know, I put in a bunch of applications … I don't think anyone's hiring though."

His Mom just ate her pot roast and smiled, "You'll find something."

"No I won't" he thought to himself.

No one wants an out of work, over the hill delivery boy on disability.

His mother started, "You know the government is hiring, you could always try and get a job with them, and once you're in …"

Mark interrupted his mother, "You're in … I know Mom. I've tried that … they aren't looking for someone like me."

The truth was that he wasn't really trying all that hard to get a job with the government. He'd filled out a few applications, but usually he'd get frustrated with the whole process and give up before it was all over. Either because he didn't like the questions they were asking, or because he just felt like he was someone they didn't really want even if he did meet the qualifications.

Frustrated, he blurted out "I know Mom, I'm looking, OK!"

"OK Mark, don't get short with me, I'm only trying to help." His Mom answered.

For the first time in the meal his daughter piped up "Yeah daddy, don't be mean to Grammy. She's just trying to help."

Mark fumed with rage at this comment, it was bad enough getting advice from his mother, but to hear his daughter reprimanding him … it was too much. But luckily, Alyssa being an expert in conflict resolution, mostly coming from having to raise four children, spoke up.

"Sweetheart, your daddy is trying very hard to get a job now, but he needs our help too, so I want you to stop talking about this unpleasantness, give your Daddy a kiss, and clean up the dishes. If you do a good job, there's ice cream in it for you."

These were the magic words that needed to be spoken. While they immediately enraged Mark, they delighted Lisa, whose enthusiasm, combined with a big kiss and hug, immediately pushed back the rage Mark was feeling. He couldn't help it; he just let it all go.

Unfortunately, the very thing that Alyssa was so good at was what made Mark even more depressed. By repressing, or not being able to express his frustrations, he just got more depressed, and pushed harder inwardly on himself. He felt like he was dying on the inside and in a way … he was.

That night his Mother put Lisa to bed, this was punishment enough for Mark, who enjoyed more than anything watching his little girl go to sleep at night. The worst he feared was yet to come, the inevitable lecture from his mother. The endless prattle on about how he needed to straighten up his life, about how much potential he had, about how it wasn't too late to make something of himself, and if not for him, then for Lisa. The fact was he'd heard it all before. It was old hat to him. He sat down and waited for it. The clock began to tick away again, he tried to focus on the ticking, to wash away all of the BS he was about to hear. As he suspected his Mom came down the stairs as usual, sat down across from him and stared … the calm before the lecture as he liked to call it. But instead of lecturing him … she just stared. It was a long hard stare, one followed up by her shaking her head, leaning across the table, and kissing him on the forehead.

"Good night Mark."

That was it? He was expecting the mild mannered Mom version of the Spanish inquisition, but instead got a kiss and a good night. Somehow though, it was worse than the lecture, and after sitting for a long time, he opened up the sideboard, and pulled out another bottle of whiskey. But tonight was different … Mark poured himself a glass, and stared at it, stared for hours. This was a first; Mark was too depressed to drink. "What am I going to do now?" he thought, "I guess since I'm sober, I'll go for a drive." It wasn't long before he was back in Old Town Alexandria, but instead of getting out of the car and walking down King street again, he just sat in his car and cried, it was a pathetic sight, seeing a man who by all accounts should be a linebacker in the NFL, sitting in a beat up old Honda, which might have been a clown car for anyone looking from outside was concerned. He just cried … sobbed his heart out, all the while realizing what a pathetic mess he'd made of his life, and how he'd just continue to live on like this … until eventually he died, and no one missed him. Suddenly he realized what he had to do. Mark got out of his car; even though it was the middle of the night he fed the meter, walked over to the railroad tracks by the Amtrak station, laid down on the tracks, and waited for the train to come.

While he waited, he played a selection from Chopin Piano Sonata No. 2 on his MP-3 Player. As he lay there on the tracks, the sun coming up over the horizon, he felt the tracks starting to vibrate a little. He was excited and scared all at once. There was still a small part of him that wanted to live … he wanted a good life, he just felt like he didn't deserve one. His heart was racing faster now, the train was approaching, the darkest part of Chopin's Sonata was playing … the part that everyone associated with death … the whistle was blowing madly now, Mark said a little prayer for the conductor … he knew what he was putting him through was wrong, but he couldn't think too much about that … the conductor was doing him a favor, and if there was an afterlife, he'd apologize someday.

The whistle was deafening; Mark's heart was racing now … he held his breath and waited … any second now. The train was coming right? Why was it so quiet all of a sudden? Mark opened his eyes, it was daylight out now. He was still lying on the tracks, but there was no train coming … it was quiet … too quiet. Mark looked over to his left and saw a man sitting there … half naked in Jeans, with 2 cups of coffee from Misha's Coffee house in Old Town. The man just sat there, expectantly. Mark looked around … the landscape was the same, Carlyle Towers looming like a dark castle attempting to overshadow the Masonic Temple. But there were no people, no cars … the noise was gone, just him and a weird homeless white guy with a long beard, no shirt, and apparently no body hair.

After a long silence waiting for the man to say or do something … he finally spoke, "Well are you going to take your coffee, or am I going to have to drink both of them myself?"

Mark hesitated, "What is it?"

The man smiled and said, "Your favorite."

He held out his hand which looked much older than his face, and Mark hesitantly took the orange Styrofoam cup from the man, and carefully took a sip … and indeed it was his favorite, Route 66 Blend no cream, no sugar. It was great … it always was.

"So what is this? Purgatory? Hell? Heaven?"

The man just shrugged his shoulders, "Dunno? It's your afterlife."

Mark looked around disapprovingly.

"I always imagined there would be more flowers in the afterlife."

"No you didn't, if you did, they'd be here." replied the man.

"Well I certainly didn't imagine there'd be a half naked, hairless white man with coffee."

The man took a sip of his coffee and smiled, "Well … sort of. Too many years of going to church and seeing images of a white Jesus has jaded you a little."

"Oh, so you're Jesus?" asked Mark.

"Um … no, actually I'm God, but he is my son, sooo … sort of. I think your Church really kind of intermingles the two concepts."

"So what am I doing here?" asked Mark. God laughed so hard that coffee came out of his nose.

254

"Uh, does "I laid down on the train tracks waiting for the train to roll over me" ring a bell? And the VRE for God's Sake … yes I'm allowed to take my own name in vain … I mean, you couldn't have waited for an Amtrak train, maybe the Acela Express train. Although I guess that would have been a little messier, but hey if you're gonna go, go out with a bang, right?"

Mark just stared at him for a minute, "Are you sure you're God, because you sure don't sound like him?"

God just shook his head, "First of all, don't call me God, it's so formal … call me Pete, I like Pete, Mark was puzzled by this remark. Finally God gave in, "Fine, call me God" second, how would you know what I sound like, it's not like I recorded my greatest hits on an album or anything."

Mark thought about this for a moment, "You mean you didn't sing on the White Album?"

God just laughed at this and said, "No, but I played drums."

Mark just shook his head and sipped his coffee … not at the same time, because that would have been messy, but one after the other.

"So now what" asked Mark?

God simply laughed and pointed behind Mark as he sipped his coffee, swallowing a little too fast and choking a little on it. Mark turned around to find he was practically nose to nose with a train of some sort. After jumping out of his skin for a moment, Mark calmed down and grabbed his chest which, he thought, had a heart that beat awfully fast for a dead guy. He calmed down and marveled at the train. It was a shiny metallic silver color, with a square plastic, window that had two giant windshield wipers covering them. It didn't seem to have many marks on it; there was an electric sign on it that displayed the destination, which read "we'll see". This kept blinking and reappearing intermittently. It also had a big yellow circle with a black "Q" written in the center. Mark suddenly realized, this was a subway train from NYC.

When Mark turned around to ask God what was going on, God was gone, instead he heard his voice coming from the opposite direction urging him to "come on". When Mark turned back around, he found himself on an elevated platform on the side of the train, God was standing there using his body to hold the doors open, as they made an annoying "ding-dong" sound, and the conductor was screaming over the intercom, "Get out the way of the door! Now!"

Mark didn't ask, he just jumped onto the subway car and the doors closed behind him angrily … that is assuming doors can be angry, but he was pretty sure that these ones were, and he wasn't about to ignore the "do not lean on the doors sign" just in case.

As the train started to move along the tracks, Mark looked around and saw that the car was fairly full of people they all had vacant looks on their faces, some of them coughed, one guy in a trench coat picked his nose and flung it at the heels of some guy, and even though it hit his shoe, neither one of them seemed to notice or care.

Mark scuttled over to sit next to God, and asked him quietly "Are all of these people dead?"

God just grinned a little and whispered back, "No … their New Yorkers. If I stood up now and peed in the corner near one of them, they either wouldn't notice, or wouldn't care."

Mark was going to protest this, but having been to NYC on many an occasion, and having ridden the subway before, he realized there was a great deal of truth to God's words.

"But why not the Metro" Mark asked?

Because if we took the DC Metro, we'd end up with a lot of concerned people wondering why we were so lost … and besides, the Q train runs express … they don't have express trains in DC … too stubborn to admit they need it. That and …"

God paused "Well nothing."

"What" asked Mark?

"It's nothing … you'll laugh."

"Come on" said Mark, "out with it!"

"Well" said God, "I really like the musical Avenue Q … I always thought that Gary Coleman was far more talented than his reputation afforded him."

Mark just stared at God for a long time. "I know" said God, you think it's stupid … I don't blame you."

After a long awkward pause Mark finally spoke up, "Huh … I just always thought that Gary Coleman's career was evidence that there was no God. I mean if anyone's life sucks … its Gary Coleman's."

God laughed at this, "Not proof that I don't exist, just proof that I don't meddle in your affairs unless it's absolutely necessary."

"What about natural disasters" asked Mark?

"Well, you're not going to like the answer, but I won't lie to you … they're absolutely necessary."

The scenery changed rapidly as they chugged along. Buildings aged quickly and either fell down, were renovated, or replaced all together with.

He called out to God "Are we traveling through time" he asked?

God just chuckled, and without looking back just said, "that would imply that time is a journey when in fact, it isn't even linear."

Mark wasn't a genius, but he did like to read, and he thought he kind of understood. "So you mean this is a "what if" kind of timeline … like, what if I killed myself, then there would be a result as a consequence."

258

This stopped God, and the train, quite literally in its tracks ... time stood still too, just enough for Mark to notice that all the roads were now pedestrian walkways, and the air smelled a little cleaner.

He turned and looked at Mark and said "Well sort of ... it's actually a lot more complicated than that. You see ... how do I put this in a way you can understand it? Oh I've got it, it's like all of time and all possibilities exist simultaneously for me. They aren't separate, and the ability to reach them isn't limited to me by the same space time you live in. It's all kind of blended together like a milkshake. The problem is that humans haven't developed the sensory organs to feel out the molecules that make up time and space ... once you can tap into these, well let's just say it changes life a lot. In fact, this is one of the key things that separate you and me, the ability to perceive and manipulate space-time. As a matter of fact if you really want to know, we're kind of the same species ... but I'm just a little bit more advanced, but at the same time, I'm much older than you ... in other words I evolved from you, but you also evolved from me ... at the same time, but ... but different times. In fact the very concept of death is ludicrous if you think about it, it doesn't really exist ... I've completely lost you haven't I?"

Mark just stared at him very confused.

"OK then" said God, "Yes it's exactly like that."

With that Mark just shook his head, God turned nervously away from Mark, and the train continued on up the tracks.

Amongst all the drab melancholy there sat a man in the corner, not so obviously homeless, but obviously out of his gourd. He just rambled on. Directly insulting people, but never getting a response.

"Oh nice day to go to Paris, don't eat the food there, gives ya the runs. Don't eat the women either, gives you all sorts of other diseases. You a French lady? You look like one of them hyped up snobs crawling with disease, sleeps with anything that'll buy you a drink, whore. How about that guy there, he looks like a fuckin' cheeseburger, why don't you squeeze him for some money, go head, he look like he could afford to lose a few pounds!"

Mark leaned over to God and said, "Doesn't anyone care that there's a rambling lunatic yelling at everyone on the train?"

God just looked at him and said, "There's always a rambling lunatic on the train in NYC. The real trick in life is not becoming one of them yourself."

As they continued on, the train made a stop at … well he wasn't sure where it was as the announcer seemed to mumble "This is wah, wah wah wah wah"

Then the doors opened and passengers who were seemingly unaware of their surroundings proceeded to get on and off the train.

All the while the crazy man in the corner kept shouting at them, "Go head get off, ain't like nobody's gonna miss you turkey headed whores, go make some ugly babies together."

Then someone vaguely familiar got on, it was a much older woman … but she looked vaguely familiar to him. She was old and frail, her hair was completely grey, she had large glasses and a mouth that looked like it had once had many more teeth in it than it did now. She sat down next to him, muscling god out of the way, she turned her head toward Mark and stared for a moment. Then she slapped him much harder than a woman of her advanced years should have been able to … it hurt enough that he started to wonder if he was dead or if he'd just woken up from a long sleep, only to discover that life was the dream. She looked at him with anger, a tear running down her cheek, and then she hugged him and started sobbing. Suddenly Mark knew exactly who it was, "Mom!" he blurted out in a sudden panic, followed by an overwhelming wave of shame. "I'm so sorry, I didn't mean to, I mean … I …"

She pulled back for a moment and said "You didn't mean to? I see, so what you're saying

261

is that someone forced you to lay down on those railroad tracks and wait for the train? Or did you just fall asleep on the tracks and for get to set your alarm for when the train was coming?"

Mark was silent, never before had so little been said to make him feel so stupid.

"Why did you do it?" asked Alyssa. Mark stammered "I don't know Mom … I just … I guess I couldn't take it anymore. No one was going to hire me anyways, so what was the point? I mean I was pretty much worthless to the world."

Alyssa just shook her head and mumbled "Just like your father … just like him."

"What's that supposed to mean?" asked Mark, who had a stunningly brilliant picture of his father in his head.

Alyssa continued, "Oh he killed himself too … but every day he lived he spent complaining about how miserable his life was. But he never really did anything about it until it was too late, until he'd killed himself."

"Wait" said Mark, "I thought Dad had a heart attack."

She looked over at the crazy man who was now eyeing God and pointing at his crotch while screaming "Come on savior boy, come get you some crabs or maybe some herpes!" Alyssa just stood up and said, "Look jack ass, I've had enough of you, we've all had enough of you. If you would just shut up for a moment and care about something other than yourself for a change, and let me talk to my damn son! This may be my last chance for a long time, and I'm not going to let a self-centered, no-nothing jack ass like you interrupt! Do you understand?"

The man retreated as far into the corner as was physically possible, bit his lip, and looked down at the ground. Mark wasn't sure, but he looked like he was going to cry.

Alyssa sat back down, and never took her eyes off the crazy man in the corner. "I don't know just who he thinks he is talking like that to everyone … some nerve!" Mark was a little startled, his mother, while a little emotional at times, was usually a rational person, someone who always taught him to respect people, especially the homeless and the mentally deranged.
Mark asked "Mom, what's wrong? Why so angry?"
She just looked at him and a sudden wave of understanding came over her face, "Oh you mean because of the way I treated him? Hmph! Trust me, he deserves it!"
She directed the next line at him "And he knows damn well what it is he did!"
She put her hand on his knee "Baby, I know I've always told you to respect people, especially those who are disadvantaged, but after you ride this train for a while, you get

to know that man … and he isn't disadvantaged at all … he's an ass hole putting on an act, and if you don't stand up to ass holes once and a while, you get to be just like him." Mark looked over at God for a little support … instead God just shrugged his shoulders and said, "She's got a point!"

Suddenly, the train ground to a halt, flinging some wide eyed tourists forward, almost into the laps of some annoyed natives who grumbled a little, but pretended not to look. The conductor mumbled out the stop, Mark could have sworn he said "42nd street", but he might have said "Hey sweet meat" for all Mark knew … was 42nd street near the East village he wondered.

"This is my stop Baby" sighed Alyssa. "But why do you have to go now?" asked Mark, "Why can't you just stay with me?" Alyssa just shook her head and said, "Because believe it or not, life goes on. Long after your body dies … and besides, I'm tired of this old body … the joints are achy, everything is sagging, and the face I have now is not my favorite model."
"Can I come with you?" asked Mark.
"No baby … this isn't your stop … but we will meet again, and hopefully I'll be prettier the next time you see me."
She kissed Mark on the forehead, and slowly wobbled out with the crowd. The crazy man in the corner, sans Alyssa suddenly got his

courage back and screamed as the doors closed.

"That's right bitch, keep walkin'. Go get you some chicken wings in hell."

Then suddenly the doors opened again, and stayed open.

Alyssa popped back in for a moment, looked right at the man and said "What did you say?"

He seemed to retreat like a wounded dog being chased with a stick, saying nothing in response.

"That's what I thought, you coward!"

With that, Alyssa turned and walked out. As soon as the doors closed, the man just straightened out, and stared out the window, now silent.

The train moved ahead now, the time seemed to pass slowly; Mark decided to ask God why bad things happened to good people.

To which God just rolled his eyes and said "Don't you people ever have anything original to ask?"

Mark was silent … God didn't bother answering.

As they were clunking along, the train wobbling to and fro, the door at the other end of the car opened … the one that was supposed to stay closed at all times. In fact the sign said they were locked for "your safety". Apparently the MTA was more concerned about their safety from lawyers that they were about actually protecting people. It was disconcerting; until Mark realized that all these people were already dead … at least he was pretty sure they were. He was a large man (Wide, but not so much tall) … very white, and very bald. He wore an old, dark colored suit … Mark wasn't sure if it was black or blue … it was just old … maybe as old as the man. He sat down next to Mark. Just close enough for Mark to realize that, well to put it nicely … he stank. The man smelled heavily of alcohol, and cheap cigarettes, and a body odor which belied a man who had never really gotten the concept of running water down. He smiled a big gap-toothed, yellowing smile at Mark and said something in some sort of Slavic language. Then off the confused look on Mark's face, he realized the mistake he'd made and spoke up in English, but still with a strong Slavic accent.

"You want?"

Mark looked into his Jacket and saw a bottle of Vodka unlike anything he'd seen, and wanted desperately to say yes. But then he remembered who he was sitting next to and politely refused.

God looked at Mark strangely and said, "Well I hate to be rude, but if you aren't going to have a drink, I sure as hell will." This caught Mark off guard and said, "You drink?"

God laughed out loud, "Amongst many other bad habits my friend. In fact, this is the most mundane day I've had in a while. I could use a drink."

The fat white man laughed, "Maybe I should have a drink with someone I never really believed in?"

God just rolled his eyes and said, "Oh come on Nikita, you and I both know that deep down in that huge gut of yours, beneath all that Communist hard line BS, you knew I was real."

Nikita just chuckled a little "yes, yes I suppose I did old friend, I suppose I did."

After a moment of contemplation, Nikita took out the bottle, unscrewed the top, and proceeded to remove his shoes and use them as glasses. Mark felt like he was going to vomit a little when he watched the two of them drink … perhaps he didn't want any after all. He looked at God in a whole new light now … with less reverence, and a little more disgust.

"What?" asked God … "If it's strong enough it adds to the flavor, and disinfects your shoes."

As disgusting as this sounded, Mark started thinking about this, and it made a good deal of sense to him.

"Fuck it." Said Mark, and he grabbed the bottle out of Nikita's hand and took a swig.

It was good.

"The best you ever had!" said Nikita. "It is Russian! Everything is better in Russia! Even this subway! It is good, but in Moscow, it is better!"

Mark wanted to argue with him, but to be honest, he'd never been to Russia, and so he couldn't tell him with any certainty.

"How would you know things were better in Russia than America, if all you have to go off of was this subway ride?" asked Mark.

"Oh, I've been to your United States. It's a lovely place … except for Los Angeles … tomatoes, bombs, and hapless movie stars … hmph … I did like your hot dogs though, very delicious."

Mark looked quizzically at God and asked "is this the Nikita I think it is?"

God nodded at him as if to say "who the hell else would it be?"

Mark just looked back and forth between the two of them, "wait, how is it that you two know each other?"

Nikita laughed hard at this and said, "How does he know me? Have you ever read your American Bible? He made everything right? So then why wouldn't he know me?"

"Sure" said Mark, "But surely you don't have conversations with everyone?"

God answered "Only the ones who don't want to talk to me. I hear enough from the ones who do want to talk. Besides Nikita and I play squash every Sunday morning."

Mark looked a little shocked and said "So when everyone else is in Church, you're playing squash with a former Communist dictator?"

Suddenly God got what can only be described as an "Uh oh" face and Nikita began slamming his shoe on the seat next to him screaming.

"I was appointed a Premiere by the government of the people, I wanted peace, I wanted justice for the world, especially America who lives in such tyranny by a government they claim to have elected, and does all it can to pacify them and keep them blind to the world at large. It was your Eisenhower who with one breath was talking of peace and prosperity between our two Governments, and in the other sending planes to spy on my country! I ask you, who is the bigger dictator, the one who cares about the people or the one who lies to them and to his friends."

"SORRY!" said Mark, "it isn't like I sent the planes myself is it? No! Sometimes you can't get everything you want out of life! You just have to keep trying until you either get what you want or die trying!"

Suddenly a big grin came over Nikita's face, and he looked at God and said "I told you I could get him to say it! You owe me a dinner at Michelangelo's!"

God rolled his eyes, and said, "Fine, we'll go Sunday after our game."

"Get me to say what?" asked Mark.
Nikita patted him on the shoulder and said,
"Mr. Smith, you are a good person, and you
know what you have to do. It is like the
black samovar calling out to the color black.
You just need to hear yourself say it
sometime. Here, you take this Vodka, a gift
from Mother Russia to Mr. Smith."
With that he kissed Mark on both cheeks,
got up and walked over to the next car.
On his way out he said, "See you on the
court!" Mark just looked at God and said,
"What the hell was he talking about?"
God shook his head and said, "I'm never
entirely sure, but he's right, you give up too
easy. You're always looking outside
yourself for the answers that are right there
inside that uncomfortable body of yours."
Mark still didn't get it and asked God,
"What's a Samovar?"
God took a swig from Nikita's shoe and said
"kind of like a tea kettle, but a lot more
complex. Come on, this is our stop."
 The train stopped suddenly, screeching to a
halt like all NYC subway cars do, apparently
unable to slow down and come to a gentle
rest like most subway cars in DC did. Mark
often wondered if this was just a New York
thing, or if the trains were really just that
badly designed. They stepped out into a
dingy hole of a subway stop. It was the City
Hall station. It was eerie to Mark who was
used to the clean and orderly Metro stops in

DC to walk into a NYC subway stop. It smelled like someone had urinated … many times … and thrown up … and then did it again and again. The heat was stifling, it enhanced the smell tenfold. To add to the creepiness of the whole experience, someone decided to add tiles that looked like eyes onto the walls … and unbeknownst to Mark, they were in the future, and these oddball eyeballs had been updated to double as security cameras. The worst thing is they followed you everywhere you went.

Mark didn't have long to ponder the effects of such unsettling surroundings as he found that he had to push his way through, or more accurately, flow like a glass of water in the ocean with a massive throng of bodies pushing him forward to the stairwell. He usually liked to at least have had a shower and a shave before he got so close to people, but there was no time, and he seemed to be the only one who noticed. Before he knew it, he was above ground right next to City Hall.

"New York City!" Mark marveled, "It never fails to amaze me how beautiful this city is." It was about this time that he realized this wasn't the present age, as he looked around, the buildings looked tall … even by Manhattan's standards, and there seemed to be some sort of walkway connecting the buildings on several stories. As well as flashing billboards that seemed to appear out

271

of thin air, always facing him directly, in fact some seemed to pop right in front of his face, trying to sell him everything from cotton boxer briefs to breast enhancement procedures. God rolled his eyes, and waved his hands, the blinking advertisements seemed to disappear instantly.

God Looked at Mark and said, "Pop ups. They're really annoying."

They walked along Chambers Street to the courthouse building, it seemed to stand out amongst the mish mosh of buildings that crowded the skyline. Not quite as tall, but older, and more majestic somehow.

As they walked up to the line for security, Mark started to take off his belt, and remove all the metal objects from his pockets, when God put his hand on Mark and stopped him. He was about to explain when Mark noticed that everyone who went through the metal detectors seemed to laugh hysterically, as they passed through.

"What is that?" asked Mark a little too loud for some people's comfort, but this being New York City, everyone pretended not to notice he was even in the room.

"Security" said God. "They abandoned metal detectors and physical searches of people a long time ago. Now you have to go through the tickle-O-tron, a machine that provokes people to laugh hysterically or cry depending on their intentions. If they're in a bad mood they cry, and they don't get through the door. The theory being that if you're a terrorist, you'll have poor intentions, and it will provoke a negative emotional response."

Mark was dumbfounded, "Wait, what if you've just had a bad day, or suffer from depression? For that matter, I'd imagine that someone planning to blow up the building would be happy as hell to come in and do his thing. If he isn't then maybe he'd just take some happy pills and walk on through … it doesn't make any sense."

God chuckled, "Yeah, its Government mandated security; it doesn't have to make sense. Besides, if people really knew how many people actually wanted to, and I mean REALLY wanted to commit some sort of terrorist act, let alone were smart enough, or level headed enough to actually go through with it, and not have anything go wrong … no one would bother with security. Besides, with the training these people get, if someone decided to go ballistic, or detonate some sort of bomb, it would be detonated before anyone had a moment to react. But still …"

And with that statement, Mark passed through the Tickle-O-Tron, a sudden wave of joy passed through his body … joy he had not felt in a very long time. Mark began to laugh uncontrollably, God followed him doing likewise. They tittered like schoolboys along with all the other people who'd gone through security, as they walked down the corridors to courtroom 14-F.

The courtroom was packed with people, there wasn't a seat in the house … not a one … except for the two up front and center that God was able to find.

God looked at Mark who eyed him quizzically, and said "What? Sometimes it pays to be the all mighty."

One of the three judges banged his gavel chuckling to himself, and as the room got quiet, you could hear not a voice, except for the courtroom personnel, who apparently had had to go through an extra layer of security and were chuckling to themselves. Apparently the head judge, who looked to be about 300 years old to Mark, either didn't go through security, or was incapable of showing any sort of emotion, as he banged his gavel and yelled at everyone to "SHUT UP!" But even in his impassioned plea, there was a distinct lack of emotion driving his words.

Judge emotionless went on, please call to order the first case.

The bailiff stepped forward, "The US Supreme Court of Appeals will now come to order, the Hon. Judge Charismatic presiding."

Mark leaned over to God and whispered, "Judge Charismatic?"

To which God whispered back, "Yeah, proof that the universe still has a sense of humor."

Suddenly Mark had another question, God leaned in and said, "The legal system has changed a little since you've been dead … not to say that a federal Supreme Court of Appeals was ever your country's smartest idea, but … eh, the people have spoken, and you'll get just what you deserve."

The first and only case of the day was called to order. It was a case about whether the state of Idaho could legally sell tennis balls to the state of Mississippi, but pay taxes in the Commonwealth of Kentucky because they had a store that straddled the border of both Mississippi and Kentucky. After he got over the shock that Tennessee had been divided up amongst the surrounding states in order to deal with the fact that California had divided up into two states in order to remain fiscally soluble, that and the fact that West VA was ceded back to VA because that state had gone bankrupt, and Puerto Rico had become a state … much to the chagrin of the Commonwealth of VA, which was doing just fine on its own, thank you. All of this because it kept the number of stars on the flag at 50 so they didn't have to replace them all and burden the flag making industry … which ironically was located entirely in Canada, which outsourced to China, which outsourced to The Democratic Republic of the Congo, now the center of the capitalist manufacturing world. After that shock wore off, he found the whole case to be boring. However God assured him that in fact the stability of the USA and the world economy actually hinged on the outcome of this case. Apparently in ways he couldn't understand. "But it's so boring, and pointless" argued Mark.

To which God answered, "Sometimes things seem that way, but believe me, the smallest detail is not unimportant in the grand scheme of things."

The trial was so boring in fact that it was halfway over before Mark noticed something he found interesting. The rather attractive young lady who was arguing on the behalf of the tennis ball manufacturers was named Lisa Smith.

"HOLY CRAP! Said Mark so loudly that he was almost shouting.

But the same urge that made him shout and stand up had been conveniently stifled, so that all Mark got out was a small, whispered, incoherent sound, with his but firmly glued to the seat. He looked over wide eyed at God and wanted to say something, but god just looked ahead in great concentration at the affairs at hand, and raised his hand while nodding his head, as if to say "Yes it is, and I know, now hush!"

But he suddenly became very interested in the plight of a tennis ball manufacturer in Idaho … in fact he found that the rest of the trial was very interesting. He felt like he was

276

watching the Super bowl all of a sudden, and the Redskins were playing the Cowboys (he knew this was impossible, but it didn't matter). His daughter was suddenly Joe Theismann. Every argument she made was a score for the Skins, and every time the opposing counsel made an argument, he wanted to scream at them to sit down and shut up! After all, his little girl was a lawyer ... a lawyer. Suddenly he felt guilty ... he couldn't explain it, he wanted to throw up ... he did, no one seemed to notice.

"I want to leave." He whispered to God. God looked at him and said firmly, "No. You're going to sit here and watch your daughter effect the course of world events, and you aren't going to say another word until the trial is over."
Mark wanted to protest, wanted to get up and leave, but he found that it was physically impossible but to do anything but sit here and listen. Tears streamed down his face as the trial continued until the court came to a decision.

The verdict was read, Lisa had won the case for the tennis ball manufacturers. Mark was happy his little girl had succeeded somehow in warding off a global war ... and he wanted to leave. But God wouldn't have it, Mark was going to go talk to Lisa whether he liked it or not. Mark protested, pleaded even.

God was firm, he said "Listen here Mark, I may not be the harbinger of doom and gloom that the world sees me as in your time. I try not to interfere with international affairs; I try not to interfere at all. But there is one thing I won't stand for, and that's you leaving your daughter who by all accounts deserves her father. Now you get your butt up and go talk to her now." Mark felt compelled to do what God said; in fact he really didn't have a choice in the matter. He walked over to Lisa, his feet moving of someone else's volition, and walked right up to her. She saw him and dropped everything. "Daddy!" she said. "But you … I mean …" She was unable to complete her sentence, as she passed out in the middle of the court room.

Suddenly people rushed to her aid from all angles, Mark wanted to help too, but he was unable to move. The room spun around uncontrollably, and the next thing he knew, he was in a dimly lit room sitting on a chair around a table with two other people sitting with him. One of them was definitely God, the other one was too obscured by darkness to see. They were both smoking, a pack sat on the table, it said "God's Finest" on the box, and had a picture of an angel with sunglasses, looking cool, with a smile and a ciggie hanging out of its mouth. The angel had its thumbs up, and was mouthing "Oh yeah." The smoke coming from their sticks smelled … well it smelled really good, and had a calming effect on him. Mark had always hated smoking, but found himself reaching for one anyways … it felt cool on his lips, and the cig lit itself. He took a drag and relaxed. "All right" he said to God, "What was the fucking point of that? Am I supposed to feel guilty that I left her? Well I do. But she seems to have turned out all right. I mean she's a successful lawyer, beautiful, well adjusted."

God added, "And she's got a beautiful family."

Mark thought about this for a moment, "so does this mean my life really was a big waste?"

God closed his eyes and shook his head. Mark went on "I mean she seems to have had a great life without me … I'm guessing it was because I left or something … so I actually did the world a favor by offing myself." God just rolled his eyes and said, "maybe … but consider this, she would have grown up the same one way or the other. That's one determined little girl you have there."

Mark was even more confused by this. "So you mean to say that I had no bearing on her life at all? Basically I'm worthless." At this, God leaned back into the darkness and disappeared altogether with into a cloud of cigarette smoke. The man who had been sitting next to God the whole time, silent, leaned forward.

"With one exception you circle jerking fuck face …"

As he leaned forward, Mark suddenly felt himself bound together at his feet, and his hands, now behind the chair were bound as well. The cigarette still hung from his lips. It was the crazy ranting man from the subway. He got up, and seemed to be enormous … there was something terrifying and familiar about him.

"You fucked up son … you really fucked up."

Suddenly Mark understood who this man was.

"Dad?"

The man stopped in his tracks, suddenly aware that he'd given himself away too easily. He took the cigarette out of his mouth and put it out on Mark's forehead. Mark screamed in agony, "Stop it!" he screamed, still unable to move.

His father simply responded, "Make me, idiot."

He walked around while he watched Mark breakdown sobbing as Mark's father began hitting him repeatedly as he circled Mark and said, "You think that it's funny abandoning your kid like that? Huh? Do you? You little shit; you don't deserve a little girl so nice. YOU DON'T DESERVE IT!"

Mark was angry now. Mark was so angry that despite his best judgment, despite being impossibly bound to this uncomfortable wooden chair, he was slowly pulling apart his bonds, fully intending to kill his … dead father.

Mark's Dad went on "Oh what? You wanna hit me? Go ahead and try. The truth is you're too much of a little girl to do anything about it. Because of you the cycle will continue. Lisa will have 3 beautiful children, 2 girls and one terrified little boy, who will grow up without a father. Why? Because when they're all no older than 6, he kills himself, just like their grandfather" for a moment, Mark's Dad stopped, and got quiet, he said so that Mark could barely hear him, "Just like I did."

Mark's Dad continued, "Oh don't look so surprised boy, I couldn't take it either, figured your mother would be better off without my lazy ass. Well I guess I was right about two out of three of my children." Suddenly Mark's Dad kicked him over on his side, and began kicking Mark.

He continued, "What are you going to do about it boy? Hit me? Well come on then do it! Get up and hit me! Get up you worthless shit! GET UP!"

With that last jab Mark managed to free himself from his bond, and was ready to jump up and clock his Dad in his face.

All he heard was "GET UP!"

281

Over and over, but there was another more curious noise that almost seemed to drown out the yelling, a loud, earth shattering rumble, followed by a horn. Suddenly his Dad's voice was replaced by his mother's voice. The floor was replaced with the train tracks, the train was about to hit him, and his mother stood off in the distance, running towards him screaming "GET UP! GOD DAMN YOU SON GET UP!"
Without thinking twice he pulled himself up and fell forward as the train grazed by him, the horn billowing all the while. He hit his head when he fell forward, rolled over dazed to see his mother standing over him in tears. She leaned down and kissed him. When she raised her face up, the world went dark.

Mark awoke in the seat of his Beat up old Honda, his daughter sat next to him; they were sipping Misha's Coffee.
"Lisa" he said, practically dropping his cup in the process.
"No" said the voice of God coming out of this little girl he knew and loved.
"Oh" he answered.
"So I'm still dead then."
The little girl looked straight ahead, emotionless and reluctantly said "No, I decided to give you another chance ... you took it."
Mark thought about this, "Oh ... I ..." he couldn't think of anything else to say.
So God answered, "You're welcome."

"Yeah" said Mark, "Thanks."
Suddenly more animated God, whose voice sounded increasingly creepy coming out of his daughter's mouth, said "I didn't want to do it. I like giving second chances, but I really didn't want to do it this time. I like you … in fact like all of you people, I love you. But you need to grow up. Life isn't about just you. Stop being so fucking selfish, grow a pair and deal with life, or so help me I will do things to you so horrible that no holy book in existence could even begin to describe the amount of pain you're going to be in."
Mark just sat silently, a lot dumbfounded.
"You have a good life Mark, stop bitching, OK?"
Mark took a sip of the Route 66 coffee, and said "OK."
His daughter smiled and suddenly sounded like herself. She leaned into him and gave him a kiss, Mark closed his eyes, felt her grab his hand, and heard her say in her own voice, "I love you daddy."

When Mark opened his eyes he saw a blinding light, and it hurt, a lot. His daughter was sitting right next to him. She was holding his hand and smiling. It was only then that he realized, really realized how great his life was.

Mark's life was never easy after that. He was forced to go see a therapist, which he felt was a waste of time because he really did see the value of his life now. But he figured it was part of his punishment for being so stupid. Actually, in the long run it helped him. His therapist seemed to know what the hell she was talking about, and she gave him tasks to do, tasks that seemed to help him keep busy, and not only realize how valuable his life was, but forced him to enjoy it. He eventually got a job at Misha's coffee house, and found he liked it so much, that he became the manager, and was even allowed to expand the franchise a little, which actually put a few Starbucks out of business.

As life and the world continued, he met a woman, got remarried, and even got to see his daughter argue the case of the tennis ball manufacturer … which really was a lot more exciting the second time around, especially taken in the context that he actually knew what the hell was going on with world affairs. He died at the ripe old age of 85 … never having led a stellar life, but a happy one. One where Lisa's husband decided to stick around after a few jarring incidents involving her father and … well Lisa was never quite clear on the next point, but something about driving with his hand stuck in the car, while he ran alongside, and some sort of vague threat about cutting off his genitals … like she said, Lisa was never entirely sure of the details.

When Mark finally did pass away, he found himself in the afterlife playing squash with Nikita, God, and some sort of Octopus like creature named Nich.

He asked God, "I thought I did everything you asked me to do … why are you torturing me anyways?"

God just rolled his eyes and said "Shut up and play jack ass."

Master Gunnery Sergeant Gary Evans

Master Gunnery Sergeant Gary Evans sat in Joe's Bar, in the same seat he'd sat in for the past … he wasn't sure how many years. Since the war ended, since his wife left him and took his kids … time seemed irrelevant to him. What was important was that this was his place in life, this was his seat. This aging relic of a man in an aging relic of a bar, which had once been new and bright, full of life, pretty women, music, laughter … was now his life, a dying shell of its former self. This was a place where the wretched dregs of a decaying society came to sit and waste the time while they slowly poisoned themselves with drugs, liquor, and pop music. It was a place where the youth came with a sense of self-entitlement and grew old too fast, where people slandered the very place he had sacrificed everything for. A place where the young whined about problems that were trivial, and the old whined about the young. It was a place where Gary watched the world he'd fought for die slowly in its own self-destructive ways. It was fitting then that Gary should be here, on V-E day.

Gary picked up his double malt scotch, a man's drink, one that he was most certain that only he drank. Gary surveyed the run down bar … Joe's

"It's a damn shame that they still call it that
… Joe's been dead for years, so have his
kids, and their kids have moved on. What
the fuck do any of you know about Joe?
Now it's just some fucking wreck of its
former self wasting away so that you punks
can piss away perfectly good lives, well you
can all go to hell!"
He drained his drink, and called out to Jeff,
the bartender, "Another one Signor!"
Jeff spoke perfect English, but because of
his Mexican heritage, he was not all that
foreign to the concept of people talking loud
and slowly to him so he understood "their"
language. Usually he would have said
something, but he'd said something to Gary
so many times in the past, that this hardly
seemed like the appropriate time.

Gary stared across the bar, "You there,
hippie kid with the dark hair and bony ass,
what's your name?"
The kid looked at him, "Mark sir."
Gary rolled his eyes, "So is sir your family
name or are you just a fucking moron?"
Mark looked around confused, only
managing to pipe back with a weak, "Huh?"
"Your last name jack ass! Don't they teach
you idiots anything in school anymore? Or
do you even go to school?"
He looked down, "Sorry sir, Mark
Lucarelli."
Gary took a fresh swig of his new drink,
"Sounds like a fucking fairy name anyway."

Mark squeaked a little, trying to sound brave, but not angry.

"It's Italian sir."

Gary drew in a deep breath as he closed his eyes and transported himself back in time back nearly 70 years, back to a time that might have been yesterday for all he knew anymore.

"My God I was only 19 years old son."

He screamed, "19 years old!"

Tears ran down Gary's inebriated, and bloated red face, and Mark was silent, shaking at this man, this ancient pariah who he'd seen in here time and time again, but never bothered to talk to, in fact he might have been furniture before tonight. But now he spoke, he had a name, and he demanded respect from everyone in that bar.

Gary went on "You've never been to Italy have you Mark?"

"No sir, but I'd like to …"

Gary cut him off, "I have. Oh God have I seen Italy … not the Italy you have today. I've seen pictures, beauty, and modern life, sacred places used as little more than tourist attractions by half-wit morons who have no respect for anyone or anything. People more concerned with what they're wearing and how drunk they can get that they don't remember. No one remembers any more. Do you even know what we went through so that you could sit here and pass off a fake ID and drink, complain about the very country

288

that exists not for you, but for everyone …
do you even understand me? Don't answer
that. You have no idea what it means to care
about anything, not another person, not
another place … hell you look like you
barely care about yourself. Yeah, I
remember Italy … Florence. It was so
beautiful then, even after days of fighting.
There was hardly anything left, but it was
still so beautiful. I killed so many people …
people that were your age, or a little older.
Boys, do you understand me? We were
boys. But we had to, it was our duty, we
were liberating the Italians from tyranny,
Understand?"

Mark just sat there silent … the whole
bar did as Gary continued. "I was so scared.
I remember I was cut off from my entire unit
… I was surprised by a lone fucking Nazi,
he came out of nowhere. There wasn't time
to react." His voice trailed off, he took
another drink. For a normal man this
evenings alcohol consumption would have
been more than enough to knock them out
… but Gary's liver was made of alcohol at
this point … and no amount of alcohol was
going to stop him from rambling. Not
tonight.

"I was alone, and in a burned out alley,
when this Nazi ... he was a kid, like you
Mark, a lot like you. We just stared at each
other, scared to death, both of us alone, and
both of us just wanted to go home. But there

we were, sworn enemies who probably had more in common than my wife and I did when we got married after the war."
Gary seemed to switch his trail of thought for a moment as he thought about his unpleasant marriage to his Ex-wife, a relationship that they had both equally destroyed.

Then he snapped back into his alcohol fueled tirade, more heated than he had been before.
"After what seemed like an eternity, we both snapped back to the hell that was our reality. Neither one of us liked it, but t was either him or me. That day, as luck would have it ... it was him. Not because I was faster, we both nearly pissed our pants raising our guns and firing, but for whatever reason ... his gun jammed, and mine didn't."

"I remember that one more than the rest of them, it's rare that you get to look them in the face, see into their soul ... As I was peering into his pack, I learned more about him than anyone I've ever killed ... I could have been going through my own pack ... porn, cigarettes, and a journal ... in Italian, I never understood a fucking word of it, but I could imagine the hell he'd gone through!"

He was now screaming at a woman in the corner who was practically in tears. Her boyfriend eyeballed him, and he knew he'd stepped over a line, but the man showed restraint. It helped that Gary backed away

290

into his seat again. He wanted to apologize, but he was a Marine dammit, and to apologize was a sign of weakness, and Gary would be damned if he was going to show a sign of weakness to some ass hole who'd never served in the military … well maybe he'd been in the Air Force, it was hard to tell the difference.

Gary stared at them all. He'd thoroughly scared everyone in the bar. He downed his last scotch of the night, stood up off the bench he'd called home for so long, screamed out, "God bless America" and pulled the trigger of his 9MM Beretta, which was pointed at his head, making a permanent mark on the bar he'd help keep in business since the war ended.

After a brief, but predictable flash of pain ... Gary just stood there.
"Why am I still standing?" he wondered.
It was as if time had stopped. There was no noise but an annoying whooshing sound; everyone's motion seemed to be arrested, except for their eyes. Everyone's eyes seemed to dance with a terror he knew would never leave any of them as long as they lived. Was this the mark he'd left on the world? Was this all he'd be remembered for? The crazy loon who shot himself after raving about a war which, despite its importance was as little in the national consciousness as President Garfield, and with time would only fade more? People

forgot too easily the sacrifices of others so that they could survive and prosper, people became self serving ... but then in a strange way, wasn't that the point?

Slowly the world faded, until all that was left was silence and darkness. This trend continued a disturbingly long time. Until Gary started to worry that this was going to be the rest of eternity, an eternal silence to persist throughout the ages.

"What a fucking drama queen!" thought Gary.

"What? That's a long time!" he responded to himself.

"OK, OK Gary, get it together. You're a fucking Marine, and God damn it if they're going to fuck with our mind ... I mean, my mind."

Damn this was confusing.

"Besides" he thought to himself, "this couldn't be any worse than the lines at the DMV!"

A half hour or so of this passed before he finally heard a noise ... it was a piercing harpy of a woman, who was obviously disgusted with the world and people at large, her voice had a gravelly quality which was befitting of someone who could have made an argument for making smoking an Olympic sport, a woman after his own heart! What the fuck was she saying? The words sounded familiar to him ... but it was like he had to relearn how to interpret language again ... it was ... it was …

"NEXT!!"

Next! Next what? Was he at the DMV? The voice came again, "SIR!!! YOU'RE NEXT!"

Gary panicked a little; he found his voice again suddenly. It was like riding a bike for the first time after a long time. True you never forgot how, but it was a little shaky at first, but familiar.

"I can't see you! Where are you?"

The voice was suddenly very quiet, and he realized that whoever it was was incredibly close.

"Try opening your fucking eyes." she said. As if this were a brand new concept to him, he suddenly opened his eyes, and found himself in ... well, what looked like a DMV office.

The walls looked like they had been white at one point, and the carpet looked like it had been a nice blue color, but this decorative choice had long since disappeared, and it all seemed to fade into a grayish color. There was a single line that seemed to stretch on for an eternity. The woman who had been gently caressing him with the verbal equivalent of a jackhammer stood behind a desk like a bank teller, the glass that protected her was thicker than his gut, but uncharacteristically clean for an office of this caliber. She had a cigarette

between her lips that looked like it had
started to burn through the filter. Her eyes
looked like they had seen more in their time
than all of humanity. Her head was
abnormally large, with her hair pulled back
so tightly, that you could see veins straining
against the weight of her hair. Her glasses
looked as if they were as thick as the glass
that protected her from what had to be a
cranky public ... and of course, she had a
long scaly tail like an alligator.

"Huh" he started to say.

To which the woman responded, "Yes it is a
tail, and yes it does look remarkably like a ...
what planet are you from?"

She flipped through a binder labeled
"Intelligent species of the local cosmos"
until she found what looked like a human.

"I guess that's what you are, though it looks
like you put on a few more pounds than this
guy. Earth? Then an alligator's tail, and
before we go any further let me just get this
over with ..."

She stuck out her tongue which was long
and slim with a split at the end like a very
long snake's tongue. She used it to scratch
her cheek before pulling it back in.

"I know, weird right? Great, now that we've
gotten that over with, what's your last name
sweet heart?"

He had to think for a moment, "Umh ...
Gary, Gary Evans, Master Gunnery Sergeant
Gary Evans ..."

She rolled her eyes, "all right, I'm going to guess that whole thing isn't your LAST name, we'll just go with Evans, First name Gary."

She stopped to read the screen, "Uh huh ... uh huh ... oh ... uh huh ... I see ... hmmm ..."

She stopped and stared hard at him before continuing matter of factly, "Really sweetheart? Had a little temper tantrum and blew our brains out in front of a crowd of civilians after several years of drinking and feeling sorry for ourselves did we? How noble."

She took a long drag of her cigarette before staring at him and rolling her eyes. She then went back to silently typing and judging him. When you put it that way, it did seem ridiculous and selfish; Gary was suddenly feeling something he hadn't felt in years ... embarrassed.

She finished typing something then printed off a piece of paperwork that said Newt on it.

"Well sweetie, for your gross stupidity, you get to come back to Earth as a newt. Take this paper down to the ..."

She spoke as she stamped the paper and started to hand it to him, when suddenly a red light started to flash next to her computer. She froze in mid sentence and stared at the light. She quickly threw the cigarette on the floor and stamped it out, as if someone were suddenly watching her, cleared her throat, and as her hands shook, picked up a phone receiver from under the desk.

With great forced politeness she said "Yes sir? Yes sir. Right away sir."

She slowly hung up the phone, and took a deep breath before lighting another cigarette and taking a deep drag to steady her nerves. Finally she snatched the paper out of what seemed to have been thin air, and tossed it into a wastebasket behind her where it combusted.

After a long moment of smoking her cigarette and quietly judging him some more she finally shook her head and said, "never mind sweetie, you either did something really right, or really wrong. You're going to see my boss instead."

She stood there and stared at him expectantly.

Finally saying, "Well move along gorgeous, I haven't got all day here!"

Gary stammered for a moment, obviously confused, "Umh, where do I go ..." he looked at her name tag pinned to her chest, "... umh Delores?"

She just leaned back against her tail, took another drag, rolled her eyes, and pointed off to the left. There was one door against an otherwise bland wall, and a sign over the door read "God, this way."

He was about to thank her when she screamed out "NEXT!"

The process seemingly repeated itself with another poor soul ... someone who looked remarkably like Stalin but with a nicer suit and scales ... with his eyes shut ridiculously tight.

Gary walked up to the old, but unassuming door, turned the knob, which was covered in dust and obviously had not been touched in a long while, and pushed it open. The door was incredibly heavy, and once he opened it, he stepped into a very dark hallway.

What was it with this place and complete darkness? The hallway was so dark, that even when the door had been open, and the fluorescent lights from the DMV flooded in, all Gary saw was darkness; it was as if there was a wall where the door was that blocked the light completely from his view. The door shut behind him, and an uncontrollable wave of fear washed over Gary's body. He suddenly, and instinctively turned around and grabbed the doorknob, ready to bolt back to whatever that perverted version of the DMV was, give Delores a huge kiss on her lizard tongued mouth, and beg her to send him to whatever fiery hell awaited ass holes like himself.

Except, there was no door ... he waved his hands around frantically in all directions, and found nothing! His sense of panic increased as he continued to flail around, and the air grew more chilled, and he

297

thought to himself in horror, "what if this is my hell?" At first Gary ran around the place looking for anything, and after a while the air seemed to cool down to a temperature that was akin to a freezer. Finally, Gary sat down and huddled in on himself. He figured, if he was going to spend an eternity here, he might as well do it frozen all the way through.

As he sat there and contemplated how fucked up his life had been, he suddenly heard a voice.

"Mastery Gunnery Sergeant Gary Evans, atten hup!"

Even though it had been half a lifetime ago, Gary's body suddenly felt hot with adrenaline and he jumped up and stood at attention! A Marine it appeared, never stopped being a Marine ... even after he died.

The voice continued, "Step forward and meet your maker son!"

Gary hesitated for a moment ... where was he supposed to step; he was surrounded by nothingness and cold.

"Sir" he started to say.

The voice interrupted with great force, "DID I ASK YOU TO SPEAK?"

Gary was silent, "HELL NO I DIDN'T! NOW GOD DAMMIT SON I SAID STEP FORWARD, AND MEET YOUR FUCKING MAKER!"

298

Gary obeyed, stepping one foot forward into the abyss that enveloped him, only to find that the abyss was gone and he had stepped into an office.

It was an old office, with wood paneling (actual wood paneling, not the cheap faux crap they started using in the 1980's. In front of him was a large desk, made out of hand carved ... well wood of some sort, what sort he wasn't sure of. And behind the desk sat a five star general, in a WWII style uniform, which was completely authentic from what Gary could tell. He was shuffling through a stack of papers, sucking on a cigar, barely paying attention to Gary, who was standing at attention, 19 again, and in his full WWII Marine uniform himself.

The General haphazardly finished some sort of paperwork, barley looking up at Gary. When he finished, he leaned back in his chair, threw his feet, clad in perfectly shined boots onto the desk, puffed on his cigar, and studied Gary silently for an obscenely long amount of time. All the while, Gary stood at attention. Something he remembered hating intensely from his days in the service.

The general spoke, "Gary, you are the most piss poor example of a marine I have ever laid eyes on."

Gary wanted to protest, but his military training kicked in, and he stood fast and silent. The General continued, "You had one mission in life son, one calling. A mission which I gave specifically to you ... a job so simple that even a half wit Air Force wanna-be jag off looser like yourself could have done in a matter of a few days. I gave you sixty five years of life to complete, and you wasted that entire time drinking, and complaining about how much you hated the world."

Gary was silent. Not only because he couldn't recall what mission in life he'd been given, but because the General was right. He had pissed his life away. Drinking, feeling sorry for himself, and worst of all, blaming it on everyone but himself, and never doing anything about it.

"Shit" he thought to himself, "I don't deserve to call myself a Marine."

As if in Response to his thoughts, God answered him, "That's right son, you don't deserve to be called a Marine. By all rights, I should kick your ass right here, strip you of your uniform, and send you back to Earth to live out a thousand lifetimes as the lowest form of life possible!"

Gary blurted out "As a newt sir?"

God stared at him, pissed off that he'd had the guile to say anything.

"No son ... that was just a warm up. I was thinking of making you a God Damn career politician! And before you open your mouth again son, remember who the hell you're talking too! But to answer your dumb ass thought, no it doesn't count when I damn myself!"

Gary stood there frozen, as God paced back and forth in his office, apparently thinking something over as he chewed on his cigar and smoked it at the same time. Finally he stopped and stomped his foot hard on the ground, turned to Gary, and said, "But the fact of the matter is, this is your lucky fucking day! You just won the cosmic fucking lottery! Son, thanks to a series of cosmic events so fucking unreal, you're getting a second chance."

Gary couldn't stand it anymore, he spoke up, "With all due respect sir, what mission did I fail to complete?"
God rolled his eyes, and said "Come on!" With that they were suddenly transported to another place, somewhere very familiar to Gary, it was Italy, in the 1940's ... it was the hospital he'd been taken to after the push to take Florence! Well if you wanted to call it a hospital, it was more like a church that had been converted to a hospital to accommodate soldiers in a triage system, it was a place where injured soldiers generally went to die, in agony. For the first time in a long time, Gary was truly terrified. Then she walked in, the most beautiful woman he'd ever had chance to lay eyes on, and the most terrifying, Donatella DiFranca.

As if to mirror his thoughts, God said "Wow! What a beauty!"

Gary answered, "Yeah, but scary as all hell. That woman gave me so much trouble; it almost made me wish I'd died that day." God smacked Gary on the back of the head and replied "That's probably because you just ruined her city, her government, and at least one of you grunts most likely killed more than one of her friends or family members in the process of "Liberating" the Italians."

Gary stood dumbfounded for a long moment.

"That's right, it never fucking occurred to you that you weren't exactly welcomed in by everyone you came across, and even if you were, it doesn't mean they didn't resent you all, at least a little for fucking up what had taken them a long time to create, a civilization."

Gary thought about this, and it nearly brought him to tears, it was something he'd considered, but never fully realized. It took the master of the universe telling him to make him really realize it.

Suddenly God's expression softened a little. He didn't look like the terrifying S.O.B. he'd been all along.

"It's OK son. It's OK to cry, it's OK to let go of it all. There are no victors in war ... only victims. That is at least as long as you let yourself be victimized."

Gary had no intention of crying, but suddenly without warning he began to ball like a schoolgirl who'd just had her pig tails yanked by a mean kid on the playground, ad God did something uncharacteristic of the Marine Sergeant persona he'd adopted, He gave Gary a hug as Gary continued to sob on his shoulder.

When he was done Gary pulled back, only to his surprise, God was no longer a Marine, he was a woman. A fairly old one at that. She had kind eyes, gray hair, and wore a long coral blue dress with a tie around the middle, loosely tightened. Her smile penetrated his heart, and for the first time since before he went into combat all those many years ago, before he killed and watched friends die in front of him on a daily basis, he felt like a human being again.

He suddenly felt like apologizing for everything he'd done wrong in life, like he needed to make amends for every sin he'd ever committed.
But she just smiled, placed her finger over his lips and said, "There's no need to apologize. Sin is a construct of man, created for the sole purpose of making yourselves suffer. Let it go, and instead of agonizing over it, move on. You have a second chance now, a rare gift few humans get. Use it wisely, and do some good in the world." Gary stopped and nodded. As God walked away into a soft glowing light that had appeared at the end of the hall in the makeshift hospital.

Gary called after her, "But what is this mission I have to complete? You never told me!" Almost as an afterthought, God paused without looking back and said, "Vittorio Lorenzo is his name. He has a mission for you; I can't express to you how important it is that you complete it. It may not make sense to you, but the fate of humanity rests in your hands." With that she stepped into the light and seemed to vanish instantly. Gary stood staring at the spot where she had been standing, dumbfounded and dazed.

Gary wasn't sure how much time had passed when he suddenly heard a voice snap him back into ... well, reality was one way of describing it, but to him nothing today seemed very real.

"HEY!" the voice snapped at him.
"You see something you like? Because if you stare any longer, I'm going to have to start charging you!"

Gary was suddenly aware that he had been staring unknowingly at Nurse Donatella DiFranca, possibly the most beautiful, and frightening woman he'd ever known. As usual, she did not look amused.

Gary suddenly realizing the gravity of his situation snapped back with what he considered a clever, witty retort.

"I ... umh ... I mean, it was just that umh." Sadly his witty retort was unable to complete the journey from his brain to his mouth; and Gary had to settle for his nonverbal stammering. Donatella simply rolled her eyes, walked right up to him, grabbed him by the ear and yanked him along and threw him into h bed with magnificent force. Of course, being thrown into bed by this woman was a thrilling experience for Gary, and something he had often fantasized about through the years. He imagined she enjoyed it just as much, just for different reasons. She suddenly screamed at him, "and if I catch you out of bed again before you are better, I'll come in while you're sleeping, and smother you myself!"

As she walked off, he hoped she would make good on her threat ... but probably she'd just threaten him again ... which was of course a close second prize in his mind. It suddenly occurred to him that he was young again, barely 19 years old; he pulled out his pocket mirror and marveled at how young he looked. It was like looking at a whole other person, or a little less than half the person he had grown into, depending on how you looked at it.

After he was done satisfying his narcissistic urges he got back to the task at hand, this mission God had talked about. Who was Vittorio Lorenzo? He met quite a few Italians on his tour of duty, but no one with that name stuck out to him. He lay there pondering for a while, when he suddenly fell asleep, the events of ... well it only seemed like a day had passed for him, but in fact a whole lifetime had, and then back again to near the beginning, wearing him down ... he was somewhat of a basket case.

As he slept, his mind entered an intense dream state. He was in the Oltrarno section of Florence, just passing the Porto Romano. As he made his way slowly up Via Romano, and turned into an alley he had one of a hundred moments that GI's who serve in combat collectively termed "dumb luck". He was just passing a cafe of some sort with the windows blown out, when from around the corner came this scared looking Italian ... kid, who had somehow gotten a hold of a German rifle, and wore a Nazi uniform. After staring at each other the kid instinctively raised his gun pointing it straight at Gary, who thought, this is it ... it's been a good run, but this really is it. But even though the kid wasn't more than a few feet away, with his rifle pointed dead on at Gary, somehow he missed ... completely.

Then as he was pulling the trigger again, his gun jammed repeatedly. Gary didn't have time to think, he just raised up his gun and shot. He hit the poor kid right in the head ... he died instantly. Another life that would never be realized, snuffed out in a flash, all in the name of fear and stupidity.

Gary was a lot low on supplies at that point; he took off his pack, and opened up the dead Italian's pack. There wasn't much in it. There was some food, a few personal Items, some great Italian porn,and various other useful items intertwined with various other useless items. Gary decided it would be quicker just to dump what little was in this man's pack into his, and sort it all out later. As he did, he looked into the man's face, trying to ignore the big hole in his head; he wondered often what these people's families would think of him, knowing what he did. Would they forgive him? I mean, this man would have done the same to him having had the chance ... but would they really care? I mean this was someone's son, maybe even someone's father. He wasn't sure, and he wouldn't have long to think about it, because as he put his pack back on, ripe with goodies, a grenade went off nearby, Gary was blown several feet back, and hit his head against a stone wall, effectively knocking himself out.

When he opened his eyes again, he was still lying on the rubble next to the wall he'd been slammed into, only he couldn't move ... he really couldn't even feel his body, as he lay there, no pain, no feeling at all!
"Uh oh" he thought, "is this still a dream, or am I really paralyzed?"
As he struggled desperately without success to feel or move anything, he had his question answered, as he suddenly heard the electronic styling of the theme to Seinfeld

playing all around him, as if in some sort of hideous stereo.

To add to the hideousness, suddenly from around the corner came Seinfeld, George, and Elaine.

George came up and proceeded to poke him with his finger saying, "Jerry, is he dead?" Jerry answered "How should I know, do I look like a doctor?"

Finally Elaine chimed in, "ewww ... George, don't touch him, you don't know where he's been!"

George responded, "What? I just wanted to see if he was still alive or not!" Elaine rolled her eyes, "George, you're disgusting."

He shot back "I AM NOT DISGUSTING! I'M CURIOUS ELAINE! CURIOUS! THERE'S A DIFFERENCE! Jerry, tell her there's a difference!"

Jerry looked at Elaine and said unconvincingly, "There is a difference Elaine."

To which she just rolled her eyes and said, "Whatever."

Suddenly from out of nowhere Kramer came running across the ruined streets screaming "Oh man Jerry, Elaine, George, THERE'S FIRE EVERYWHERE!!!" He then ran off.

All three of them rolled their eyes as Jerry said "All right, all right, let's go get a Latte or something, this is WWII, no place for a bunch of unarmed Jews to be wandering

308

around." George and Elaine half-heartedly agreed, and started off on their own, George continuing to argue with Elaine that there was a difference between being disgusting and being curious. Jerry told them to go ahead, and that he'd catch up.

As they walked out of earshot, he got uncharacteristically serious and stared at Gary. He knelt down to eye level and said, "The man you killed was Vittorio Lorenzo, his book needs to be delivered back to his family. Sorry to be blunt, but really, you are a bit dense."

Jerry then got up and started to walk away saying, "I wonder if I can get a good leather jacket while I'm here. As he walked off the closing electronic blips and bops from the Seinfeld theme played out, effectively ending his dream.

Gary jolted awake from his nightmare. It was the middle of the night, one of many nights where Gary would wake up from nightmares. But this one stuck with him. It was too weird to just be random. Most of his nightmares involved flashbacks to the war, but never once had he ever dreamt of something as frightening as Seinfeld. He'd only watched it once, and as far as he was concerned, it was a show about a bunch of whiny New Yorkers who lived like kings and complained about it. But there was that name again, Vittorio ... he wondered if he really had killed Vittorio.

Gary slid his pack out from under his cot;
he rummaged through it, and marveled at all
the items that were now collector's items, all
like new. Including a pack of cigs without
the filters ... Man he'd be smoking those in a
hot second, especially now that he knew a
lifetime of smoking wasn't going to get him
lung cancer.

As he took a drag of his cigarette, using
the light from the tip to illuminate the inside
of the bag a little better probably not a good
idea considering there might be live
munitions in the bag, but he figured he'd
already died once today, this way might be
even more spectacular! Then he felt it. A
leather bound book, he remembered this
book suddenly from this very moment in
time. He very clearly remembered looking at
it thoroughly and thinking it was somehow
very significant, but as he never really
learned more than rudimentary Italian ...
mostly "I want", "that one", and "how much
baby" as well as a plethora of swear words
that he would remember for the rest of his
life, he had thrown it away, never bothering
to even try and make a connection with it.
But then he was a Marine, and Marines
weren't big on things like making emotional
connections with books.

He flipped through it, trying to make
sense of the Italian words written out before
him. At least the hand writing was legible,
as a matter of fact; it struck him that it was

310

immaculate. Either the person who wrote this was a genius, or some sort of serial killer ... or both. Still none of it made sense to him, and if it hadn't been for the last day's strange events, he would most likely have thrown it out again. But this time around, he figured, he'd better try a little harder.

"Who do I know that speaks Italian, isn't trying to kill me, and I can trust to translate this for me?" He wondered.

"Nurse DiFranca!" the thought suddenly sprang to mind ... but wait, "Is she trying to kill me?" he wondered.

Finally he decided that maybe she was, but the fact that she was bound by an oath to save him at the same time kind of canceled that urge out. He was about to jump up and go find her, but then he remembered it was the middle of the night, and seeing as how he needed her help with a matter that wasn't a medical emergency ... maybe it could wait till morning. Gary spent the rest of the night staring at that book, smoking cigarettes, and wondering how anyone ever found Seinfeld funny. Now The Bob Newhart Show, that was funny!

At some point Gary must have dozed off, he knew this, not because he experienced any more strange dreams, but because he awoke to a sharp slap across the face from nurse DiFranca!

"What'd I do?" were the words which instinctively came out of Gary's mouth.

311

"What did you do?" asked Donatella, "Look all around! There are too many cigarette butts on the floor! And I catch you with this one thoroughly in your mouth, like you were still smoking it! I am a Nurse, Not your mother!"

She continued to yell at him much quicker in Italian, but Gary only caught bits and pieces, meaning there was a lot of swearing at him involved.
Finally she switched back to English, "If you want to burn down this whole damn place then just set off a grenade! Otherwise smoke outside!"
She chucked the cigarette butt in his face and stormed off.
"Great!" he thought, "now she'll really help me!"

As much as he wanted to get started with the task at hand, he found himself joyfully reacquainting himself with some of the things he'd lost along with his youth. Things like hair, of course he had a lot of hair as an adult, it was just that most of it had migrated off of the top of his head, and was attempting to colonize every square inch of his back. That and the ability to simply look down and see his toes, or getting aroused every time he even so much as thought about a beautiful woman. In fact he reflected later on as to how strange he must have looked spending the day patting or staring at certain body parts and giggling like a schoolgirl.

Eventually the novelty wore off, and he got down to business. So the question was how to get Nurse DiFranca to help him. If it were a normal woman, he might have offered to buy her dinner and take her to a movie, but seeing as how she hated his guts, he supposed a date was out of the question. "Flowers it is!" he finally decided after some careless thinking.
It wasn't so much that he didn't want to take the effort to think of something more original, it's just that he wasn't that original himself. Plus, like most men, he didn't have a clue when it came to women ... he just knew what mass media and his ex-wife had taught him, that they all liked pretty things and desired nothing more than flattery and ... well ... pretty things.

So when no one was looking, Gary snuck out of the hospital and snagged some flowers from a nearby flower shop ... which he of course had to break into, but for all he knew the owner was never going to re-open it anyways. He haphazardly arranged them into what was, in florist's terms, an absolute mess. But it was as good as it was going to get with his skill set.

Thinking himself quite clever, he snuck back in and went to his cot, only to find Nurse DiFranca with a less than pleased look upon her face.

"Donatella!" he blurted out trying hard not to have his voice sound any more screwed up than it already did.

She said nothing, she just stood there staring for a long time, her almond eyes penetrating his soul and making him wish he'd taken God up on his offer of being reincarnated over several lifetimes as some of the lowliest creatures on the planet.

Finally she spoke, "Where the hell have you been?"

As young as Gary thought this whole experience had made him feel, suddenly he felt like he was eight years old again, and his mother was about ready to beat him for having caught him coming home from sneaking out with some of his friends to go drink in the woods.

The only thing he could think to do was stick out his hand with the paltry, and he now realized, sickly looking bouquet of flowers he had arranged. She snatched them out of his hands took one look at them, and threw them back at him.

"What am I am supposed to do with these things hmmm?"

Gary stammered back, "I ... uh ... I mean, I just thought I could do something nice for you ... you know, to thank you for your help."

Donatella looked infuriated, "So this is supposed to be a thank you? You come into my country, my city, and without my

314

permission, bomb the shit out of the whole place, and yet I still help you out, even though I hate you and all your GI Joe buddies. For this you give me heartache and grief, then sneak out, and steal flowers to say thank you?" Gary shot back, a little too confidently, "I didn't steal them!"

"Bull Shit you didn't steal them! The only flowers in a ten mile radius are at the flower shop down the street, and you have the nerve to tell me that you didn't steal these? You see that's the problem with men, you're all such terrible liars! That and you're ungrateful little shitheads too! If you really want to say thank you, then stop fucking around here and get better, if you really want to say thank you, go rebuild my house and my city while you're out there! Go make sure that people are fed and happy and stop being a little um, what is the word? Ah yes, piss ant machismo ass hole, and start doing something constructive with that overdeveloped body of yours."

Gary was speechless, and although he was clearly more than a foot taller than her, he might as well have been an insect looking up at her as she held her foot right above his head.

She continued, "Now if you don't mind, I have some real sick people to attend to."

And with that, she walked off, leaving him standing with a pile of flowers resting at his feet.

After the stun factor wore off, Gary
slowly picked up the flowers off the floor,
and found an empty, well he wasn't sure
what to call it, but it was big enough to work
as a vase, and that'd have to be good enough.
Apparently not all women liked flowers.

As he lay in his cot, hoping he'd die again
soon, he heard a voice coming from two
beds over. It was another soldier, an army
private, his head was bandaged, and his eyes
were covered, it was probably a good thing
since he was missing his legs and his left
index finger, a fact that he most likely
wouldn't grasp until his sight came back ... if
it ever came back.
"Hey buddy" he whispered, "over here."
Gary walked over to the poor man and sat
by his bed side.
"Hey soldier, you looking for a good job
with great benefits, where you can get paid,
be a hero, and serve your country?"
As if to complete his thought, the man shot
back, "Then Uncle Sam wants you!"
They both chuckled for a few moments at
this, and then were silent for a moment.

The man went on, "So you in the Army
too?"
"No, I'm a Marine" Gary answered.
"OH! A SAILOR! Well pardon me!"
Now usually this sort of talk might have
escalated to an all out brawl after a few
drinks, but considering the man's condition,

Gary swallowed his pride for the moment. "Yeah, something like that."

"Say" said the man "You got one of those ciggy's on ya? I'd get it myself but you know, doctor says I gotta stay off my feet!" Gary looked horrified at the remark, but the man just said "Oh come on pal, laugh! I know I ain't got no legs, there's no use in being down about it ... doesn't do much good!" The man started to laugh at his situation; his laughter was so infectious that Gary couldn't help but laugh with him.

The man continued, "There ya go pal! It ain't so bad, hey at least I get to go home again and see everyone! And yeah Doc says my eyes should heal up just fine, I may not be able to see all the fine details without squinting, but I ain't gonna be blind!"

He was right, Gary knew he wouldn't be out of this hell hole for some months to come, and many of his friends wouldn't go home at all.

Gary went and got one of his cigarettes from his bag, placed it in the man's mouth, and lit it with a strike anywhere match ... something else modern society had banned. The man seemed to relish the thing as if he'd been in the desert for days without food or water, and suddenly came upon an ice cream shop.

After more contemplative silence the man said "So I gather you're trying to get on the good nurse's good side?"

"Yeah" said Gary, "I need her help with something, but right now, she hates me, and I don't know what to do. I don't get women at all, you try and do something nice for them, and they crap all over you."

The man continued to smoke, using the space between his missing digit as a cigarette holder and said, "You know she's lost a lot of her family in the war right?"

Gary looked at him bewildered, "Uh, no ... I didn't"

The man went on, "Yeah, both of her older brothers, and her father, all killed by guys wearing uniforms just like ours."

Gary thought about this for a bit and said "Wow ... she must really hate us."

The man answered, "Not entirely. She's a smart woman, and while she wants to kick the shit out of every American she sees, she knows it weren't nothing personal. She sees men come through here every day, many of them leaving in body bags, and figures, instead of trying to kill every GI who comes through here, maybe she can refocus her energy on saving someone else's father or brother. She really is an incredibly compassionate person."

"Wow" thought Gary, he never thought a soldier, let alone some Army Grunt was capable of such deep, complex thought. And yet, here he was.

The man went on "Maybe instead of shallow gestures, you need to try listening to her; I mean really listening to her. Maybe instead of treating her like some kind of Italian dame, you need to treat her like a real human being, help her heal her own wounds. Maybe what she really needs is a sympathetic ear."

Gary was dumbfounded; this had to be the smartest, most sensitive man in the entire armed forces ... of any country.

Gary started, "Hey soldier ..."

Just as Gary was about to ask for his name, Nurse DiFranca came from seemingly out of nowhere and stared at him, but this time it wasn't so much in anger like the last time. This time there was a look of concern on her face. Still the shock of her last tirade lurked deep in his soul and he sat there frozen, as if his not moving would keep her from knowing he was there.

She reached out and felt his forehead. Then looked him in the eyes carefully, finally saying the last thing Gary thought she'd say, "Are you OK? Do you know this man?"

"Not really, we were just shootin' th shit. I was just about to ask his ... name."

Gary stopped cold as he looked at the man, who no longer had a cigarette in his mouth, and was obviously in a coma.

319

He looked at Nurse DiFranca with a look of stunned confusion on his face, "But ... we were just talking ... I mean ... he was Just speaking to me a moment ago!"
Nurse DiFranca looked at him with great empathy, and linked her arm around his, taking him back to his bed and lying him down.

He started, "But he was just talking ..." Before he could complete his sentence, she shushed him gently, and held his hand saying, "This place does a lot to a person. It can make you a little bit crazy. It's this damned war. People, lives, and livelihoods disappearing right in front of our eyes, the real casualties being the ones who were left behind. For us, the suffering has just begun." Gary was silent, thinking about what the man had said to him.

Finally he spoke, "Still it must be harder on you, I mean it's your country that's ruined, and you must really hate us for ruining it."
Nurse DiFranca sat quietly thinking for a while, and then said, "It's true, I could be mad at the USA for coming in here and destroying my home, my city. And I guess I wouldn't be human if I wasn't a little upset by it. But really, it's just a few buildings, a broken field here and there, a few items gone. But all of these things can be replaced, all of them, with time, will come back somehow. This war will end, and somehow

we will rebuild. But the people are what are most precious, we can't replace the people, nor can we erase the horrors that those who have survived them will relive for the rest of their lives. In that way, your country is as much a victim of this war as any other country caught up in it. In the end, we all have to go home and deal with the consequences. I could be mad at the world, and create more misery, or I could make sure you go home to your family, and maybe that way there is one less victim."

Gary thought long and hard about what to say next. He felt a little like he was at a therapist's office, only he wasn't wasting his time for once.

Finally he blurted out, "Do you have any family?"

Suddenly Nurse DiFranca squeezed his hand tight, tight enough that it went from being painful, to completely numb. She stood up, kicked the chair she'd been sitting in over and stormed out mumbling obscenities in Italian as she did.

As Gary sat there trying to wake his hand up which had gone so numb that it literally hung lifeless from his arm.

"Damn" he thought, "I guess it's time to come up with a plan B. Maybe I should try singing to her?"

He thought to himself, "Wait, no, I'm trying to get her to help, not change her mind on the whole Hippocratic Oath thing."

321

He continued to come up with more plans on how to woo the good Nurse, each one worse than the last one, and just as he was contemplating a clever plan to trap her in a contraption similar to the one in the game Mouse Trap, she came storming back in with a handbag, walked right up to Gary and told him to "sit down!"

"I'm already sitting" he pointed out.

"Well" she started, "sit more than you already are!"

Gary was visibly confused, but he decided that the best course of action was not to argue, but to try and "sit more." So after a little adjustment Nurse DiFranca looked satisfied that he had followed her instructions and proceeded to open her handbag.

First she pulled out a carton of cigarettes, it was an Italian variety, one he wasn't familiar with, and knowing how bad Italian, and indeed European cigarettes were, he didn't really want to know. Much to his dismay, she took out two, lit them both in her mouth, and shoved one in his.

"You smoke these" she said, "They'll make you live longer."

Gary wanted to protest the inaccuracy of her statement, and refuse the cigarette, which already tasted like ... well if stale were a taste, that'd describe it. But he thought it best simply to thank her and smile, while he puffed away at something that would be more useful as kindling for a campfire.

Next she pulled out a photograph, stared at it for a few moments, and then handed it to Gary. He looked at it, and instantly recognized Donatella DiFranca in the middle of a group of people, who looked like her family, either that, or she found a group of people who bore a striking resemblance to her and gathered them all up for a group picture. Gary reflected on the fact that no one smiled in pictures back then ... or now ... whenever he was. But still, there was something so much lighter about her in this picture than the woman who stood in front of him. She almost seemed to glow. She still looked stunningly beautiful, with almond eyes, wavy blonde hair, and a beautiful body, but she looked much older than she was, sad in a way that seemed to manifest itself physically.

"Your family?" he asked.
She took a deep drag and said, "Yes, my family. My Poppa and my two brothers, they're both dead, killed in Palermo, as your General Patton attacked us in Sicily. I'm not sure what was worse, that he died at the hands of people who should have been our allies, or that he died defending Sicily!" Tears started to well up as she recanted about her father and how he used to call her his Principessa. She went on, "He told me that no matter what, I was not to blame the

Allies for whatever happened to him, our family, or our country. Not that many of us consider it much of a country, but as far as the world is concerned, we are. He told me to take care of my youngest brother, but he was so headstrong, even though he was only 17, he insisted on joining the army. He wanted to prove himself a man, like his brother and his father ... no one knows where he got this trait. We are Florentines first! Not Italians and certainly not Sicilians!"

She then proceeded to spit on the ground in disgust. "So you see, if I blame you for my brothers and father dying, then I have to blame all of America, then Italy for getting involved in pointless conflict brought about by our own greed and arrogance, then I would hate the army, then my father, then my brothers, and finally myself! So I choose to do what no man had the balls to do, to stop hating everyone, and start healing. Someday we are all going to look back on this time as the most stupid time in history!"

Gary was not a soft man, but in all his years since the war, and now being thrust back into it, what she said made more sense to him than a 2 for 1 deal at Denny's. Being at a bit of a loss for words, he finally asked her, "Where did you learn to speak English so well?"
Donatella reached down and felt her stomach instinctively as more tears came to

her eyes; my Boyfriend was an English man, a professor. We were to get married, but ... well he's no longer around."

Gary reached up, and grabbed her hand, and just sat next to her in silence as she cried. He didn't know what else to do, so he sat there, never saying a word.

Finally she wiped away the tears, and composed herself. As if suddenly snapping back into reality, she snatched the picture of her family away from him, and looked him dead in the eyes saying, "Thank you for your kindness, but if you ever tell anyone any of this, I'll slit your throat while you sleep! Abbia Capito? Do you understand?"

A little taken aback at her sudden mood swing, though not at all surprised, he answered, "I got you."

Donatella wasn't exactly sure what that meant, but he got the idea. As she was about to get up he stopped her, touching her gently on the arm, "Wait, I ... I need help with something, something not medical."

She stared at him for a long time trying to decide if he really needed her help, or if this was some sort of pathetic attempt to hit on her. She decided to sit down and listen anyways; she figured she always had the option of slitting his throat as he slept if his request wasn't serious or amusing enough. Gary's hands were shaking a bit, but it wasn't because he was old anymore, he was nervous, more nervous than he had ever been in any combat situation. Without a word, he reached into his sack and rummaged around, a little too long maybe ... or maybe not, he was pumped full of adrenaline which made time seem to come almost to a stop. Finally his shaking hands reached around the leather bound notebook, and pulled it out.

As he handed it to Donatella, she noticed how scared he looked, and rubbed his hands as she took the book from him looking right in his eyes and smiling.
This was all Gary needed to begin relaxing, he pulled himself together and said, "I don't know what this is, that is, I can't read it, but I know it's important ... somehow."
She looked at him a little puzzled, but she opened the book and began looking through the pages. She seemed entranced by whatever it said; she flipped through the pages like a woman possessed. Each page seemed to bring a different, emotion, sometimes joy, sometimes sadness, but always a sense of satisfaction at the end of each page. Finally she closed the book tightly and stared at him.
"Where did you get this book?"
"What is it?" he shot back.
"I asked you first!" she said.
"Yeah, but I asked you before you even read ..."

He stopped right there, it was apparent from the look on her face, he wasn't going to win this juvenile argument.

He stammered for a bit, trying to get the right words out, finally settling on, "I took it off of a dead man, one of your countrymen, even if he was wearing a Nazi uniform ... but I swear it was in self defense, and I was really just looking for supplies, I just didn't have time to sort through everything, I mean, all I remember is standing next to him, then an explosion, and then ... well I woke up here."

Donatella did not look pleased with his answer, but figured it would have to do for now. She closed her eyes, swallowed, placed aside all her judgment for another time, and said, "It is a book of poetry and short stories. Some of the best I've ever read. Whoever this man was, he should have won an award for his brilliance, not ended up dead."

Gary looked shocked as he sat on his bed, "I'm sorry" he said. "I didn't want to kill him ... I didn't want to kill any of them, it's just ..."

"... this damn war, I know." she finished.

He went on, "Vittorio Lorenzo is the author isn't he?" To which she replied, a little bit surprised, "it is."

This information seemed to shock and please Gary more than if Donatella had told him she wanted to have a threesome with him and her even more attractive female

327

friend. "Right" he said ... "and there didn't happen to be an address listed in there?" Donatella flipped through the book and suddenly replied, "Yes! There is!" Just as Gary was beginning to think this would be the easiest thing he'd ever done, she went on, "It's in Cinque Terre, but unfortunately it doesn't say where in Cinque Terre, that part is torn out."

"All right, a little bit challenging, but I can deal with a little challenge." He thought to himself.

"Where is Cinque Terre?" he asked.

"A little bit north and west of Florence." she replied.

Gary blurted out with genuine excitement, "Oh great! That shouldn't be too hard to reach!"

"Well ..." she replied "maybe it's not so easy to go to, even when the war was off. But now, the train is not running, and walking there would surely mean death. The only way in now is by boat, and this is dangerous as well, the Germans do not trust us since the armistice, especially with most men in that area openly working against the Nazi's in the Italian underground. They frequently shoot any boat leaving Genoa simply because they are paranoid of the resistance. Even fishermen do not dare to venture out. In short, if you are thinking of going there, don't, its suicide."

328

Gary was silent for almost a full minute finally he spoke out, "Well, believe it or not, I've already committed suicide once and lived to talk about it. But ... and this will sound even more crazy ... I'm on a mission from God, I must deliver this book to this man's family. Nothing is more important to me right now."

Donatella considered his words for a much shorter time than he'd expected before saying, "OK, I'll help you then."

Gary was shocked at how easy this was said "Wait ... you believe me?"

She grinned and said, "Not the part about the mission from God, but your determination seems to be impeccable, and your mission seems like a selfless one. If I can help you and put the minds of the family of this fantastic author at ease and do something other than pointlessly kill other people, then I will. More than that, the passion you have moves me. We will talk more about it tomorrow. But rest now; you will need all your energy."

For the first time since he had been a child, Gary slept well that night. No bad dreams, no tossing and turning, just sleep. He woke up feeling completely refreshed, in fact he was feeling so much better, that his commanding officer decided to pay him a visit. Colonel John Walker was a beast of a man, even among the beastliest of men, a man who feared nothing, and who it was rumored, grew hair on his hair he was so much of a man. His mere presence made those who had lost their legs in battle attempt to stand at attention for him. Gary was no exception to this rule. He instinctively stood up so straight, you would have thought someone had shoved a steel rod so far up his ass that it had replaced his spine.

The Colonel let him stand at attention for an uncomfortably long time until finally saying, "At ease Marine."
As if he were talking to every Marine in the hospital, suddenly the whole room settled down.
The Colonel went on "Well Private, you look like something the cat puked up, ate, and puked up again but we weren't all born pretty. What you don't look like to me is a Marine who's been seriously injured. So if you're done with your stay at the Holiday Inn, I suggest you get your ass back to work! Gear up, and meet me out front in 15 minutes." "Yes Colonel!" Gary replied to the Colonel who was already walking out, but before he did, he turned and threw something at Gary.
"Oh and by the way, the US Marine Corps was impressed with your little bout of dumb luck, congratulations; you're now officially a Corporal. Keep getting lucky, and maybe someday you'll make it to Master Gunny! Or

better yet, maybe you'll lose your virginity
to a woman! But don't hold your breath."
The Colonel then attempted to smile at
Gary; it was a hideous sight to behold, as the
smile looked like it had been forced open
with steel wire and one he hoped he'd ever
have to see again. In fact, as he remembered
things, the Colonel wasn't going to live too
many more days.

In the hallway outside, Gary suddenly
heard the voices of Donatella and the
Colonel sparring angrily, He wasn't quite
sure what was said between the two of them,
but he heard enough to know that there was
a lot of swearing involved. Suddenly
Donatella came storming in, furious, and
heading straight for Gary. He wasn't sure
who was more frightening, Donatella or The
Colonel.
She got straight to business, "That man is ...
he's ... he isn't a man, he's some sort of
gorilla in a monkey's uniform."
Gary couldn't help but chuckle a little at this.
Despite all his Marine pride and Machismo,
he had to admit, the Colonel was a bit over
the top.
She went on, "He can't just stroll in here like
he owns the place and ask wounded men to
march to certain death! This is ridiculous ..."
She then went on a tirade in Italian that was
so fast and furious that Gary couldn't even
be sure it was in any known human
language. "What, are you just going to

blindly obey him? Walk out of here and kill more people until another bomb finishes the job that the first one was unable to complete?"

"I don't want to go." said Gary, "But if I don't go, I might as well kill myself now, because even if the Nazi's don't, I'll never be allowed to go home."

Donatella shook her head, "well, so much for your mission from God! Perhaps you think your pride will protect you from God? And to think I actually took you seriously! Well, go on then, Go stand up for what you really believe in."

Gary really wanted to smack her, but he wouldn't. Not only because he'd never hit a woman, especially one who was bound to hit him back even harder, but because she was right. He was being a coward in fulfilling his mission.

"Fine!" he said, "but what am I supposed to do about it. Even if I do run away from my unit, what do I do then? Are you going to help me?"

She studied his face for a moment and said, "Fine! If you are serious, then you will meet me at the port in Genoa in 3 days, from there you will sail to Cinque Terre."

Gary was about to protest or at the very least whine a little, but before he could get a word out Donatella slapped him hard across the face, hard enough that he thought he saw

God sitting behind his desk in full military garb.

"That's just in case you are lying!"

Then as he recovered his composure and raised his finger in protest, she grabbed him and kissed him so passionately, that he was pretty sure that he saw God again, but this time the softer, gentler female version ... as comforting as she had been to him before he started his little adventure in altered reality, she wasn't really the image he wanted in his head as he experienced this particular emotion. Although she was pretty hot for an older woman.

Gary wasn't sure whether he'd experienced more stars when she kissed him, or when she hit him, either way, any doubt about what he had to do was gone from his head.

"I'll see you in Genoa" he said. With that he grabbed the rest of his gear and walked out, never looking back.

The next day was a grueling hell on earth, as they marched up the Italian coastline on foot towards Pisa for 20 straight hours, from there they were to head Northeast towards Milan, where if they were lucky, they would be able to push the Nazi's out of Italy for good. Gary however had other plans; he was going to ditch his unit in Pisa and head straight for Genoa. How, he wasn't sure of, but he just decided to have faith that somehow he could. It was funny,

333

even though he found himself in his much younger, much stronger active duty Marine body, his stamina and will power seemed to belong to the old man who'd spent more time sitting on a bar stool drinking himself to death than reaching down to touch his toes ... something he was able to see again. So while the rest of his unit marched vigorously along, he found himself constantly wanting to sit at a bar and have a few drinks, maybe a steak dinner. He wasn't sure if everyone else was thinking the same thing, but he just seemed to suffer more in his earthly desires than the rest of them.

They reached Pisa under the cover of night, it was of course raining and cold, two more feelings Gary had hoped never to experience in this extreme again simultaneously, but well, here he was slopping through the muck, freezing his ass off.

"At least I know that if I go to hell it won't be any worse than this" he thought. "At least it will be warmer than this."

With that he heard a company halt, they were in Pisa, and would take shelter in an abandoned church. The city looked beautiful at night, there were hardly any lights on, and the quietness of the city made Gary fall asleep quickly, despite him being wet and miserable, even his sleeping bag was wet, and the stone floor wasn't much of a comfort either. He wondered how he got through the war the first time around.

As he slept lightly, he dreamt of heaven. Not the crappy DMV heaven he'd gone to after plastering his brains all over Jeff, the poor Mexican bartender ... something he regretted almost more than the suicide itself. The only hard working decent person in that fucking place, even if he didn't speak English all that well. No, the heaven he dreamt of was the one he'd always imagined. It was a large castle made of pure diamond sitting on top of a mountain surrounded by clouds, and all around it was a village, but the village was actually sitting on top of the clouds, he could walk through the air on top of the clouds through the village, and there were people everywhere, just going about their daily business, doing various jobs and errands that you'd expect to see people in a little town or village to do, bakers, street vendors, shoppers, mothers and fathers with children, all living out their daily lives.

What Gary found unsettling was that he seemed to know all of these people ... even though he didn't recognize a single one of them. More than that, they all seemed so ... happy, but not because any of them looked like they were particularly wealthy, in fact some of them looked downright dirt poor, all of them were in fact covered in dirt to some degree or another. But they all danced and sang, as if everyday life were some sort of quasi-musical adventure. They all smiled at him and greeted him as he walked by saying things like "welcome back old friend" as they passed him.

He felt this immense sense of kinship with all of them as if they were indeed old friends.

Just as he was beginning to wonder where the hell he was, the doors to the castle opened wide before him, and a red carpet rolled out from it, stretching all the way to his feet.

"I guess this means I should go in?" he thought to himself.

As if to answer his question for him, the carpet slipped under his feet and yanked him forward at an incredible speed. He fully expected to fall over at any moment, but as it pulled him, the laws of physics seemed not to apply to him, and he stood comfortably on the rug as it brought him to his ultimate destination, never feeling so much as a light breeze.

It was the middle of a great hall, one adorned with beautiful frescoes of everyday life throughout history, and far, far into the future. There were many scenes of war repeating itself over and over until ultimately, well the story told by the paintings seemed to stop, and there was an endless expanse of darkness on what looked like it should have been wall space for more paintings.

In the center of the room, sitting on a pillow, sat the old lady who had revealed herself to him as God earlier. She gestured to a pillow on the other side of a table she sat next to, and said, "please, sit."
Gary happily obeyed, and sat on a comfortable pillow.
"Tea?" God asked as she began to pour herself a cup from the ornate tea set sitting next to her.
"Um, no thanks, I really don't like tea ma'am" he politely refused.
But he found the smell to be overwhelmingly delicious. As if she had read his mind, she simply smiled and poured him a cup. Gary just grinned, a little embarrassed and took a sip; it was the most wonderful thing he'd ever tasted, but unlike anything he'd had before.
After a few moments of enjoying the tea, Gary asked, "Ma'am, is it OK if I ask you, where am I? And why am I here now?"
God smiled and said "You may ask anything you like. First of all, this is the Treasure tower on Eagle Peak, your home from the remote past, and through the distant future, though you may not remember it, and yes, the villagers are all your comrades. As to why your here, well that's more complicated. It's rare that you would return before you fulfilled your vow to me. But if you are here, it must mean that you are at a

337

crucial point in your mission, and you need some guidance."

Gary took another sip of the delicious tea, answering only with, "Um ... what?" God smiled, "Don't worry about it too much; it will all make sense to you again at a later time. The important thing to know is that at some point in the remote past, you gathered here with all your comrades out there, and made a vow to me. Each one of you has a mission to fulfill in your respective lives. For some it may take many lifetimes to realize and carry out that mission. You are well on your way to carrying out yours. The book you are delivering ..."
She paused as if trying to think of the best way to explain. She went on, "You see the walls here contain a history of the world as it is, as it was, and as it shall be. The details of everyone's daily lives are up to them, but the ultimate destiny is recorded on this wall."

Gary looked around at the wall, he did indeed see moments throughout history, both ones he recognized and ones he didn't. Then he saw the end, it was the world consumed in flames.
"Not much of a future if you ask me ma'am." said Gary.
"Please don't call me ma'am, it bothers me ... makes me feel old. Please, call me Clarence."

Gary opened his mouth to explain to God that this was a boy's name, but then, he was sure she knew, and besides, he was sure it didn't matter to her.

"OK ... Clarence, so ... guide me."

God studied Gary for a moment then finally put down her tea and gestured to the end of the world, the last mural and said "You see this is how the world will end for humanity if you don't deliver that book. But these black walls, if you succeed, will be filled with color and life, even some of the horrible things that happen in between will change to light pictures portraying happiness and progress. Understand?"

"Not entirely" Gary replied, "Why does it matter so much if I deliver a stupid book?"

"Why?" laughed God, "because you are my disciple, and you promised me you would, right here, in front of the great gathering of common mortals ... you promised me that if it cost you your life, you would do this one thing. Just like Vittorio promised me he'd write the book."

Gary still looked confused.

God sighed, "You see that book contains poetry and stories that will survive the next Great War ... the one you wouldn't have lived to see even if you hadn't committed suicide. From the ashes of that war, which will devastate humanity in ways you can't even imagine, new societies formed, and civilization began anew. But the writings in that book, along with a few other great books, manage to survive, only because they were where they ended up after you took them there. Preserved for all humanity, and based on his writings, and a few other surviving texts, the world is finally able to develop a society based on peace, culture, and humanism. From this one simple but selfless act, humanity is able to flourish, and take its place amongst the universe as one of the great species."

"But if you fail. If you decide it's too hard, or that you just want to survive and live out a happy life, concerned only with pleasure and narcissism, you may, and this mural will remain the same, leaving humanity to become nothing but a footnote in galactic history, if even that!"

As Gary contemplated his fate, and sipped his tea, God continued, "I know, it's pretty heavy, right?"

Gary answered, "Yeah, tell me about it ... Clarence."

God chuckled a little and got up to give Gary a big hug.

"Now" she said, "it's time for you to get down there and complete your mission."

As Gary continued to sip his tea, he looked right into God's eyes as she opened her mouth and strange sounds came out of her mouth ... pinging and whooshing ... it sounded a lot like...

Bullets! Gary bolted awake from his dream, it was dawn, and he heard the distinct and unmistakable sound of bullets flying through the air.

"What the fuck!" he screamed out as men everywhere attempted to scramble and arm themselves ... it was an ambush. Despite all the craziness happening around him, Gary was thinking about the dream ... was it real? Did he go into the afterlife again somehow, or was he just stressed out? As if to answer his question, he reached over for his gear and his gun, only to find the tea cup he had been sipping from moments earlier in his dream was sitting next to him, warm tea still in it. Gary quickly took a sip, and was satisfied. That it was not a dream.

His fascination with the tea cup quickly ended as a bullet whizzed by him, and shattered it. Gray was suddenly terrified, because in his first go around at this life, he had been unable to travel with his unit up to Pisa, since he was still recovering from his injuries, only to hear that his entire unit had been wiped out, save for 2 people (the Gunny being one of them) in an ambush in ... Pisa.

"Oh crap" he thought to himself as he quickly geared up and gathered with the other Marines in a well protected corner of the stone church they were holed up in. Several bodies, and soon to be bodies littered the floor, some of the poor bastards never even got the chance to wake up and defend themselves.

The Colonel and the Gunny were up front, arguing. The Colonel wanted to head out the front door and break left to a row of shops that held a more promising defensive position. The Gunny wanted to stay behind and wait out the enemy a little, sneaking out the back of the church as cover and shooting from both sides of the building.
Finally the Colonel said "Look Gunny, I don't have time to argue this with you, I'm taking these men to that row of shops, and we're gonna wipe out this contingent of Nazi Bastards, and either you come with me, or you and anyone else who wants to can stay behind and face a god damn court martial once I'm through! Now Come on everyone, let's move out!"

As the Colonel and the rest of the Unit moved toward the row of shops, sustaining minimal casualties along the way, The Gunny and four other Marines stayed behind ... with Gary, who had not so fond memories of coming up to Pisa with another group of marines, including the Gunny, and one of the other four Marines who were all currently disobeying a direct order, only to find the bodies of everyone who had just moved near the remains of what looked to have been shops.

Gary's heart raced as he watched the men pour into the shops and start to take up defensive positions, and as the Gunny was about to concede and take the remaining group with him, there was a sudden, jarring explosion, and in one fell swoop, save for the five of them, Gary's entire unit was now dead.

The five of them pressed themselves so hard against the wall of that church; you would have thought the church itself was God. They were all silent, and after a full minute of agonizing silence, they heard German voices ... laughing. Coming out of hiding, there were only seven of them ... they had laid the perfect trap. The Gunny signaled them to be dead silent, and they crept quietly out the back. The Nazi bastards were standing over the burnt corpses of their comrades, and congratulating themselves on a job well done, as they did, the Gunny and the other four marines, quietly snuck up to the very defensive positions the Nazi's had been using, and proceeded to kill them all ... The Nazi's fought back, managing to kill on Marine, and injure another one, a wound that would eventually prove fatal. But ultimately it was just Gary, the Gunny, and a Private first class named Joe Johnson.

"GOD DAMMIT, GOD DAMMIT, GOD FUCKING DAMMIT" screamed the Gunny as he picked up a piece of rubble and tossed it in the general direction of where the Nazi's had been standing.

He went on, "That arrogant PRICK! Why the hell was he leading a combat unit anyways, he should have gotten a fucking desk job somewhere; more of us would be alive now!" The Gunny ran towards the rubble of the fallen shops and screamed "WHY WOULDN'T YOOU JUST FUCKING LISTEN TO ME FOR ONCE!"

As the Gunny continued to hurl profanities both at the Nazi's and the dead Colonel, Joe and Gary just stood there, dumbfounded unable to speak, the initial adrenaline rush wearing off slowly, and the reality of their situation beginning to sink in. "What do we do now Gunny?" asked PFC Johnson.

The Gunny rushed Johnson knocking him to the ground, and stared at him face to face as if he were ready to kill him where he stood for daring to speak. Johnson just stood there, unable to move amongst the Gunny's steely gaze.

Slowly the Gunny's posture and expression softened. Whatever demon had possessed him a moment ago seemed to vanish.

He closed his eyes and said, "Now we go back to Florence. It ain't safe here."

Johnson panicked a little, "What about all the bodies? We can't just leave them here without a proper burial for Christ's sake!!!"

The gunny pulled a cigarette out of his pack, lit it and said, "If we stay here, they're gonna have to send someone to bury us as well. Look, we go back, get reinforcements, and come back in full force. I promise you, we'll bury every single one of them. We will be back."

This seemed to be enough to pacify Johnson somewhat, who started gathering supplies for the march back with Gary. In half an hour they were ready to go, having gathered food and other supplies from their fallen comrades, and the dead Nazi's. As they were about to leave, Gary announced, "I'm not going back with you."
This alarmed Johnson greatly, and he started protesting wildly, but the Gunny just stood there, and stared at Gary calmly while he smoked his cigarette, contemplating what Gary had just said, and finally grabbed Johnson and yanked him so hard that it shut him up. "Fine" the Gunny said, "You wanna stay here with these guys and die ... be my guest. Hell, I admire your sense of duty. But I'll tell you one thing, if I come back here and you're just another corpse to bury, rest assured, I ain't gonna be the one to bury you son." Gary stood his ground, "fine! But I'm not leaving!"
The Gunny just smiled and said, "Suit yourself, Corporal." and with that, he turned around and started the long walk back to Florence.

Johnson seemed unable to decide for almost a full minute, looking back and forth between Gary and the Gunny like some sort of lost puppy dog.

Finally Gary said, "Go. Get your ass back to Florence, and get home ... open that bar you always wanted to open, just come up with a more original name than "Joe's". It's really dumb to name a restaurant after yourself when your name is Joe."

PFC Joe Johnson just looked at him dumbfounded and muttered "How did you know ..." Gary had a small moment of panic realizing that he hadn't told him about his bar yet ... in fact it was on the trip back to Pisa on his first go around at life with reinforcements that Joe had confided this dream of his to him. A trip Gary wouldn't be making this time around.

Gary stammered, "You talk in your sleep. Now get the fuck out of here!"

Again looking like a lost puppy, Johnson ran after the Gunny. Gary gathered a few more supplies, as well as a map of the region. He of course had no plans to stick around.

Gary headed Northwest towards Genoa as fast and as quietly as he could. While he knew from experience that the Nazi's had pretty much pulled out of this area, you never knew when a rouge group of them would be wandering around, more than happy to kill another American. Gary made up his mind at the outset of his journey from Pisa ... there would be no more killing, not

346

unless it was absolutely necessary to completing his mission. Gary had had more than enough killing for one lifetime; he certainly didn't need any more in his second go around.

Gary moved swiftly, determined to get to his destination, taking advantage of every shortcut and bypass he could. He was going to get there in time, if not early. There was just one small problem, Gary was actually headed East ... you see, as it turns out, Gary was horrible with maps. As much as he hated to admit it ... he knew from the lack of shoreline, and the endless hills that he was lost.

Gary came across a tiny village ... he was sure it had a name, but there really wasn't much of a way to tell since the only sign in front of the village had apparently rotted out completely until all you could make out was the letter "S" and the letter "A". It was afternoon now, and people seemed to be taking a siesta of some sort. There was one man sitting in front of a stone house drinking wine out of an old mug. He was muscular, hairy, and had a disproportionately large belly for a man so physically fit otherwise, and he had a strange black mustache that protruded out from his face to a point on either end, along with slicked back black hair. Gary wasn't sure which one had more grease. As if to add t the stereotype, the man was wearing high water khaki pants held up by suspenders, and a dirty white tank top that only covered half of his enormous belly.

The man didn't move he didn't look surprised; he simply sat there and stared at Gary as if he were a tumbleweed going through an old western town. Nothing special, it just caught your eye for a moment, and rolled on to wherever tumbleweeds tumbled. Gary spent most of his life in temperate climates, so he wasn't sure where they went ... for all he knew, they wandered the earth forever. Gary walked up to the man, and attempted to speak Italian to him. After a broken attempt to ask for directions, the man just stared at him ominously as f nothing Gary had said registered with him. Finally the man burst out into laughter which, while it was uncontrollable, was better than the dead silence. Despite his violent fit of laughter, he never moved out of his seat even an inch.

Suddenly in perfect English, the man said, "So you want me to help socks find a home for a pasta dish then? Or maybe you wanted something else?"
Gary was incredibly embarrassed and confused.
The man responded to his confusion saying, "In English please."
Gary swallowed his pride and finally said "I left Pisa this morning, I'm trying to reach

Genoa. Can you help me? I need to get there by sometime tomorrow!"

The man laughed again, and said "You have a terrible sense of direction sir! In order to get to Genoa by tomorrow, you need transportation, maybe a horse and carriage, or maybe a motor car of some sort."

The man continued to sip his wine as Gary waited anxiously for the man to continue, which of course he didn't. The man simply went back to his chair and wine.

Finally Gary asked, "Well ... where can I get something like that?"

The man smiled at Gary saying, "I have a truck my friend, and would be more than happy to help you. The question is, how badly do you want to go?"

Gary let out a heavy sigh ... he was pretty sure he was going to have to humiliate himself in some way in order to get to Genoa in time. He mumbled, "I'll do ... anything."

The last word of this phrase came out like a man with severe constipation issues. The man smiled broadly showing what few remaining teeth he had in his head. Gary wondered if he shouldn't have played a little harder to get, but it was too late, the old man had him.

Gary's mind raced through the list of awful things this man could do, trying to decide what the worst of them was, and just as he was imagining himself servicing a

349

sheep somewhere in the pasture for the man's pleasure, he said "make me an offer."

"Huh?" Gary responded.

The man finished his wine saying, "You American soldiers are so daft. I'll be more bunt with you ... if you want me to take you to Pisa, I require payment. What is it you can give me that would entice me to risk my life and my truck to take you there?"

Gary was still reeling from the complex nature of this man's English skills.

Who used "daft" in a sentence anymore? He snapped out of it reaching into his pocket and pulling out a handful of US money, $10.42 to be exact, it was a king's ransom in Italy back then.

The man snatched the money out of Gary's hand and snapped at him, "Don't insult me! This is hardly enough for my services!"

He quickly stuffed the money into his little change purse he had stuffed in his sock, and tucked it away with no intention of returning it. Gary rolled his eyes; maybe he had picked the wrong point in time to decide not to kill anymore. Gary turned his thoughts to the mission at hand, sucked it up, and pulled out an unopened pack of American Cigarettes, his last full pack. The man's eyes sparkled all of a sudden.

"American Cigarettes!" He snatched them out of Gary's hand and held it like it was his first born child saying, "They are fresh!

Unopened! This is indeed an intriguing offer! Still, it is not enough."

The man stuffed the cigarettes into his shirt pocket and leered at Gary like a spoiled rich kid on his birthday that gets enough presents to satiate an entire third world country, but still it isn't enough. Gary flipped through his pack and found one more item, quietly deciding that if this didn't work, he may just have to go back on his promise not to kill anyone. He pulled out what during his entire tour of duty with the Marines had been his prized possession, a set of pornographic magazines, some of the best the USA had to offer. Gary suddenly hoped that the man didn't have a preference for sheep.

For the first time, the man simply stared at the latest offering in Amazement, his hands shaking as he slowly reached out for the small stack of pornography.

"May I?" he asked irreverently, staring at Gary like he was a God.

Gary sighed, "Go ahead."

The man slowly thumbed through the magazines with childlike wonder, and a teenage boner, finally saying, "This is worth risking my life for!"

As the man rushed into his house to get his keys and hide the magazines somewhere his wife, or mistress, or maybe sheep, wouldn't find it; Gary mumbled to himself, "Yes it is." one of them contained a nude layout of Betty Grable after all.

351

The man rushed back out of his home, now wearing a strange leather cap and a pair of ridiculous looking mismatched leather boots, and said "Avanti! To Pisa!"
He then drained the remnants of his wine bottle, very quickly, and grabbed Gary by the hand, pulling him around back as they ran. Gary hoped this wasn't where he kept his sheep.

To his relief there was a ... well it was a vehicle of some sort around back. It resembled a truck, but only sat one person, uncomfortably in the cab. Then there was a small flatbed connected to the back for hauling small loads, and of course, it only had 3 wheels. Before Gary could ask where he was to sit, the man shoved him into the flatbed and threw him a set of goggles, saying as an afterthought "So your eyes don't get any bugs in them, OK?"
As he said this he smiled his strange, barely toothed grin and held two thumbs up, finally saying, "Oh and you may want to keep your mouth closed while we drive!"

Gary was going to protest this, but before he could, the man was in the cab and the "truck" roared to life, making more noise than a Chevy without a muffler, and spewing black exhaust out of the back. Immediately Gary started to choke on the exhaust, quickly putting on his goggles as if it would somehow help with the smoke. At least his eyes didn't burn anymore. He pulled out a kerchief to cover his mouth and nose. It got better as the vehicle moved. Hopefully there wouldn't be any traffic.

The journey would have been pleasant, except for the jarring jolts he got from the combination of the engine's vibrations and the unpaved country roads. Not to mention the fact that the man was stinking drunk and veering all over the road. Gary tried hard to concentrate on the scenery, which worked for a while, but eventually the motion was too much to handle, and several times he found himself hurling over the side of the truck. A fact that seemed to amuse his host as he would laugh hysterically every time it happened, stopping only when he realized he was about to crash into something.

Gary wasn't sure when, but at some point, he passed out from exhaustion and hunger. He woke up to see the man's mostly toothless grin only inches from his face as he said "Wakey wakey!" Gary bolted awake and grabbed his pack. "We are here Mister Gary!" Gary hauled himself out of the bed of the vehicle, and steadied himself as the man shoved a napkin into his hand with a small croissant of some sort wrapped in it. Gary was suddenly very thankful to this man, as they arrived just in time to see the sun rise, and after that trip, the croissant tasted like heaven itself ... and Gary knew what heaven tasted like!

They were in a garage of some sort ... it looked like it had recently been abandoned, all the tools had been ransacked, but it was clean enough, and the lights worked. The man had even brought them Coffee to wash it down with in little porcelain cups. Maybe this guy wasn't so bad after all. After breakfast Gary thanked the man profusely and asked him if he knew the way to the port.

The man laughed saying, "Please, if you can't find the port in Genoa, you aren't really looking all that much. But to make sure you could find it, I took the liberty of arranging a guide ... although he may need a small payment, he can show you to the port."

Gary was liking this guy more and more as he shook his hand and headed towards the door, as he was about to exit he asked the man what his name was.

"Gunther" the man answered.

It seemed a little odd that this man had a Germanic name, but he thanked him all the same and headed out the door.

He walked into the city just as the sun was coming up. It was glorious, and still relatively untouched from the war. Gary could smell the fragrant aromas, good and bad, coming from the city, a city that was still alive and kicking, something he missed dearly. Just as he was about to head out into the city, with or without this so called guide Gunther had provided, he felt the unmistakable jab of a gun butt being pressed into his back. Suddenly he was surrounded by three German soldiers, one of whom was disarming him as he instinctively put his hands in the air. One of them was clearly and officer and he smiled saying in perfect English, with only a slight hint of an accent. "Welcome to Genoa Herr Gary."

Gary sighed with a suddenly deflated sense of self worth, "You're my guide, right?" The officer smiled and said, "Very observant of you sir! And now we will take you on a guided tour, to your new home, yes! We hope the accommodations are comfortable." "Fuck" Gary said as the two goons with guns escorted him through the city, which for now at least was firmly under Nazi control.

The officer talked to him like he was a child, "Now don't feel so bad Herr Gary, Gunther is one of our best bounty hunters, an Italian agent if you will. He is a master at tricking unsuspecting sops like yourself. We pay him handsomely."
Gary shook his head and said, "Tell him I want my magazines back."
The officer didn't say anything back, he just smiled.

They took him to some sort of municipal building, bound up his hands and feet, and threw him into a room that looked like at one point or another it had been responsible for dispensing real justice. They tied him to a chair to make sure he wouldn't go anywhere, and left him, never once uttering a word.

"What a fucking mess" thought Gary. As he looked around the room, he noticed his pack was just lying there unattended in the corner. He chuckled "Well no one ever accused the Nazi's of being brilliant."

He scooted his chair slowly over to his pack, with the intention of recovering his knife and cutting himself free of his rope bindings. Unfortunately, halfway there his chair fell backwards and he knocked himself unconscious. When he woke up, the room was much darker, the sun was going down, and he was still lying on the floor. For some reason all he could think was that Donatella was going to find him and kill him if he didn't get out of here right now.

With that, he desperately tried to right himself, but before he could even tip the chair to one side, the door opened. Gary had fallen in such a way that he couldn't see who it was, but he heard several footsteps coming his way, and then the unmistakable voice of the Nazi officer who had kindly escorted him to his cell said, "So is this an example of your American freedom? You'll be lucky if you win the war Herr Gary!"

Suddenly Gary got very angry, "Listen you little Nazi parasite one day we're going to march right into Berlin with the hand of God him ... or herself, and we're going to wipe your little girl Nazi tea party off the face of the Earth, and your glorious leader is going to chicken out and kill himself at the last minute as your country goes up in flames! You hear me scumbag!!!"

The room was filled with chuckles as the officer leaned in closer to Gary and said, "Well, for all of our sakes, I hope you're right about that." Gary retorted, "You're damn right I'm right about that, I ... wait ... what?"
Everyone seemed to laugh hysterically now as if there were some big joke, and Gary was the only one not in on it. He was suddenly sat up right, and a table and more chairs was brought in, as someone cut him free from his bonds.

He stood up instinctively and looked around to see several armed men in the room, all of them very Italian, and dressed in everyday clothing, except for the Nazi officer, who was still very much in uniform. Several of the men sat at around the table as the rest of them brought out a feast of pasta, bread, wine and selected cheese and meat dishes, even setting out a place for Gary who was encouraged to sit down and eat.

This was even stranger than the Seinfeld dream, and Gary had to wonder if he was awake or not. He sat down cautiously and said, "Is this a dream? Did I die again and no one's told me yet."

With a slightly perplexed, but overwhelmingly jovial look on his face, the officer said, "I assure you, you are very awake, and very alive. Please have a seat; we are waiting for one more guest."
Gary still wasn't sure if the officer was telling the truth or not, but after all his recent experiences with the afterlife and dreaming, he decided it was best just to go with the flow.

Having barely eaten in the past few days, Gary was voraciously hungry, and found himself stuffing his face without saying a word. The Nazi officer just sat patiently nibbling on some meat and cheese, and sipping on wine waited until Gary was satiated enough to listen to him. As he was about to speak, the door opened, and in walked Donatella DiFranca.
She looked at Gary and chortled, "I'm glad you like the dinner, but please, try and chew with your mouth closed, OK?"

"As I was about to say" the officer stated, "Welcome to the Italian underground. We've been expecting you." He went on, "We have the privilege of operating as the local Nazi authorities, a clever ruse don't you think? But enough about us, tell me, how did you find Gunther, a swine of the lowest order, who lives I believe in the countryside somewhere East of Pisa?"

358

The reality of his situation suddenly sinking in, Gary answered, "Either divine intervention, or dumb luck. Take your pick." Donatella kissed him briefly on both cheeks and said, "Usually I would say dumb luck, but in your case I will make an exception and say it was divine intervention. Either way, I'm happy to see you kept your promise."

"Won't they miss you in the hospital? Gary asked.

"Maybe a little" Donatella started, "But the war is moving north now, so less and less. Plus ... your cause moved me. At first I thought you were just a creative liar trying to get into bed with me. You wouldn't have been the first. But when your men rushed back to Florence and told everyone what had happened in Pisa, and that you had stayed behind to die, I really believed you ... and even if it is a creative lie to get me in bed with you, it certainly deserves a prize, and perhaps the desired result for the creativity level, and effort involved."

Gary laughed, "I'm not THAT creative, but maybe I'll take you up on your offer later."

Donatella smiled at his advances, but before the conversation could get any more intimate, their host interrupted. "I'm so happy that you two star crossed love birds have found each other at last, but as I recall, Donatella said you were on some sort of mission of mercy, no?"

Donatella suddenly snapped back into reality, "Umh, yes ... it seems Gary here has something valuable to return to a family in Cinque Terre."

The officer was suddenly interested, "What is it?"

Before Donatella could answer Gary replied, "The last memory of their son. A man I killed in combat sir."

He pulled out the book and tossed it on the table for the officer to examine. He thumbed through the book and read a few pages, and with tears welling up in his eyes he said, "Please, call me Marco." and he handed back the book, looking more determined than ever to help Gary.

"Do you know who this man is? Or where in Cinque Terre he lives?" asked Marco. "All I know" Gary answered, "Is that his name was Vittorio Lorenzo, and that he lived somewhere in Cinque Terre. It can't be that big being so isolated ... can it? Marco frowned a little and looked around at his comrades who were equally as dissatisfied. Marco finally answered, "Individually Cinque Terre is small, but it is a group of five villages spread over a long, mountainous coast, now completely cut off from civilization."

Gary's stomach sank. This was going to take forever.

Marco saw how upset Gary was and began to laugh, "Please my friend, do not despair. I know of the Lorenzo family. They live in the town of Riomaggiore."

Gary was a little shocked, "You know of their family? I know Italy isn't that big in the grand scheme of things, but come on!"

Marco leaned in close to Gary and said, "I make it a point to get to know everyone who is involved in the Italian underground intimately, and this man, Vittorio, his family has given more for the cause of freedom than most, three sons to be exact."

Gary shot back. "No way, the man I killed was trying to kill me! Trying to kill American soldiers! The man I killed wasn't a member of your resistance movement!"

Marco considered this a he sipped his wine. "I know of this family, and I assure you, the man you killed was not Vittorio Lorenzo. All three brothers were executed as traitors, rather hastily, and in front of many witnesses. So I will say it again, the man you killed was not Vittorio Lorenzo!"

Gary wanted to argue with Marco, point out the obvious flaws in his logic, but at this point Marco had pushed himself nose to nose with Gary, and spoke like a man possessed. Besides, explaining to him that he knew it was Vittorio Lorenzo because God told him through a dream with the cast of Seinfeld sounded a little crazy. Besides, Gary knew from experience that such men were not to be argued with, even when they were wrong, and especially when they were armed.

Gary simply sipped his wine and apologized, "I'm sorry, I didn't mean to offend you. I'm sure from his poetry, he was an honorable man."

Marco suddenly seemed to realize just how stressful the current situation was to all involved, and regained his composure.

"I am sorry myself ... I just ... I get passionate about the men under my care. They are like my own brothers ..."

Gary continued for him "I understand that all too well. I feel the same way about my fellow Marines."

Marco did not look too pleased but despite his unease, he raised his glass and said "To fallen comrades ... how do you Marines say it ... Sempre Fidelis?"

Gary laughed, "Semper Fi will do sir."

That night, Gary slept in a bed. It wasn't the cushy mattress he'd had in his home before he committed suicide, in fact by his modern standards it hardly counted as a mattress at all, but after the last few days, it was heavenly. As he lay there in his underwear, in the dark, in came Donatella. She opened the door, quietly shut it behind her, and crawled into bed with Gary and began kissing him. They made love, and they held each other, all night without saying a word.

As they were falling asleep, Gary whispered to her, "What did I do to deserve that?" She answered, "That was for good luck. Marco is taking you to Riomaggiore tomorrow by himself, this world is to unpredictable for me to hold back feelings. I love you, and if we only have this night, at least you knew that."

Gary looked into her eyes and wanted to open his mouth and say something, but the communication that occurred between the two of them in bed at that moment was more than anything either of them could have said. Besides ... Gary wasn't exactly a master word smith, and he didn't want to screw this up.

Gary woke up to the sun coming into his room, and the sound of church bells ringing. Donatella was gone, and he would have thought it all a beautiful dream, except that there was a note next to his bed. When he opened it a necklace fell out, one with an emerald stone attached to it, her necklace. The note simply read "For good luck. Please return soon."

Gary smiled and after he got dressed, placed it in his shirt pocket.

At breakfast Donatella was nowhere to be found. When Gary asked, he was told that she left early this morning, before the sun had come up. Apparently there was another makeshift hospital popping up in Genoa, and casualties were coming in. Gary wanted to go say goodbye to her, but there wasn't any time.

"Besides," he told himself, "I will be back for her, so there's no sense in saying goodbye."

He went with Marco to the dock disguised as a fisherman. He kept his belongings bundled up in a sack, and headed down to the dock. Marco brought him to what looked like a boat made entirely of wood from rotted trees. He was shocked to find out that the boat had an engine ... apparently, like the ship's construction; it was put in as an afterthought. As he and Marco set up the ship to get underway, Gary felt a little sick to his stomach, and more than a little afraid for his life.

Marco saw his fear and said, "Don't worry, it will get us there!"

"Alive?" Gary asked.

Marco seemed a little insulted, but gave out a little chuckle, "yes, alive."

Gary's mind was not put to rest.

The Journey to Riomaggiore did not help any more to set Gary's mind at ease. The seas were choppy, and while Gary was not prone to seasickness, the sounds the ship made combined with the amount of water they had to constantly bail out in order to stay afloat, put knots in his stomach that made him return the contents of his stomach to the Mediterranean. Marco was silent for the majority of the journey. Occasionally he'd poke fun at Gary's gift giving to the sea.

They pulled into a narrow channel as the sun was coming up. The sunlight illuminated a beautiful, magical town that seemed to have been built on a mountain that ran straight into the sea. The homes were colorful, pinks, reds, Azure Blues, all blended together perfectly. It was a modern marvel. Gary wondered how they got all those houses up on top of a mountain like that. Truly there was a reason God wanted such an important book to rest in a city that could have been built by her own hand (Gary didn't imagine the drill Sergeant version of god was capable of such a thing).

They were greeted by a group of friendly looking fishermen who looked like the type of people who would help a stranger get back on their feet regardless of the cost to their own well being, except that they were armed to the teeth with rifles pointed straight at them. But Marco, with his hands raised shouted out something in Italian ... a musical limerick of some sort, he wasn't sure, but one of the men sang back the rest of the tune, and all of a sudden, the rifles went down, and the smiles lit up their friendly faces. They were escorted through the streets of Riomaggiore, which was a confusing and tiny maze, the type of place you wouldn't want to be in close combat in. They were led up to a small apartment

365

building that had at one time or another been a house, and buzzed in by the occupants.

When they reached the top of the steep stairs, a door opened and they were led in to a small apartment. The man who'd let them in the apartment brought them into the dining room. It was colorful, with cheery paint covering over possibly hundreds of layers of cheery and not so cheery paint. Gary was seated at a large wooden table, while the man who'd escorted them took Marco off into another room.

Gary admired the table; it looked magnificent compared to their meager surroundings. It was a sturdy, dark wood stained table that sat 8 people comfortably, but with some doing, could most certainly seat 12. The chairs looked to be hand carved, with an ornate looking seal carved into the backs, and cushioned seats that were well worn, and covered in purple velvet. Whoever had sat in this seat regularly was about the same size as Gary.

They sat for a very long time, made to feel all the longer by the fact that there were two ornate clocks in this room, one hanging on the wall, and the other a freestanding grandfather clock in the corner, both would tick and tock incessantly, almost eerily in sync with each other. Gary was tempted a few times to get up and try and find out when someone was coming, but he felt compelled to stay. He'd killed people before,

366

but he'd never then gone to their family homes for the purpose of telling them that he had killed their son and now wanted to make up for it by giving them one of his belongings. He wondered if they'd ask him to dinner.

After what seemed like an eternity, where Gary had managed to count all the flaws in the stucco wall and then categorize them by severity of the flaw, and then tried to see faces in them, suddenly a group of people came in with Marco, all looking very somber. One of them, a very tall, and intimidating looking man marched over to Gary, and looked as if he were about to crush his head with his bare hands, a feat Gary was certain he could easily carry out had he wished to. The man just hovered over him, as a strikingly beautiful woman, who could have passed for 25, but her silver hair and some very fine lines said she was much older. The woman came over and stroked the man's arm, seeming to calm the beast in him down enough that he wouldn't kill Gary. Instead he spit in Gary's face, and walked to the opposite end of the table where he sat silently staring right into Gary's soul. "That must be Mr. Lorenzo" Gary thought to himself as he wiped the spit off of his face.

With them were two more beautiful, but much younger women. None of them smiled, all of them stared expectantly at Gary. Marco sat next to Gary and said, meet the Lorenzo family. Gary politely said hello, although he wasn't sure any of them understood English.

They listened intently as he tried to explain who he was attempting to use a strange combination of English words, Italian words, and words he thought were Italian. The two younger women, who were Vittorio's sisters, bit their lips hard attempting to suppress laughter.

Finally Marco stopped him, saying "They know who you are, and if I am not mistaken, they speak perfect English."
Gary wondered if everyone in this damn country spoke English and just thought it would be funny to make up another language to piss off American soldiers. The oldest of the three women spoke, silencing the giggling of the two young girls.

"We do speak English here. You are not among commoners, though our surroundings may seem humble. Before the unification of the Italian peninsula, we were a noble family, based out of Genoa. But as time has passed, and the need for royalty seems to have diminished, we find ourselves here, in this beautiful village at the end of the world."

"I see" Said Gary, a little bewildered by this news.
"Then you also know why I'm here?"

The mother began, "Yes, I understand that you came here to somehow make amends for ..."

She was cut off by Mr. Lorenzo, who stood up like some giant ogre and said, "... for murdering one of my sons in cold blood!" Gary started to get a little defensive and stood up himself, a little pissed off at this jackwad, who he'd come here to apologize to, not fight with.

Gary screamed, "Listen up sir. I didn't want to kill your son any more than I've wanted to watch some of my best friends die in my arms, or in mid sentence as they talked about their families, or their dreams, or watch them explode in front of me, killed by someone we'd never see, and who'd probably die without ever knowing their killer! I came here sir, to apologize, not to be ridiculed by someone who I don't know and whose situation I can't change. War is hell sir; I'm just trying to make a little more sense of it."

The man might have leapt clear across the table, killed Gary, and thought nothing of it, had not one of his daughters stood up and looked him in the eye, saying "Papa, please. Nothing can bring back Vittorio, Stefano, or Giovanni! Certainly not killing this man, who despite everything is at least attempting to do something decent in a world gripped by madness. Please." The father looked at his daughter, who seemed to

369

have magical powers over him, and instantly calmed down.

His daughter and wife held him as tear started to flow steadily down his stern looking face, his other daughter just sitting, and looking uncomfortably down at her lap. Gary had a similar emotional reaction, except instead of crying, he was more embarrassed at his lack of control.
He sat down, and eventually the Mother spoke. "I am Elena, this is my husband Vittorio, and these are our two daughters Francesca and Leonora. Please, while I appreciate your gesture ... perhaps you should be quick about it."

Gary nodded understandingly, and quickly produced the small book he had been holding on to, and handed it to Elena. Realizing instantly what it was, they all drew closer to it. Elena covered her mouth as she gently traced the outlines of the book and began to cry uncontrollably along with Francesca, who had been the one to calm Vittorio down moments earlier. Leonora just seemed to stare at it with morbid fascination and awe.

It was Vittorio who now calmed his family down. He stood up and looked at Gary, deadly serious now. "You had better leave now. I appreciate what you have done, and in time it may help to heal our family, but so help me, if I have to look at your face too long, eventually I will no longer be able to restrain myself. I will kill you, and this time my daughters will not be able to stop me."

Gary didn't argue this time ... he understood, and got up to leave without saying another word.

Suddenly Marco put up his hand and stopped him, asking Vittorio, "Sir, if it is possible for you to restrain yourself a little longer, may I see a picture of Vittorio?" Vittorio Sr. hesitated at this question, it seemed like an odd request, but at some point he decided it was not unreasonable. He went into the other room, and came back with a large family photograph where of course, no one was smiling but somehow everyone looked happy.

Marco held out the picture to Gary, and said "Which of these men was the one you killed?"

Very uncomfortable with the whole situation, Gary stared at the picture of the stony faced clan, all of whom bore a strong resemblance to their mother ... except for the women. Even though they were all dressed in formal attire, with slicked back hair, and completely shaven, save for the large handlebar mustaches, which made them all look like stereotypes from a 1920's silent film in NY, it was plain to him which one he'd shot on the streets of Florence.

"None of them" remarked Gary.

There was a sudden and palatable change in the mood of the room, as if a dark, heavy cloud was suddenly being lifted to reveal a sunny day.

"None of these men look even remotely like the man I killed." said Gary.

Marco smiled, "you see, it is as I said, the brothers Lorenzo were caught and executed as traitors ... or should I say, patriots."

Mr. Lorenzo, now with tears in his eyes stared at the journal which had belonged to his son while his wife held it even more tenderly in her hands. Suddenly Mr. Lorenzo stood up, marched over to Gary and hugged him so hard that he thought he might die again. Then he grabbed a glass, poured some of the table wine for everyone, all while still holding on to Gary like a rag doll, and announced "Now we toast! To my family! My boys who died protecting Italy, to my daughters who hold the keys to our future, and to Mr. Gary! We may have been strangers in the past, but God himself has brought you to us, and now you are like my son as well, Salute!"

They all raised their glasses and toasted, "Salute!"

The evening that followed was one of revelry and a lot of drinking. More than even Gary was used to, but at the end of the night, while Gary was ready to pass out, the Lorenzo's seemed to have more than enough energy. But understanding that their "new son" came from a place where they didn't celebrate like this, they offered him a bed, while the party went well on into the night.

As he slept, he was transported into a dream state, and again found himself in the city on Eagle Peak, where he was carried off by the townspeople into the great hall, and God hugged him with tears in her eyes. Gary remarked to himself at how beautiful the old woman looked every time he saw her.
She said one thing to him, "You have fulfilled your vow."
Gary had so many questions, so much to talk about, he felt like a different person. But before he could ask, his eyes opened, and a dull pain ravished his body, a pain he was all too familiar with, Gary was hung over.

He found himself in a spare bedroom, one with a closet full of clothes, and with a dresser that had pictures of the Lorenzo's on it. In the drawer of the dresser he found a sheet of paper with a poem written in English on it.

> I flew amongst the clouds today
> Whilst from the ground
> The birds looked upon me with Envy
> But I did not lament nor shame them

Instead I lifted them
up higher than me
And in the process
exhausted myself
Though I fell to the
ground in pain
The birds will fly for
all to enjoy
And my spirit will
soar with them
For eternity

"He wrote it as a child" A voice said coming
from the doorway. It was Mrs. Lorenzo.
"It isn't his best work, but for an eight year
old ... well, we knew he had a gift."
She came over and took the poem from
Gary's hand. "Why did he have to leave?
Why does a child need to waste his life so
pointlessly for ... for nothing?"
She stared at Gary as if she were looking for
an answer to this question, that only he had.

He contemplated this for a few moments,
feeling as if he owed her an answer.
Finally he said, "As boys we feel compelled
to prove ourselves, whether we have the
heart of a poet, or the soul of a warrior. As
we get older we learn that we need not prove
anything, but for many of us, it's already too
late."
Mrs. Lorenzo stared at him, "You talk as if
you were already an old man, but you can't
be older than 20!"

Gary suddenly remembered, he wasn't as young inside as he was on the outside, and said "War ages you very quickly."

After a large breakfast, with plenty of coffee, the initial side effects of the hangover had passed, and Marco, who must also have been hung over, groggily said, "Come, we must return to Genoa, I have a resistance to run, and my presence will be missed if I am gone too long."
Marco and Gary gathered up what few belongings they had and were off to the docks. There was a great deal of hugs and kisses, and pinches, as the Lorenzo's and a handful of other strangers who seemed to know what had transpired here as if they had all been in the dining room with them, saw them off.

They boarded the old rickety fishing boat, and took some extra goodies from the townspeople with them to eat. Goodies that would no doubt be returned to the sea at some point, and they set sail.

When they were a good twelve hours out, and as Gary munched on some sort of delicious chocolate treat the Mrs. Lorenzo had given him, Marco came up and sat next to him saying, "Not so bad eh? You did your good deed, and made a deserving family very happy!"
"Yeah" Said Gary "Not bad at all. I'm just not sure what to do now. I mean, essentially I've abandoned my unit, and am now

375

AWOL. I can't go back, and I certainly can't go back to America. It's better that they think I'm dead!"

Marco laughed at this, "Well It's better to have lived your life than to have simply lived it out to its conclusion."

Gary thought about this, and how he'd lived out his life the first time, and agreed that even if he died today, this life was much better.

Marco went on, "Well you do seem to have the heart of that woman Donatella! This is no small feat from what I understand of her. She does not give it away freely."

Gary couldn't help but smile when he thought of Donatella, he'd loved a lot of women in his time, but none of them as passionately as he'd felt about her.

Marco got serious for a moment, "I wonder though if you could now do me a favor. "Sure!" said Gary, "You certainly seemed to have stuck your neck out for me for no reason. What can I do for you?"

Marco's voice got even more serious and a little bit shaky now, "I wonder if you would look at this picture now, and tell me what you see?"

Marco pulled a photograph out of his back pocket and handed it to Gary, his hands were trembling now.

"Calm down their chief! I'll look at your picture!"

Gary pulled the picture out of his hand and studied it. It was a picture of Marco, in full Nazi uniform, standing in front of an old WWI prop plane. His arm was around another man, also in Nazi attire. A man who looked very familiar to Gary for some reason ... suddenly Gary dropped the photo and leapt to his feet, only to find Marco standing in front of him with his pistol drawn and pointed right at Gary's head.

"I thought so" said Marco.

Gary piped up, "That's the man I killed ... the one with Vittorio's book. You knew him?"

Marco was in tears now, his hand shaking, but still firmly in control of the pistol.

"His name was Friedrich!"

Gary blurted out "Your brother?"

To which Marco replied, "No! He was my lover!"

With that, he shot Gary in the head, the world spinning around him, the last thing he saw and heard was Marco standing over him with his arm extended saying "Hail Hitler." As he spit in Gary's face, then ... darkness.

"Damn" thought Gary, "I seem destined to end my life with a bullet to the head."

Gary woke up on a beautiful bed, adorned with rich purples and yellows, with satin sheets and an open canopy, the sun streaming into the room. It was the castle on eagle Peak.

"Great" he thought, "so much for happily ever after. But still, this is a little nicer than the DMV."

Just as he finished that thought, a woman came into his room, her thick glasses and permed hair made her unmistakable. It was Delores from the DMV. She had a tray with breakfast for him on it.

She rolled her eyes and said in her raspy voice, "Here you go sweetheart, compliments of you know who."

Gary stared at the silver platter he was handed, as it seemed to hover over his lap, it had a warm croissant, some fresh fruit, juice and Coffee.

"Thanks" he said.

Delores stuck her long, snake like tongue out and whacked it against her earlobe, as if there was something on it she wanted to remove and said, "don't mention it sweetie."

"Wait," said Gary "I thought you worked at the, well whatever that place that looks like the DMV is."

She shot back, "I got a lot of jobs. I like to keep busy. Plus I got lot of kids to look after, I love the little buggers, but they ain't cheap!"

She walked out waggling her dinosaur looking tail behind her muttering something about needing a cigarette. Gary suddenly felt a little sick to his stomach trying to imagine who in their right mind would purposefully knock up Delores ... more than once. He finally decided that for all he knew, she was a looker in her species. Besides, he loved her attitude.

As lovely as this version of the afterlife was, Gary noticed that he was again, old. But this time he wasn't as fat and unhealthy as he had been. It was as if he had lived out a different life all together, one where he drank less alcohol and ate a few more vegetables.

He ate the croissant, which stayed warm, along with his coffee no matter how long he let it sit. After breakfast he wandered outside of his room into the main chamber ... he suddenly realized, while he was still in the Castle on Eagle Peak, it was different. The murals had changed, they showed a different path for humanity, not one completely free of war and conflict, but one where ultimately the human race didn't completely blow itself up. One where we spread out into the stars, and eventually created whole new species and civilizations on other planets, and then ... well the mural stretched on farther than Gary could see.

He suddenly noticed something odd out of the corner of his eye, a minor little detail, but one that gave him a small chuckle that turned into a giant laugh. It was PFC Joe Johnson opening up his bar, it looked so bright and shiny, just the way Gary had remembered it, the only difference (besides the absence of Gary's permanent impression on his bar stool) was the name … "Gary's Bar". Gary laughed so hard that he had a couple tears streaming down his face.

"He never was that inventive, but at least he listened to me."

Suddenly Gary heard a voice pipe up from behind him, "Welcome back brave soldier!"

Gary didn't feel very brave.

"Basically I abandoned my fellow Marines to go on some damn side mission to deliver a book. How is that brave … Clarence?"

God just smiled and gestured at the mural, "but because of your actions, you made all this possible. You stood against everything that should have been right for a greater purpose, despite the obstacles, and the outcome you knew it would have for your life. That's real bravery."

Gary rolled his eyes and marveled at humanity's new history.

"But no one will ever know I did all this, I mean, my life isn't even a footnote in the society page."

God smiled, "I know, and I appreciate it … you made a vow to carry out this mission, and where there is unseen action, there is visible reward!"

Gary chuckled. "You mean like a bullet to the head from a Nazi Jackass while floating in a wooden death trap on the Med?"

God shook her head, "You don't seem to understand what would have happened to you if you'd have stayed. You would have been caught by the US Army; court marshaled, and then spent a good portion of your life in jail. By dying this way, the Army thinks you are a hero, who died staying with fallen comrades, and Donatella will have been spared the pain of knowing you were alive and she'd never get to see you again." Gary sighed, "Well, I guess I've done my bit for King and Country. It's done, and there's no sense in whining about it now. Besides I hate whiners. The question now is … what's next?"

God smiled, "Now you get your reward." She reached into his shirt pocket, and pulled out the necklace Donnatella had given him. "Or don't you recognize me in my old age?" Suddenly she put the necklace around her neck and transformed, aging backwards until Gary suddenly recognized her, "DONATELLA?" he screamed out.
She laughed, "Like I said, call me Clarence!"
Gary couldn't keep quiet, "But that's a boy's name! Besides, Donatella is so beautiful!" God blushed a little bit, "OK, if you like Donnatella, then you can call me Donnatella." She pulled Gary, who was now a young man again, close to her, and they kissed passionately. When he finally pulled away, they were in Joe's … or rather, Gary's bar. The tables were lined with his companions he'd lost in the war, all of them

with women, and in some cases men, at their sides.

The Juke box sparked to life with a lively tune, and Donatella said "You asked what now? Now … we dance! And later … we do whatever we want, and go wherever we want!"

As they were about to dance away eternity, Gary had a horrible thought. "Wait, I have to ask you something ... you aren't a big fan of Seinfeld, are you?" Donnatella suddenly understanding his concern answered, "No, not at all. I find them to be whiny jerks that live like kings and do nothing but whine about it." Gary was relieved but still a little confused. Donnatella smiled and shook her head, "You want to know why I used them in the dream, right?"

Gary nodded. Donnatella went on "I was in the middle of making a big dinner and talking on the phone, and it was on the TV in the background. I was too distracted to think about it. I just sort of sent them down to tell you about Vittorio. But no, I definitely don't like that show."

With this major point cleared up, they lived happily ever after, until he discovered she wasn't really a big fan of Bob Newheart. Not that she didn't like it ... she was just lukewarm on the whole concept of the show.

www.ingramcontent.com/pod-product-compliance
Lightning Source LLC
Chambersburg PA
CBHW060150260626
47160CB00001B/203